"I wish to warn you of what is to come."

He had seen the sensual, enticing, womanly Marguerite at first. This was the angry, controlling, warrior-like Marguerite.

Was there some other plotting going on? He took a breath and asked, "And what is to come?"

"My lord Henry is simply putting me in my place. He wishes me to know what he could do if he is displeased with me. I fear you have been caught up in a lovers' quarrel."

"Henry will call off the wedding today?" His instincts told him there was much more going on here.

"Of course he will! He loves me and will not give me away to some northern lord who never attends court." She must have seen his look of disbelief, for she added, "I was raised as consort for a king, not some…some…"

"Barbarian of mixed blood, my lady?"

* * *

The King's Mistress
Harlequin Historical #735—January 2005

Praise for Terri Brisbin

"A lavish historical romance in the grand
tradition from a wonderful talent."
—*New York Times* bestselling author
Bertrice Small on *Once Forbidden*

The Norman's Bride
"A quick-paced story with engaging
characters and a tender love story."
—*Romantic Times*

The Dumont Bride
"Rich in its Medieval setting...Terri Brisbin has
written an excellent tale that will keep
you warm on a winter's night."
—*Affaire de Coeur*

"Beautifully written and well researched,
this book is a perfect ten in many ways."
—*Romance Reviews Today*

TERRI BRISBIN

THE KING'S MISTRESS

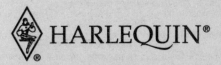
HARLEQUIN®

TORONTO • NEW YORK • LONDON
AMSTERDAM • PARIS • SYDNEY • HAMBURG
STOCKHOLM • ATHENS • TOKYO • MILAN • MADRID
PRAGUE • WARSAW • BUDAPEST • AUCKLAND

ISBN 0-373-29335-6

THE KING'S MISTRESS

www.eHarlequin.com

Printed in U.S.A.

Please address questions and book requests to:
Harlequin Reader Service
U.S.: 3010 Walden Ave., P.O. Box 1325, Buffalo, NY 14269
Canadian: P.O. Box 609, Fort Erie, Ont. L2A 5X3

This book is for Gail Link, romance author and bookseller extraordinaire, who was one of the first authors I ever met and continues as a friend to this day! Thanks, Gail, for the hours of enjoyment you've given me with your books and for your ongoing support!

Prologue

Anjou Province
November in the Year of Our Lord 1177

The slippery satin of her floor-length gown swished around her legs as she turned to face the king in anger. Unable to believe the pronouncement made by him, Marguerite of Alencon gasped.

"Sire! Surely you cannot mean to turn me away from your affections."

"You will always bear my love, fair Marguerite, even as you bear my child. But you must be clear on this point—you will never take the queen's place in name or in honor."

"You have made her a prisoner, Your Grace. You have stripped her of her wealth and power. 'Twould serve you well to seek another as your queen and wife."

Only after the words escaped did she realize the danger in teasing the Plantagenet temper to rouse. So caught up in her own plans and desires, she stepped too far in voicing these thoughts.

"'Twould serve many well to remember that I am the one who made her prisoner and that I am the one who controls her wealth and power. 'Twould serve many well not to meddle in the affairs of this kingdom.''

With his fists clenched in anger and his head thrown back as he spoke, his words echoed through the chamber and sent shivers through Marguerite as she reconsidered her approach.

"Sire, I beg your forgiveness for my brazen words. I wish only to love you and to give you pleasure and heirs as you desire. I carry one now within my womb and simply want to share my joy at the honor with you."

Nothing inside her could make her take back the words. She wanted to be queen. She carried his son now. Her blood was noble enough to take her place next to him. Bastard or not, the blood coursing through her veins could be traced back to Charlemagne.

But she was a realist if nothing else, and so, gathering her pride in a bit, she lowered herself into a deep curtsy at his feet and tilted her head down until she was lower than his hand. After a minute in that humbling position, she raised her head and lifted his hand to her mouth. With a reverent kiss on it, she touched it to her forehead and whispered to him.

"I am yours, Henry. I live to love you and to serve you only."

His manner calmed for his heavier, angrier

breathing slowed and he did not pull away from her. Instead, he assisted her to her feet and he guided her to a chair. Once she'd taken her seat, he paced across the chamber without speaking. Marguerite had seen this behavior before in him. When first confronted with news that was neither pleasant nor wanted, he exploded, his temper getting the best of him. Then, when given time to acclimate himself to the news, he dealt with things in a fairer way.

Ridding himself of the disgraced Eleanor would take some maneuvering with both church and nobles and Henry was probably thinking of ways around the objections that may be made to it. In spite of their age difference and her perfidy to him in matters of family, he was most likely seeking a benevolent manner to remove Eleanor, yet one without losing the wealth and lands she brought into the marriage as her first husband had.

Marguerite reached over and, to soothe her parched throat, took a sip of the sweet wine still in her goblet. Watching the king pace back and forth, she knew he was beginning to agree with her assessment and ideas. She relaxed against the back of the high chair and waited. There was no sense in interrupting Henry now. Just as she began to get nervous over his silence, he stopped and turned to face her.

"Several years ago, I supported a monk from Sempringham in his battles against the revolt and the charges of his lay brothers," the king said. She knew not where these words led, but waited for his explanation. "The order now thrives and is under my protection. One of their lay houses would be a good place for you to remain until you give birth.''

He was banishing her?

''My lord, do you mean to send me to a convent?'' She could hardly draw a breath at the thought. ''I only want to...''

''I understand, Marguerite,'' he said, smiling that charismatic smile that had entranced her from their first meeting. '''Tis best to have the babe before any other plans are made between us.''

A small measure of fear crept up her spine at his words. Something within her knew that he was twisting her words and her desires for his own. But then, was that not what kings did when given the choice? She had not reached the level where she was now by avoiding the difficulties, and so she pressed her suit before he could leave and not give her some commitment to hold on to.

''And marriage, sire? Will there be marriage after the babe?''

Henry walked swiftly to her and pulled her to stand. The goblet dropped from her grasp as he wrapped his arms around her in possessive embrace and brought her mouth to his. His mouth took hers in a lustful, claiming kiss like the many they had shared for months and months between them. Over and over, he tasted her lips and his tongue played against hers as she felt her resistance to him and his ways diminish. When she was breathless, he drew back from her, tilted his head so that he met her gaze with those clear, Angevin eyes and he smiled at her.

''Oh, fair Marguerite, there will be marriage.''

Chapter One

Abbeytown
Silloth-on-Solway, England
July in the Year of Our Lord 1178

"My lord!"

Orrick turned at the brother's call and stopped in his stride to his horse. Brother David, large and lumbering, approached him without calling out again. A message then?

"Good brother, what do you need of me?"

He knew most of the brothers by name because he had spent time since he was a babe here both with his father and alone on his own tasks. This one had been a member of the community for nigh onto ten-and-four years and in charge of the abbey's vast assortment of clerks.

"The abbot requests another moment of your attention, my lord. In his office chamber."

Orrick nodded to his men and, with his helmet still in his hand, followed Brother David to the abbot's office. 'Twas something important or the abbot would not summon him back so soon. A few minutes brought him face-to-face with Abbot Godfrey.

"Come in for a moment, my lord. There is someone to see you and I thought you might want some measure of privacy."

Orrick ducked lower to enter under the short doorway and straightened to his full height when inside. The royal envoy, wearing the insignia of the Plantagenet king, stood before the abbot's table that was already strewn with papers and scrolls. The abbot left quietly without looking at either of them.

"My lord," the man said, bowing before him. "Abbot Godfrey thought to save us both some travel. This is from the king."

The sealed scroll lay in the air between them and something within Orrick made him hesitate to touch it. Not expecting word from the king who was in Anjou at the present, he could not imagine what tidings were carried within this roll of parchment. And part of him did not wish to know.

Pushing off his mail coif and tucking his helmet under his other arm, he reached out and accepted the messenger's duty. The waxed seal cracked off the parchment in his hand and he stepped back away from the man to unroll the parchment until he could read the words. Then he stopped breathing as the words began to make sense to him.

Henry wanted to reward him for his father's past and his current service to the Crown. A woman, nay, a wife, befitting his standing in the esteem and respect of the king. More gold for some service already performed. Another title.

Orrick swallowed as the words struck him. His father had been no fool and neither was he. He knew, plain and simple, that he was being bought. And the price being paid was high enough to make him worry. If Henry was stepping into the affairs of his nobles, Orrick knew he should be worried. Especially when it happened in the remote area of England where he lived and breathed. And when it brought him the likes of a bride named Marguerite of Alencon.

The messenger asked if he should wait for a reply and Orrick shook his head. "My answer will be my attendance on the king's call, sir."

"I shall convey your willingness to him, my lord."

The man's words were said almost as a question rather than a statement. His call to wed the king's vassal was obviously not a secret at court for even the envoy knew the contents of the letter. And the words contained some doubt that he would agree. Not permitting any question to remain between them, Orrick replied to the envoy's unspoken words.

"I am the king's dutiful servant, sir. I live to serve as he needs me to."

The messenger nodded and bowed before leaving the chamber. Orrick watched in silence as Abbot Godfrey walked slowly back in and waited for his reaction to the news he'd received. Godfrey kept his counsel in good times and bad and Orrick did not hesitate to tell him this life-changing pronouncement of the king's.

"I am to marry at the king's behest."

"Marry, my lord? Did the king speak of whom you marry?"

Orrick knew that the marriage agreement was more important than the people involved, but he nodded to the abbot. "Lady Marguerite of Alencon."

"Do you know the lady?" Godfrey asked, looking over Orrick's shoulder at the king's words. Free in his examination, the brother reached over and took the parchment from him, reading the words several times. 'Twas their practice since Godfrey knew Orrick would miss some of the important details and Orrick knew Godfrey would not. "Marguerite of Alencon.... The name seems somehow familiar to me. Mayhap your lady mother would know of this woman?"

"If she belongs to Henry's court, my mother will know her name and her history, fear not."

"'Tis true, my lord. Your lady mother has an inordinate amount of knowledge amassed about the king and his people. If she would turn her interests to other matters, her soul might gain some wisdom."

Orrick knew Godfrey disapproved of his mother's hunger for courtly gossip, but the years of being separated from her extended family and many friends in Normandy had not lessened the urge to follow the goings-on of those she'd left behind. In this instance, it might help him decide if he were being rewarded or punished with this marriage gift from the king.

"I will speak to her about her weakness, good abbot,'' he said as he rolled the parchment up and slid it safely into the tunic he wore beneath his chain mail.

Godfrey cuffed him on his shoulder and laughed. ''You will ask her what you need first and then reprimand her for her weakness, will you not, my lord?''

''You know me too well, Godfrey,'' he said, acknowledging his plan. ''Why waste valuable information without finding it first? This is my future I speak of. I should discover what I can before answering the king's call and taking the wife he offers.''

Godfrey's wizened face lost its joking expression. ''Orrick, make no mistake in the flowery language of his message or in the beauty of the woman he names. You are ordered to take this wife. And to take her now.''

Orrick matched his seriousness. ''I did not miss that part of the message, Godfrey. I understand the intent within this.''

''Then go with God, my lord. I will keep you and the lady Marguerite in my prayers until you return safely to our lands.''

He reached out and shook the abbot's hand and then received a blessing from him. 'Twas the way of Godfrey. Without another word, he made his way to his men and mounted his horse. The journey would take nearly two days unless they pushed. Now with the need to return home and prepare for his travels to the king's court and a wife, he did urge his men faster.

First though he must tell his mother and make arrangements for her comfort elsewhere within the keep. His wife would need to have a certain hold on the way things were done and he suspected that his mother, familiar with the keep and its people for over three decades, would not relinquish her power without challenges. There would be time for all of that, of course. First he needed to go bring home his bride.

The journey seemed to speed by as he thought about the woman who would be his wife and the mother to his children and heirs. He was not some green youth with no idea of what was to come. Marriage had been on his mind for some time, but always one matter or another came up and interfered with it. Now, the king had given him a way to do it simply and plainly.

So, it was with great anticipation that he and his men rode into the yard of Silloth Keep and approached the stairway to the great hall. He had taken no more than three or four steps when his mother's voice rang out to him, squashing any belief that the king's orders would work out for the best.

Lady Constance came tearing around a corner and faced him as her ladies and various other servants caught up with her. The redness in her face and her labored breaths spoke clearly of her agitation. But what was she upset about?

His stomach sank as she waved several parchments in his face. Without any attempt to lower her voice, she addressed her most pressing concern to him.

"Swear to me that you will not marry Marguerite of Alencon!"

How had she known? They had just arrived at the keep after a strenuous ride back from Abbeytown. The king's messenger reported to him there without traveling here. How could she have known?

"Mother, the king has ordered our marriage. I go now to answer his summons and to bring her back here. How did you know her name?"

He watched as the confusion and anger and frustration filled her face. She turned to several of her ladies and none gave her the answer or reassurance she sought from them. Orrick was becoming convinced, as Godfrey was, that his mother spent entirely too much time fretting over gossip and other womanly worries such as those. Mayhap his new wife could help to distract her from such ways?

"You cannot marry her."

This was getting out of hand. This was why he should not have delayed his marriage this long and why his mother needed to take her place within his wife's household. But her sorrow over his father's death had driven him to mercy and her excellent skills at chatelaine had won out. 'Twas time to change that and his wife would be just the person to do so, with his guidance and control.

"The king has gifted me with Marguerite of Alencon, as you apparently know. And the king is generous in doing so...." His words drifted off as even he experienced an uneasy feeling over the amount of gold being paid to take this woman as wife. Damn, but his mother knew what was at the heart of this matter and now he feared asking her. But he must know what he faced from the king. ''Tell me now, for I would hear all of it.''

Steeling himself for what was to come, Orrick took a deep breath and faced his mother in the midst of all who looked on around them.

''The king is truly generous, Orrick, but not in this instance. He pays you gold for he seeks to give you his mistress as wife. Marguerite of Alencon is the king's whore.''

The king's whore?

Now that he'd heard his mother's words, he turned and sought his chambers. Orrick needed to prepare for this summons and prepare himself to take the king's refuse as his wife.

At least now he completely understood that he was being punished for some sin committed by either himself or his father. What other reason could there be for such an insult as this?

Chapter Two

"Henry will not do this to me. You are wrong," Marguerite argued. "He loves me."

But the words sounded hollow and unconvincing even to her ears. Marguerite turned away from her companion and looked at the elaborate dress spread on her bed. It could not be. It simply could not be true that Henry had given her in marriage to someone else.

"You know him better than anyone, Marguerite," Johanna replied in a bland tone of voice. "If you say he will claim you before the marriage can happen, I believe you."

Her temper flared and she flung the dress from the bed onto the floor. Grasping the edges of it, she tore it open and pearls and gems went flying all over the room. Before she could rip it into the pieces she wanted to, another voice called out to her from the doorway.

"Is this how you treat the gifts of the king?"

Marguerite turned as Lord Bardrick, Henry's steward and henchman here at Woodstock, entered her chambers. Johanna made a quick curtsy and escaped, though Marguerite was not sure if her own temper or the steward's lecherous gazes at the woman's ample bosom made her run from the room. The door slammed and she was alone with one of very few men who had Henry's confidence and knew the king's secrets.

"My lord," Marguerite said, dipping gracefully as she knew she could to the floor in a curtsy, one that shared a glimpse of her own now well-endowed bosom with him. "I fear I am overwrought with excitement over my impending marriage to Lord… Lord…" She pretended not to remember the name of her prospective husband for a moment until Bardrick said it.

"Lord Orrick of Silloth."

"Just so. Lord Orrick of Silloth. I mean no disrespect to the king. Indeed I am always pleased by his attentions and his gifts."

They both knew the gift most recently given to her by Henry. The babe had been a girl unfortunately, and of no use to Marguerite in her plans to make a claim for Henry's further attentions and affections. At least a boy would have been accepted and graced with a title and a position of power and wealth as Henry's other bastard son, Geoffrey, had been. Through a boy she could have some hold. But the girl born a few months ago was worthless to her and remained behind at the convent where she had given birth to her, a nameless noble, nay a royal bastard, to be raised by the nuns there. Her own sister stayed behind to oversee the baby and to answer her own call to a life of service to God.

Bardrick walked to the door of the room, opened it and spoke to one of the servants waiting outside. "Take this to one of the seamstresses and have her see to it. And quickly, girl," he yelled, pushing the servant to move more rapidly. "The wedding is on the morrow and it must be ready."

Marguerite watched with a sense of amusement as the girl gathered the pieces of the dress together and stumbled from the room. She had not moved from the spot in which she stood.

"The king plans on carrying out this farce then, Bardrick?" she asked.

"'Tis no farce, lady. You will marry Lord Orrick and Henry will brook no refusal on your part."

"And if I do not?" Marguerite could not believe this was the end. Henry would reclaim her. He would object, mayhap even at the last moment, and save her from this unspeakable match.

"The last three people who refused the king's generosity are not alive to tell you the stupidity of doing so. Think on that tonight as you prepare yourself for your marriage in the morn."

A shiver shook her and, even though she tried to hide it from this weasel, his smarmy grin told her of her failure.

"Aye, lady. The prudent thing to do would be to acquiesce to Henry's wishes. His loyal subjects who do usually live longer and better than those foolish enough to stand against him."

Fight it though she did, she nodded slightly in his

direction, never meeting his eyes since she knew the satisfaction she would see there at her surrender. Bardrick bowed to her and backed to the doorway, the way he did when she was the king's favorite. The insult of it was clear—she was one of the many who had sought the king's bed and now were to be used as rewards for services rendered to his faithful.

"Sleep well, Marguerite."

The sound of his laughter and scorn as he made his way down the corridor away from her was the worst of it. It broke her resolve and she fell onto the now-empty bed and let the tears flow.

This could not happen to her. She had been groomed throughout her life to be the consort of a great man. Her blood was of royal stock and she deserved a husband of the same. She did not expect to be given instead to some barbarian of mixed blood in the north of England. This Lord Orrick lived as far from the court and the king as anyone could get. His lands were in some godforsaken place where there was never sunshine as in her own homeland. He was simply some minor lord over a few keeps and a mongrel group of villeins. She deserved more than this, more than him.

She deserved the king.

Marguerite waited for her grief to pass. There was still time. Henry could still, would still intervene before the words proclaiming her Orrick's wife were pronounced. He could step in at anytime and call off this farce and gift this "lord of the north," as he was called, with some mealy-mouthed chit more of his class. Someone content to suffer his touch and his life in the rough place he called his own.

She remained in her chambers for the rest of the evening, waving off her servants and her meal, preferring not to suffer the pitying looks of everyone around her over this match. As sleep was finally overtaking her, she prayed that Henry was simply making a point to her about overstepping her place and that he would keep her as his own.

Surely that was his plan?

"If you tug that once more, I will have your head!" Orrick said through clenched jaws. "I am not some maid who needs these kinds of clothes."

"But, my lord, the king will be present at your wedding this morn, along with the most important of his court. You must look your best."

Orrick began to mumble, but realized the futility of it. His own servants' efforts were being complemented by some of the king's men in order to make certain that every order and direction of the king was being followed to the smallest of detail. The king's steward here at Woodstock had visited him several times over the past two days in order to convey Henry's pleasure over his quick arrival and his agreement to the marriage.

The woman must have made herself into some kind of problem if Henry was this anxious to rid himself of her. And in but a few hours, she would be his—his wife and his problem to deal with.

"Finish it, Gerard. Finish it now," he growled under his breath.

His man must have recognized the end of his limits of putting up with so much frivolity for he urged the others to complete their assigned tasks and leave the room. Gerard gave him one more look before also leaving.

Orrick shook his head and found himself alone.

He looked down at the elaborate tunic and the thick chains of gold that lay on his chest, and worried. He hated this much attention. He hated being at court. He hated all of this. But as a loyal subject of the king, he had no choice but to persevere until he could return to his own lands and sink back into the anonymity that the distant, wild north of England offered him.

And take his wife with him.

They would meet for the first time in less than an hour—a courtesy granted by the king at the request of the lady. She knew nothing of him; most at court could probably not describe him or even know they spoke to him as they did. But no one here hesitated from speaking of her. He had listened to the tales since his arrival; indeed he could hear the accolades in his mind even now.

She was beautiful. Her long, rich golden-brown hair reached nigh to the floor and flowed in generous curls over her lushly endowed body. Poems had been written about her gloriously blue eyes and sculpted red lips.

She was well educated—her family had provided the most learned tutors of the day—and she could speak most of the languages of the continent and could read and write in at least five, including Latin and Greek.

She was well pedigreed—in spite of her illegitimacy, her bloodlines reached back to Charlemagne and the great Frankish kings. She had connections to most of the royal families in the Christian world on the continent of Europe.

And she was the king's whore.

Orrick sought out the window in his chamber. Pushing it open he observed the activity beneath him in the yard. Enjoying the familiar frenzy, he breathed in deeply and tried to allow the coolness of the breezes to soothe his concern. He wished he could talk this over with someone, but there was no one he could trust with his doubts over this marriage. There was so much more to this than a simple agreement and an order of the king. Was he being humiliated for being only an English nobleman and not one of the king's favorites? Had his father or mother sinned against the Plantagenets and he would bear the cost of it now?

He planned to do nothing here in the severe scrutiny of the court other than accept Marguerite as his wife and take her back to his lands. Any problems between them would be worked out there, where no one questioned his authority or power. No one except the woman who pushed her way into his chambers now.

''Have you met her yet? Has she been presented to you?'' His mother had followed him to Woodstock as he had expected but her presence here was not helping him. Instead her questions and veiled comments caused him more concern.

"I meet her in less than an hour, Mother," he said as he turned away from the window to face her. And to clear up any doubts, he continued. "Alone."

Orrick watched as his mother did momentary battle with the words she wished to say. Her face, not bothered yet by the wrinkles of life, tightened in worry. When had her pale blond hair begun to change to gray? She still had the full, robust figure he'd always known, but she was beginning to favor her mother in appearance. Now that he looked closer, Orrick could see the softening of her green eyes.

"Alone? But your family and hers should be present at such an important meeting. I must—"

"You must do nothing, Mother. I will meet Marguerite alone first and then you may attend the ceremony with the others." His words sounded harsh, but he must speak sternly to her or she ignored him and went on her own merry way.

She looked as though she would argue for a moment and then a different expression filled her eyes. He saw the tears gathering and, for once, he knew these were not just a ploy to gain his sympathy or support. Her words confirmed it.

"I only wish your father could be here to see this. He had hoped you would consider marriage years ago, but…" Her words drifted off.

Orrick regretted his tone. "I delayed and now he will not see it. I am sorry for that, as well." He left the window and walked closer to her.

"Things will be different," she whispered.

He heard the fear in her voice. She would lose her standing with the arrival of his wife. Instead of being lady of the keep, vital to its efficiency and safety, she would now be an interested onlooker with no power or control that he or his wife did not grant her. Did she realize that she had given him the opportunity he had searched for to speak on this issue before his marriage?

"Mother," he began, unsure of his words. "After the marriage…"

"If you would arrange an escort, I will move to my dower property near Ravenglass. It may be easier if I go directly there and you can have my belongings delivered to me when you arrive in Silloth."

Although she said the words calmly, Orrick could almost feel the rapid beating of her heart. He could hear how she held her breath waiting for his words that would determine her fate. He knew his mother and she wanted nothing less than to be resettled in her dower keep since it was even more removed from life than his corner of England was. There must be a way to soothe her fears and not set up too awkward a situation in his own home.

"Your keep in Ravenglass needs some work and is not suitable for you to live there at this time. While repairs are done, I think you should remain at Silloth and give guidance to my new wife. Things will be strange to her and you might help her become accustomed to our ways and our people."

After an uncomfortable moment of silence that seemed to stretch on for days, his mother's exhaled breath and relaxed shoulders told him that he had said the right thing.

"I will only stay as long as the new countess needs my assistance, Orrick. I will not remain where I am not wanted."

Orrick strode to her and gathered her in his arms. "I know you will not interfere, Mother. I know you mean well."

Both of their words sounded hollow even to his ears. His mother, the Lady Constance, was a meddler and manipulator. She poked and peeked into every aspect of life at Silloth and at his other properties. She lived to meddle. But today, on his wedding day, he would accept her words as truth and hope for the best when they found themselves back at Silloth.

He stepped back from her, holding her shoulders as he moved away. "Now, I must finish my preparations and meet my bride face-to-face."

She looked as though she would say something else, but a frown settled on her brow and her lips tightened as she held the words within her. Since he would rather hear any more disparaging remarks here in the privacy of his chambers, he waited. When she spoke no more, he leaned closer and kissed her forehead.

"All will be well, Mother. Truly."

His mother offered him a bow of her head but no other words as she turned and left his chambers. He let out the breath he had not realized he held and felt some of the tension within him ease. The first of many strained meetings that faced him at Woodstock, and the one that in some ways he thought the worst, was done and now he could move on to meeting his bride and facing the king as he married the woman who was the king's mistress.

Lady Marguerite requested that they meet at terce and, as that hour approached, Orrick left his chamber and proceeded down the corridor to a smaller room designated for their encounter. The bells calling the religious to prayers began to echo from somewhere close by as he entered the chamber. Knowing the practice of women to be late, Orrick did not dream that she would be waiting for him.

As he closed the door behind him, he realized that the gossip about her beauty and gracefulness had not been an exaggeration at all. As she lowered herself to a deep curtsy before him with her head bowed demurely and even more womanly curves and contours revealed to him, the baser part of him responded, as well. This could work after all. She would not be so difficult to bear as a wife.

Chapter Three

"My lady," he said as he acknowledged her obeisance and held out his hand. "Please rise now."

The softness of her fingers against his work-roughened hand sent fire through him. And when she finally raised her gaze to his, he knew he was lost.

Her hair did indeed reach nigh to the floor in spite of some decorations and jewels that were woven into the curls surrounding her face. His hands itched to touch it, feel it, even bring it to his face and inhale the fragrance of her that was carried by it. When she moved her head, her hair cascaded in flowing waves over her shoulders and arms and down her back. In an instant, his mind pictured her how she would be later in the night—in his bed, naked, with only her hair to shield her.

Shocked by his carnal reaction to simply meeting her, Orrick knew he must tame this beast within him or appear the barbarian she surely thought him to be. Stepping back and motioning to a bench, he allowed her to sit. A few steps across the chamber and he felt a bit more in control. Until she spoke.

"My lord Orrick, I am pleased to have this chance to meet you privately. My thanks for granting what must seem a strange request by a bride on her wedding day."

Soft and incredibly feminine, her voice carried within a hint of huskiness and once more his body betrayed him. That underlying tone would be evident as she cried out her pleasure in his bed. He saw her naked and writhing against him as he filled her with his seed and as their satisfaction poured forth from both of them in loud cries. He closed his eyes for a moment and then realized her power.

Orrick had come to this day aware of the gossip and the tales told about her ongoing liaisons with the king. He had armed himself with a healthy measure of suspicion so that he did not become anyone's fool in this. Believing that he did not make decisions with his cock, he had felt completely at ease with his ability to assess the lady and the situation and handle all of it.

Fool!

In but a few moments, her beauty, her blatant sexuality and her silent promises about what would be his ensorcelled him. With a curtsy and a nod, with a shake of her hair and an enticing scent and with simple words she had ensnared him in her trap. Now he stood before her, hard as stone and wanting her more than he had ever wanted a woman. The urge, the need, to touch and taste and hold and have and fill and claim and mark her as his own grew until he feared it might overwhelm him. Looking around the chamber, he spied a small table with a jug and some goblets. He used it to break her spell.

"Wine, my lady?" He poured some for himself, managing not to spill it in spite of the way his hand shook. Without waiting for her reply, he filled a goblet for her and brought it to her.

"My thanks, Lord Orrick," she whispered as she lifted the wine to her mouth.

He watched as she finished her sip and as a drop of the sweet dark liquid began to trickle down from the corner of her lips. Even as his body moved forward to her, Marguerite used the tip of her tongue to catch it. He could not allow this to continue. Pulling his control around him, Orrick stepped back.

"And the reason for this meeting?"

"Why, to meet you, my lord! I know 'tis not so unusual for those of our status to marry without ever setting eyes on each other." She paused and let her gaze move over him in a provocative way. Just as he could almost feel her touch, she continued. "But His Grace, the king, allowed this breach of etiquette because we have long been friends."

"So I have heard, my lady."

There! He needed to let her know that he was no man's fool, not even the king's. He might be forced to take Henry's cast-off lover as wife, but Orrick would not pretend he did not know the real relationship between Henry and Marguerite. Not even to her, not even to assuage his own pride.

Her reaction surprised him. She stood and handed him the cup. Walking to the door, she faced him.

The soft expression on her face changed to a much harder one, one that sapped most of the beauty from her features. She stood taller and stared at him with a look that sent icy chills down his spine.

He had seen the sensual, enticing, womanly Marguerite at first.

This was the angry, controlling, warriorlike Marguerite.

"Although I owe you nothing, Orrick of Silloth, I know that you are forced to this marriage as I am and want you to know the truth."

He lifted the cup to his mouth and swallowed the wine in one mouthful. "And which truth would that be, my lady?" Did she plan to admit that she had shared the king's bed and mayhap even had his love?

"This marriage will not happen. I am somewhat sorry that you have been drawn into this misunderstanding between the king and me, so I wish to warn you of what is to come."

Was there some other plotting going on? Did the king have some punishment in mind for some imagined wrongdoing on his or his father's part? Why this sham of marriage if Henry planned to arrest him on some charge? His gut tightened and he worried about what would happen to his people if he were imprisoned or hanged. Finally, he took a breath and asked.

"And what is to come?"

"My lord Henry is simply using this charade to put me in my place. I overstepped myself and he wishes me to know what he could do if he is displeased with me. I fear you have been caught up in a lovers' quarrel."

The roiling in his stomach lessened a bit as his own suspicions grew. Would Henry go through all of this very public display of giving her in marriage and then default at the last moment? Orrick had signed most of the papers involving the transfer of property and titles and, indeed, had received a portion of the gold promised already. Aye, a king could undo all of that with a word, but would he?

"Henry will call off the wedding today?" he asked, searching for something more. His instincts told him there was much more going on here.

"Of course he will! He loves me and will not give me away to some northern lord who never attends court." She must have seen his look of disbelief for she added, "I was raised as consort for a king, not some...some..."

"Barbarian of mixed blood, my lady?"

Oh, her words had been duly reported to him just after she'd uttered them. He had chosen to ignore them for in the strange situation it was sometimes difficult to discern who said what to whom about whom. The challenge had been offered and accepted—there would be no more of the courtly niceties between them in this conversation. She did not soften her stance at all; indeed she seemed to be strengthened by the fact that he knew how she felt about him.

"Just so, my lord. Surely the king will find a more suitable match for you from among his English nobles. I fear I am far too accustomed to living at court and in my own country that it would make me too sad to move so far from it."

And too far from Henry. Those words remained unspoken, but they echoed in his head as though she had shouted them.

"Is your purpose in telling me this to force me to Henry with a request to call off this arrangement? Is that what you hope for?"

She looked away as though she was not going to answer and then turned back and met his stare. "I was simply trying to save you the humiliation of facing the court at a wedding without a bride at your side. I thought you should know that Henry will claim me and not allow you to marry me as you've been asked to do."

Her voice was soft and he could almost believe that she was sincere. For a brief moment he did believe her, and then a stab of pity tore at his heart as he realized the truth of the matter.

She believed it.

Marguerite believed that Henry would step in and stop the wedding. She was either ignorant of the arrangements already in place, or she was simply denying it to herself. He guessed that, after years of being the king's favorite, 'twas too difficult to admit that she no longer held his affections or that unofficial place of honor within the court. The gossips had not named a new paramour to the king, but it would simply be a matter of time before one was identified and took her place.

How could it feel to have lived less than a score of years and already be considered a castoff? Loved, abandoned and now given away to a stranger. From the look in her eyes and the tilt of her chin, she did not want pity from him or anyone else. So, he would give her none. But as she had warned him, he would offer one of his own.

"I, too, believe that humiliation will be the order of the day, Marguerite, but fear you will feel its bite and not I. I suggest you prepare yourself and protect your heart if you wish to survive it."

She blinked rapidly as though trying to understand, and he knew it was time to leave. He put his hand to the knob of the door and she stepped aside, allowing him to pass without comment.

There was nothing else to say to her. They were both pawns, playing out the moves of the game in front of the Plantagenet court and before the game master himself.

God help them all.

Marguerite smoothed the elaborate gown over her legs and stood motionless as the women crowded around making adjustments to her hair and dress. It did not bother her for she had been raised this way—servants carried out their tasks and nobles took no notice. Apparently they reached that point when they were either satisfied or ran out of time, for a long polished looking glass was positioned before her and she had her first look at the fruits of their labors.

If her eyes seemed a bit too bright or her skin a bit too pale, no one noticed but her. The pale blue satin-and-silk gown and undertunic brought out the creaminess in her skin and the iciness of her eyes. The double-thick length of gold chain that surrounded her waist twice and then rested on her hips reflected the brightness of the many candles in the room. Matching gems and ribbons had been threaded through her hair, which now fell almost past her ankles as she moved.

'Twas appropriate as an unmarried woman to show her hair thus, in all its glory and richness. If the marriage truly happened, 'twould be the last time it would be displayed openly to be seen by one and all. After seeing Henry's reaction to it unbound, and now Orrick's, she began to understand the power of such a feature. She nodded at the servants holding the heavy glass and they took it away.

Her visit with Orrick had been startling in its results. He was not as barbaric as she thought he would be. Tall and muscular, he looked fairly attractive in his court garments. His pale brown hair fell to his shoulders and he wore neither beard nor mustache as many men at court did, and it left the masculine angles of his face exposed. His cool green eyes showed intelligence when they gazed at her, and his voice was deep and rich. In many ways his appearance pleased her. But it mattered naught for she was not for him.

She gave away no sign of her anticipation of Henry's arrival, but she knew he would see her before the planned ceremony. He would explain his arrangements to keep her at his side and everything would make sense to her. She had paid a price for her presumptuous behavior, and now duly chastened, she would return to court as Henry's favorite. The knock at the door startled her from her thoughts. Before she could say otherwise, a serving woman pulled the door open. Her uncle entered, alone, and bowed to her.

Ah. Marguerite understood that her uncle would take her to Henry before the ceremony and put an end to this. Without a word, her mother's brother offered her his arm and they walked through the corridors of one of Henry's favorite palaces. Servants, guests and enemies lined the great hall to witness her fall from grace. Acknowledging no one, Marguerite focused her gaze on a place ahead and walked steadily alongside her only male relative in England.

Sooner than she would have thought possible, they reached the front and climbed to the raised dais. The maid assigned to her on her arrival at Woodstock stood off to her side to assist her as needed. Other than those two people, she was alone.

Uncertain if she should look for Henry, Marguerite gathered her nerve and looked from one side of the dais to the other. Lord Orrick stood with several of his retainers and an older woman who must be his mother. Roger, the bishop of Dorchester, who would perform the ceremony, sat in one of the two chairs placed in the center. She looked to the larger, more ornate chair and finally saw the king for the first time in several months.

He exuded a force of life unlike anyone else she had ever met. In spite of the personal battles he fought within his family and those he waged on behalf of his kingdom, he appeared invincible to her. If his hair was a bit grayer or if his waist had gained a few inches, it did not detract from his appeal.

His piercing gaze captured hers and for a moment

she lost her breath. Marguerite knew that nothing had lessened his desire for her...not the time that had passed, not the babe she bore him and not this farce of an arranged marriage. A smile tugged at the corners of the lips she knew so well and she answered it with one of her own.

She had been a fool to think he would not intervene. Lord Orrick's words earlier had caused her to doubt the man she knew. But now, as she could read in his expression, she still had his love and his passion. He would never give her away.

Content now with how this would end, she let out a breath and relaxed. Of course, when he made his announcement of an alternate arrangement for Lord Orrick, she could not allow the victorious feelings within her to show. While in public, she must behave as a chastened woman so that Henry's pride was satisfied and so that he knew she had learned the lesson he taught.

Lord Orrick now walked to her side. The bishop's clerk began to read out the betrothal agreement to those assembled. His booming voice echoed to all in the great hall and went on for several minutes as their properties and titles were announced. Henry had been generous to both of them or should she say *would* have been generous if the marriage was in truth. This "lord of the north" was to gain much by agreeing to marry her.

A pang of hurt pierced her as she realized two things: that she was nothing to this man Orrick except the gold and titles she brought him, and that Henry had made this bargain overly attractive so Orrick could not refuse it. No nobleman in search of power and wealth could.

Taking a deep breath in and letting it out, she purposely chose another explanation of this agreement, one that made more sense to her mind and her heart—Henry was demonstrating her worth and value to him by the amount he was offering Orrick. Henry would stand and put an end to this soon, but so long as the agreement stood, it was a significant sign of his affection for her.

The sudden silence startled her from the thoughts meandering through her mind and brought her back to the ceremony before her. Marguerite looked up and noticed Orrick approaching her side. Holding out his hand to her, he waited for her to place her hand in his grasp.

She looked to Henry for now was the time for him to speak. He nodded at her, looked only at her, as he did so. She fought the victorious smile that threatened to break out as she nodded back.

"My Lord Bishop," he said, standing now as he spoke, "let the exchange of vows begin now."

Chapter Four

'Twas luck alone that his hand was already offered to her, for Orrick knew that she would have stumbled or, even worse, fallen at the king's words. Everyone on the dais could see the blood draining from her face at his order to begin. For a moment, he even thought she would faint. Now he prayed that her shocked condition would continue through the ceremony, for her legendary biting tongue and fierce temper would not help matters.

Confusion and disbelief filled her blue eyes as he guided her forward. He repeated the bishop's words sealing their marriage and squeezed her hand when her words were needed. Like a trained animal, she stuttered out the vows required. She trembled beneath his hand and he slid his arm around her waist to keep her standing.

Part of him wanted to chastise her for not heeding his words of warning. Part of him wanted to turn and walk away from this devil's bargain. But the duty-bound part within him kept him at her side and even helped her to kneel to receive the bishop's blessing as they were pronounced husband and wife to Henry's court.

Whispers tittered behind them as the crowd knew not how to respond. Orrick stood and drew Marguerite up as the king also now stood once more. Henry clapped loudly and called out to his courtiers.

"Huzzah! Huzzah!" Henry shouted.

The cheering and clapping increased now and was loud enough to gain Marguerite's attention. Orrick knew he would have to get her away from the king and this crowd quickly to preserve any remaining dignity for himself or her. Motioning to his mother, he introduced Marguerite formally and then asked his mother to stay with his new wife. He must speak to the king and gain permission to leave. Orrick had no desire to stay and subject his family to the farce of a bedding or the morning-after fiasco.

He approached the king and asked for a moment in private and then followed Henry to an alcove in the corridor outside the hall. This would be a tricky conversation between king and vassal, between the lover and the husband of the same woman.

"Sire," he said, bowing his head to Henry, "my thanks for your attention to this matter." Henry surprised him by laughing out loud at his words.

"You may not be grateful once the lady regains her ability to speak."

Orrick held his own tongue rather than express his thoughts. His only intention was to save his family and his wife from the open ridicule that would occur if either of them lost control in front of the court.

"I do wish to ask your permission to leave Wood-stock now."

"Now, Orrick? And not stay for the feast I ordered to mark the occasion?"

He hesitated, not certain of how to answer, but then he decided that the direct method was the correct way to approach this personal matter. He dragged his hand through his hair and let out his breath. The only way was man to man.

"Your Grace, we both know the truth of this situation. We both know of your relationship with Marguerite. We both know why you arranged this marriage between the lady and me. There is no need to drag out the public display any longer. All who witnessed the ceremony know and understand the message you gave."

Henry's face turned red and Orrick feared he had spoken too bluntly. "Think you so?" Orrick nodded. "And what, pray thee, was my message?"

"That you are king and your will shall be done."

His diplomatic way of saying that the king would punish any who overstepped their place in his world must have worked, for Henry's eyes lost their angry glare.

"Your party may leave at will, Orrick," the king said as he turned to walk away. "One day you may thank me for the gift I give you now."

Thinking the king referred to his granting permission for them to leave and not face the continued embarrassment of a wedding feast and bedding, Orrick bowed to Henry and followed back into the hall. Approaching his retainers, he gave orders for their departure as soon as arrangements could be completed. Then he faced his bigger challenge. Marguerite.

She stood nigh to completely still, except he noticed that her hands shook in spite of the way she clasped them in front of her. The pale shade of her complexion was unusually gray and the blankness in her gaze told him all he needed to know. Nodding to his mother, who thankfully did his bidding without question, he escorted his new wife from the hall and back to her chambers.

Marguerite did not move from the place where he stopped and neither did she look at him as he called out orders to the servants there. If she knew what was going on around her, she gave no indication. In a way, he was grateful for this shock that enclosed her in its grasp. He had much to accomplish before they could leave Woodstock and the prying eyes of the court and king. Orrick wanted to put as much distance and time between them before resting his head for sleep.

"Mother," he called out, "would you see that Lady Marguerite's belongings are moved to our wagons? She should be packed for the most part already."

His mother moved into the room and began to organize the servants' activities. And still Marguerite stood in the middle of it, looking neither left nor right. Pity for her filled his soul. He could only imagine what it felt like to be so wrong about someone and to discover that truth in front of so many others who awaited your betrayal and downfall.

"Marguerite," he said in a low voice to her. "Marguerite, do you have a maid who will travel with you to Silloth?"

She said nothing and he was about to shake her to gain her attention when a young woman came to his side and curtsied.

"My lord, I am Edmee, the lady's maid. I will travel with her."

"Help your lady change into something that can withstand traveling and be ready in half an hour."

"Yes, my lord," Edmee answered. Before she could step away, Orrick reached out and stopped her.

"Do you speak English?"

"Nay, my lord. Only Norman and French, my lord."

"Prepare your lady now."

Orrick shook his head—another problem. His people, other than his mother and her few ladies, spoke English and a smattering of other local tongues like Gaelic. Was English one of the languages Marguerite spoke? Surely it was.

There was no time to spend fretting over these minor details and so, confident that his orders were being followed here among the women, he returned to his own chambers and found his men efficiently preparing for their trip. Within an hour, his group was on its way out of Woodstock and toward northern England and his home.

If Orrick had known the problems he would face on the road, he might have delayed leaving after all. The weather conspired against them, slowing their progress with days on end of rain and wind. Although the hospitality of local lords was extended to them, his party was unable to travel quickly due to his wife's condition. *His wife.*

Marguerite had not stirred from her befuddled state since their departure from Woodstock. His mother reported that she barely ate or drank at all, and spoke not a word to anyone, including the young maid Edmee. The lady cooperated and followed instructions, but did not do anything more than was asked of her.

Orrick stood from where he'd broken his fast and considered what could be done for the severe melancholia that had beset Marguerite. Although certain that the surprise of the wedding being accomplished and the realization of her situation caused it, he was also sure that the rigors of the road were worsening it. Now, with less than a day's travel left, he felt a small measure of relief and hopefulness that once they arrived in Silloth and once the lady had a chance to accustom herself to her new life, it would all work out. Orrick also knew that, if needed, the village healer was accomplished in her skills.

At his orders, the lady was escorted to him and he helped her mount. His hands slid along from her waist to her ribs and he noticed the change in her form. Taking his place on his horse next to her, he guided hers as they made their way on the road west.

He called on his long-unused skills at diplomacy and court behavior and tried to engage her in conversation. His attempts were unsuccessful. He asked her questions about her family and tried to elicit some information from her about her life in Normandy. He failed. Even his efforts to describe Silloth and his lands and people met with no change in her empty expression.

Still, Orrick talked about what she would see, those she would meet and what was expected of her as lady of Silloth. He hoped some of it would seep through and she would gain some information from it that she could use on her arrival.

Passing by Abbeytown, Orrick rode straight for home. It was just before sunset that their group reached the village outside the keep. The enthusiastic greetings of his people made him smile. He had not realized how uncomfortable he'd been in Henry's court until he caught sight of the open gates of his home. He urged his mount faster and soon they were before the steps into the keep. A glance at Marguerite revealed a gaze that was no longer empty. Now it was filled with horror and she looked around her and back at him.

Before he could dismount to help her, someone pushed through the gathering crowd and reached her first. Orrick did not react fast enough to reach her first. The tall, Scottish warrior lifted Marguerite from the back of her horse as though she were a child and held her out in front of him as he examined her from the top of her head to the bottom of her feet.

Orrick leaped from his horse and stepped over to his friend's side. "Gavin, put her down."

"She doesna look very sturdy, Orrick. Are you sure she's the right one?" His pain-in-the-arse foster brother's evil grin told him that Gavin was enjoying the mischief he was causing. But the expression on Marguerite's face, now gray with fear, concerned him more.

"Lady Marguerite has had a difficult journey, as have we all. Put her down so that I might escort her to the chambers."

Gavin did lower her to her feet, but her legs gave out as she tried to stand. Instead of giving way to him, Gavin scooped her up in his arms and turned to Orrick. Marguerite pushed herself as far from her *rescuer* as she could manage and then did the most unexpected thing.

With a strength that belied her frail condition and petite size, his wife let out a scream that had most of those witnessing the scene grimacing in pain from its loudness and shrillness. Gavin, the instigator of this mess, did not shrink back from it at all. Indeed, he laughed out loud, nearly losing his hold on Marguerite as his body shook with the force of it.

Orrick stepped closer to try to soothe her, but her screams ended on a strangled cry and, as he watched, her eyes glazed over, rolled back into her head as she fainted.

"Mayhap she has a bit of pluck after all, Orrick," Gavin said as he handed the lady over to him. "She'll do."

"You misbegotten cur of a—" Orrick began in a furious whisper.

"Hold your tongue, friend. I wanted only to welcome your wife to your home."

"Damn you, Gavin. If that had been your intent,

you would not have caused this fiasco in front of the entire village.''

Wasting no more time berating his friend, Orrick climbed the steps into the keep, calling out for his wife's maid to follow and giving his own instructions as he went. By the time he'd reached the room adjoining his own, servants followed, bringing hot water, the lady's trunks and food and drink. Orrick laid her on the bed and stepped back so that her maid could attend her.

Exhaustion of body, mind and spirit was overtaking him, as well. Now that they were home, this could all be sorted out. Obstacles that seemed so large on the road would be conquerable now. Orrick turned, deciding that everyone needed some time to rest and refresh themselves.

His steward and his mother waited in the corridor outside the chamber and neither looked pleased. He would hear his mother's concern first then deal with his steward.

Leaning toward her, he asked her quietly, ''What is it, Mother?''

Her answer, in a like tone, could have been shouted at him for the force it carried. ''Is she carrying the king's bastard?''

Orrick reeled back as though struck and he turned back to see Marguerite still prostrate and unmoving on the bed. 'Twas one scenario he had not thought of. Leave it to his mother to come up with it. Well, the truth of her condition would be known with her first menses or with its absence, so he may as well ask his mother now.

"Did she bleed on the trip here?" Orrick rubbed his forehead against the growing pain there. His mother's tight-lipped grimace gave her answer. "I suppose that we must wait to discover that, then."

His mother began to turn away, but with a hand on her arm, Orrick stopped her. Looking at one then the other, he commanded, "Say nothing of that suspicion to anyone here. If word gets out that she is breeding, I will know from whence it came."

He released Lady Constance's hand and held her gaze, waiting for her acceptance of his order. When she nodded, he added, "I suspect that the long journey has simply exhausted all of us and, with some good food and rest, we will all regain our senses."

Both his mother and Norwyn, his steward, nodded again and began to leave, but there was one more thing he needed first.

"Lady Marguerite's maid speaks no English. Can you find someone to help her? Her name is Edmee."

"Doesn't Marguerite speak it?" his mother asked.

"I fear I did not ask her that question when last we spoke. 'Twas not a concern of mine then. Now I suspect that it is not in Marguerite's temperament to teach her servant even if she knows the language."

"None of my ladies will play servant to a servant, Orrick. You must know that."

The pounding between his ears increased and he was certain that his jaw would lock in the clenched position in which he held it for so long. His control was at an end, and just as he took a breath and prepared to let his displeasure show, Gerard spoke from the shadows.

"My lord, I could teach the maid."

Orrick thought on this offer and realized that it was the only way, at least for now. "Fine, Gerard. Show her what she needs to know about the keep and teach her some of our words. Norwyn, she will need additional help, as well. Assign—"

Norwyn waved his hand at Orrick. "Already done, my lord. The chambers were made ready and servants were assigned to see to the rooms and to the lady."

"Fine, then. I need—"

"In your chambers, my lord. Wine and food for you," Norwyn answered. "Hot water for a bath is on the boil and will be ready shortly. And when you are ready, we can review my notes and your orders about the estate."

He could not fault Norwyn for his thoroughness. The man had learned at his father's knee about the duties of being steward and, although still new to the position here, Orrick had found him to be more than competent and resourceful in managing the keep, village and lands of Silloth. Surely the man could hold things together for a short while longer while Orrick bathed and ate.

Back in his chambers, after removing his mail, peeling the sweaty tunic and stockings from his body and sinking into the steaming bath that awaited him, Orrick waved away his servants. As he slid into the soothing heat, he wondered if anything about this marriage would ever work.

Chapter Five

Her eyes would not open.

Marguerite had tried for some unknown amount of time to force them, but her body would simply not follow her mind's commands. Since every bone and muscle and place on her body ached with unrelenting pain, she simply decided that it was not yet time to awaken. The warmth of the chamber and the softness of the mattress upon which she lay pulled her back into sleep's embrace.

The noises of a large group of people wakened her and this time she was able to open her eyes and sit up. Pushing her matted hair out of her face and stretching to remove the painful tightness in her back and legs, Marguerite looked around the large room and realized where she was.

Inside the black tower of Silloth Keep. This would be her prison for the rest of her life.

She slid from the bed and crossed the room to reach the one window in it. A seat with a thick cushion had been fashioned from the alcove surrounding the window and Marguerite sat down there, exhausted from just the few steps she'd taken to reach it. Examining the carvings that decorated the walls next to the window, Marguerite knew that this would be a pleasant place when the sun shone through the window and warmed it.

The walls are ten feet thick in the keep and it is one of very few stone-walled castles in northern England.

She heard Orrick's voice as he told her of his home. All she could think of when she saw it for the first time was that it was once of the darkest and most primitive buildings she'd ever seen. With its square shape and unmarked towers, it looked sinister against the sky behind it.

It was built of stone to withstand the power of the sea over which it stands and the winds that buffet it constantly. A wooden keep could never survive the forces here on the cliff.

Thinking on his words, she leaned closer to the glass to try to see out, but the darkness outside thwarted her efforts. She would need to wait until morning before she would see the extent of her prison. Tears gathered in her eyes and soon streamed down her face.

Why had Henry done this to her? She had pledged her love to him. She had promised to obey his every command. She had given herself, body, heart and soul, to him. She had even acknowledged her sin of overstepping her place with her demands. And still, Henry had not relented in this.

Now, she was married to this northern lord and

taken as far from Henry as she could be in his vast kingdom. What was to become of her now? Out of favor and out of the king's sight, she would be forgotten in the wilds of England and never regain her place in the king's household and court. And some newer, younger, richer, more beautiful woman would take her place in Henry's life and in his bed.

The sobs grew within her and finally, unable to hold them in, she let them out. Sliding onto the floor, she laid her face against the cushion and cried out her sorrow and fears. And when the tears no longer flowed and she was even more exhausted from giving in to the emotions, she fell asleep as she sat.

The noises that woke her next were those of servants moving around the chamber. Marguerite opened her eyes this time to find the strong early-morning sun streaming in through the window and shining on everything in the room. And without remembering how she had accomplished it, she was back in her bed, covered by several blankets. Trunks filled with her clothes lay scattered around the chamber and two young girls worked under Edmee's guidance in emptying them and putting her garments in the large wooden chest. Even though she watched silently, her maid noticed her.

"My lady. You are awake! Have we been too loud in our work? Your lord husband thought it might give you some measure of comfort to have all your belongings settled when you woke."

"Is that what he thought?" she asked. It was exactly what was being done—her clothes were put away and her looking glass, her brushes and hair combs were all neatly arranged on a small dressing table next to the window. She wasn't certain how she felt about it.

"I beg your pardon for not being here when you awoke last eve, but your lord husband ordered me to go the main hall and eat."

Edmee continued to explain her absence, but all Marguerite could do was wonder how she had gotten back to the bed from the window seat. She looked at the two girls who went about their tasks without acknowledging the conversation. They did not understand their language!

"Edmee, do they not speak Norman?"

She watched as the two exchanged a few furtive whispers, but gave no sign of knowing that they were the subject of her questions. But before her maid could answer her, a knock on the door interrupted them. The door opened and servants entered carrying a large wooden tub and buckets of water. With a method that spoke of efficiency, a bath was poured for her, platters of food placed on the table and those who had brought everything were gone without a word. Marguerite blinked several times, almost not believing that it had occurred at all.

The sight of Orrick in the doorway told her she had not dreamed it.

"My lady, allow me to welcome you to my home," he said with a bow. He spoke English, which she refused to acknowledge. Not willing to lose all that she was, she gave him a blank look and waited.

"I had hoped, when I heard that you were gifted

with the ability to speak and read several languages, that one of them might be English,'' he said now in the Norman dialect of her homeland.

She gave a quick warning glance to Edmee so that her servant would not reveal her knowledge and then answered him.

''No, my lord. I speak my Norman dialect as well as *langue d'oil* and *langue d'oc,* Latin and some Greek and Italian. But I do not speak English. I am fluent in those tongues used on the continent, where I expected to live.'' She aimed her words at him and his pride, hoping to remind him of how much this place was not a desirable location in the Plantagenet world.

If her sting was successful, she knew not, for he simply nodded and waved the servants out. Edmee hesitated for a moment but at Orrick's dark expression, she curtsied and left with the others. Then he closed the door.

''My lady,'' he began as he approached her, ''with your obvious gift for spoken languages, I would ask that you learn the one that is mine and my people's. As their lady, you will need to converse with them.''

''I will not be here long enough to worry about such a thing,'' she blurted out. There was a part of her that still believed that Henry was simply drawing out the lesson he taught her and that he had not abandoned her at all.

Lord Orrick stalked her across the room and towered over her, forcing her to tilt her head if she wished to look into his eyes. She did not, so she lowered her chin and turned her head away. All it took on his part was two fingers under her chin and she faced him in spite of her decision not to. He was as strong as he looked, and fighting him would simply leave her bruised, something she did not wish to experience.

"I had hoped that when you awoke from your melancholy state and, after you regained your strength from the long ordeal of journeying almost the length of England to get here, you would realize the folly of your belief. Be clear on this matter— Henry has rid himself of you. He has graciously, as only kings can do, taken his problem and made it my own."

He could not have hurt her more if he had delivered the blow with his hand instead of his words. He understood her deepest fear and her deepest desire and used it against her. Marguerite willed the tears not to gather again, but her efforts were unsuccessful. All she could do was look away from his gaze.

He released her and stepped back. She dared a glance at him now that there was some distance between them. Although his voice had softened with his horrible words, his face and eyes had hardened.

"Marguerite, there is much we will need to work out between us, but there will be time for that. For now, refresh yourself and rest." He pointed to the tub and the food. "Join me at the evening meal in the hall and I will present you to your people."

He did not wait for a response from her, which was probably a smart thing on his part. So many thoughts, so many replies were racing through her mind that she could not have chosen only one as an answer to his request.

Marguerite knew only she did not want to be here. She did not want to be married to Orrick. She wanted to return to the court and seek to repair the damage done between her and the king. But for now, she must bide her time and plan an escape from this unbearable place and marriage.

Orrick pulled open the door and called to her servants to assist her. As they hurried into the room to do her bidding, she caught Orrick's gaze for a moment. The pity she saw there struck at her and she resolved to remove it. Any other emotion was acceptable—anger, disappointment, even hatred. But not pity.

Suddenly exhausted from the exchange of words with Orrick, Marguerite allowed Edmee to take control and soon found herself sinking into the first hot bath she'd taken since the day of her...the day she left Woodstock and the king.

"Is the lady coming to break her fast here?" Gavin asked as Orrick made his way to his chair at the long table. His foster brother was enjoying his discomfort much too much for Orrick's liking.

"She is not," he answered as he sat down. "The lady is still exhausted from the journey. She will join us for the evening meal."

Gavin laughed heartily and Orrick fought the urge to wipe the smile from his face with his fist. Waiting until the servant filled his cup and moved away, Orrick held his tongue.

"'Tis partly your fault for scaring her to death in the yard." He said it, but he knew it for the lie it was as soon as the words left his mouth.

"Did you tell her you were leaving on the morrow?"

"Nay."

"What did you tell her? Did you ask for the truth?" Gavin lowered his voice. "Is she breeding your king's bairn?"

"I did not ask her." Orrick busied himself choosing a chunk of bread and another of cheese.

"What did you say, then? You must get to the truth and soon."

Gavin meant well; he knew that. But the doubts that had plagued him before his marriage plagued him more now, and being questioned over this was not to his liking.

"We had a brief conversation which consisted of the lady offering insult after insult and me trying to ignore and rationalize them."

"I will tell you what she needs. The *lady* needs to be reminded of her dishonor. The *lady* needs to remember why she is here at all. The *lady*—"

"Will learn all those things in good time, friend." Orrick clapped Gavin on the back. "There is no need to crush her into the ground on her first day, is there?"

Gavin did not look certain, as though part of him thought that grinding her resistance down quickly was the best way. But his friend was not cruel at heart and he knew Gavin would support him in anything he did, even taming his wife's unruly spirit.

Before turning the conversation back to his impending visit to the abbey, Orrick drank deeply of his ale.

"I should be no longer than two days at the abbey."

"That long?"

"The journey to Woodstock and back took more time than I expected and there will much to catch up on with Godfrey. Would you accompany me?"

"Are you taking Norwyn?"

"Nay, he will stay here."

"Then so will I," Gavin replied. "After all, I am a hostage here."

"And when did your status as hostage ever prevent you from coming with me?" Orrick noticed the gleam in his friend's eyes and realized his aim. "I do not want her abused, Gavin. Not by my mother and not by you."

Gavin began to sputter a reply, but Orrick stopped him. "She answers to me and to no one else. Do you understand?"

"Aye, Orrick. I do."

"Marguerite is on her own for the first time in her life, with no one to protect her by name or position. She is testing to discover my limits. You know better than anyone that I have them, and so will my wife."

Gavin nodded and the meal was finished in silence. There was much Orrick needed to do before he could leave again, and at least one conversation with his wife that he would rather not have. But as lord of these lands, 'twas his responsibility to carry out his duties, no matter his personal wants or needs. And his oversight of the abbey's lands and lucrative salt lathes was part of that and could not be avoided or ignored.

Orrick stood and took leave of Gavin who was busy flirting with one of the servants. He'd postponed his meeting with Norwyn last evening and now needed to review the records here and give instructions for his absence for the trip to Abbeytown.

All through the day, as he met with his steward, the captain of his soldiers, and discussed the coming harvest with those who oversaw his farmlands to the south, his mind drifted back to the woman in the keep. Drawn by the vulnerability of her soft crying, he had watched her as she sobbed out her sadness. With the door between their rooms opened but a crack, he waited until she fell asleep and then carried her to her bed.

Although he had had his share of women, he was not experienced in the ways of love. He'd search his mind for words to say to her to make her understand Henry's actions, but there were none. She was obviously so much in love with the king that she could not comprehend that his heart, if it ever were involved, had changed toward her. His plans for her certainly had and Orrick understood all too clearly his selection as her bridegroom—good bloodlines, loyal and far enough away to keep her out of the king's sight and way.

Until she accepted that this was not a temporary stay, but her home, there would be no peace between them. Any hopes that Orrick had for a happy marriage depended on *her* giving up her hopes of the king calling her back to him. Lady Marguerite was not about to do that. Not now, and probably not for a long time.

He may not know love, but he knew the ways of the Plantagenets. Orrick's father had watched them before him and, although he had no wish to be involved in the intrigues of the court, he knew them nonetheless. The king was a decisive leader, and once Henry had made the decision to give her in marriage, she was gone from his thoughts and certainly from his heart.

Now, all that had to happen was for her to learn that hard lesson. Tonight's dinner would be the start of it.

Chapter Six

Pride filled his heart as he surveyed the hall. His people had put forth their best efforts in trying to impress their new lady. The rushes on the floor were new and freshly scented with herbs. The tables had been scrubbed clean and everyone present seemed a bit cleaner and shinier to him, as though they had all washed and dressed in their best. Even Gavin had shaved and looked more like an English nobleman than a Scots warrior-chief.

Now, they waited for Marguerite to arrive. She was late for the announced meal time, but Orrick was willing to give her a few minutes. He was drinking his second goblet of wine when she entered.

The wait had been worth it.

No longer the road-weary traveler, Marguerite had chosen a rose-colored gown that complemented her complexion. Now restored by a night and day of rest, she walked confidently to the dais and then up the steps until she stood before him. Her beauty nearly made him jump over the table to reach her instead

of walking around it. Gavin must have known the
impulses surging through him or seen the lust he
knew must be clear on his face, for his friend cleared
his throat loudly and Orrick understood the message.

Control.

Dignity.

Hell!

Orrick strode quickly around to her and held his
breath as she lowered into a curtsy before him, as a
dutiful wife would before her lord husband. He took
her hand and helped her rise, still surprised by her
behavior. He had expected some sulking and un-
pleasantness. Instead the perfect woman presented
herself to him and his people.

He lifted her hand to his lips and kissed the inside
of her wrist, watching her eyes to see her reaction.
Marguerite startled, but not enough that anyone but
he could see it. As she moved to stand at his side,
he entwined his fingers with hers and held on to her
hand. He turned to the others.

"I thank you for your efforts in making this meal
and this occasion a special one. Now, I ask you to
make welcome my...wife, the Lady Marguerite of
Alencon." His voice broke slightly as he referred to
her as wife for the first time before his people. Some
of his servants had been with his family since before
his birth and he felt a nervousness not known before
as he tried to impress them.

Marguerite's gaze met his and he saw the puzzle-
ment there. Then he realized he had spoken in English and she probably had not understood a word of
it except her name.

"My lady, I thanked them for making your first meal in our hall a special one. They have worked hard to make your welcome a good one," he said in Norman. Continuing once more in English for his people, he said, "My lady does not speak our language, at least not yet, and so I ask you for your assistance in making her welcome."

His throat tightened as the clapping began in the back of the hall and spread forward, getting louder as it did so. Some called out her name and some called out "Huzzah." He smiled as he looked at her.

Marguerite lowered her head in an acknowledgment of their welcome and then returned his smile. Leading her to their seats, he was surprised again when she stopped near his mother and curtsied to her, as well. This sign of respect was not missed and the crowd cheered again. Marguerite hesitated only a moment when she caught sight of Gavin, and then she continued toward the center chairs.

Finally, they were seated and, with his wave, the servants first approached with a bowl of water for washing their hands. Then they surrounded the table to place platters of fish and fowl and beef and mutton before them. Warm loaves of white flour bread and tubs of freshly churned butter were delivered to the table, as well. Cabbage and peas, stewed with mustard seed and pepper, and boiled turnips completed this course. Orrick nodded and everyone began to serve themselves, each two sharing a trencher between them. Because of the occasion, Orrick had ordered that the silver platters he owned be used as well as the silver spoons for those at his table.

The meal commenced and he spent his time offering Marguerite the choicest of the foods placed before them. She smiled and accepted them with a grace he had not seen before. Conversations swirled around them and he translated for her. Soon, the main dishes were removed and the cook delivered some treats that he had prepared especially for this meal. A warm tart of apples and pears filled the air with the smell of cloves and cinnamon as it was brought to table. It was his favorite and he told Marguerite of it.

This was proceeding far better than he thought it would and Orrick found himself relaxing as he finished his wine. His wife was a changeable woman. Mayhap she had accepted her fate? Could this work out between them?

With those thoughts, others broke through. He had been aware of her throughout the meal. He noticed the smell of the soap she'd washed with and the softness of her skin when she placed her hand in his. Her glorious hair, wrapped into two long braids, still made his hands itch to touch it. When she leaned closer to share a quiet comment with him, he was sorely tempted to turn his face and take her lips in a kiss.

But one glance at his mother's worried expression and he remembered what he wanted to forget—she might be breeding and he must know before he bedded her. Otherwise, as his mother's words had warned, he would raise the king's bastard as his heir and never know. Another whiff of her enticing scent and the sound of her husky whisper near his ear and

Orrick was not certain that his mother's way was the right one.

She was his wife and any son she gave birth to was legally his heir. Since he had raised no objection to the marriage, he had no recourse but to accept any child she bore as his. And if she carried a child by Henry and he made it known, only he would suffer embarrassment for her role as Henry's mistress was known.

Marguerite raised her eyes to him and he reached over and pushed a stray tendril of hair off of her face. She did not flinch at his touch and even leaned into his hand, turning a casual touch into almost a caress. Heat raced through him and he felt a certain part of his body harden in response to her acceptance. His blood pounded in his veins and he knew that he would have her this night and not wait for an answer to the question his mother had raised.

His bride was no cringing virgin. She knew the ways of physical love and seemed to welcome his attentions. Mayhap 'twas best to get this first joining over quickly so that their fears and nervousness would cease?

Aye. He would not wait. He would have her.

As if she'd read his thoughts, Marguerite leaned closer and spoke to him.

"May I have your permission to seek my chambers, my lord?"

The urge to kiss her grew until he thought he would die if he did not taste her mouth. She smiled and waited for his answer.

Orrick cleared his throat and nodded. "Of course,

my lady. Mother, would you accompany Marguerite?''

Although his mother's face hardened, she nodded and rose. Marguerite stood and curtsied to him. He noticed a blush creeping up from the fair skin of her chest where it was exposed by the cut of her gown, onto her neck and cheeks. He stood and kissed her hand once more and then watched her leave the table and make her way to the stairs that led to their chambers. His mother glanced at him before she followed his wife out.

He knew of his mother's concern, but nothing could change the fact that Marguerite was his wife. He must take this important step in establishing their relationship.

''I guess the lady's temperament has improved with some rest and good food, then?'' Gavin's words interrupted his thoughts.

'''Twould seem so.''

Gavin grabbed his arm and pulled him to his seat. ''You must not appear too eager or you lose your advantage, Orrick.''

''What advantage?''

''You are lord here. Even when hot with lust, you must appear to be in control of your actions.''

''She is my wife and it is my right to have her,'' he answered. Focusing his attention on his friend, he was puzzled by Gavin's words. ''Say whatever it is you hint at.''

''Do not be fooled by the display she presented to you and your people. There is more to her than a biddable wife.''

"And that would be…?" he asked.

"I do not know yet, but tread carefully with her."

"Are you saying you think her a danger to me or to Silloth?" It was absurd, but he had learned to trust Gavin's judgment. "Tell me what you suspect."

Gavin took a deep breath in and let it out, looking around at those still at table and in the hall. Then he shook his head and spoke quietly. "Go. Wear yourself out in her bed. You are thinking with your cock now and my words will mean nothing until you have satisfied your need for her."

He should not have been surprised by Gavin's candid words, but he was. He began to argue, but Gavin stopped him.

"Your pardon, Orrick. Go. May you find joy in your marriage bed." Before Orrick could speak, Gavin grabbed the jug of wine from the table, handed it to him and strode off.

His body reminded him of the woman waiting for him and he took one more look around the hall before leaving. The expressions of his people told him that they knew his condition. With nothing more to do or say, he carried the jug of wine with him and made his way to his chambers.

Her skin itched where he had touched her. Marguerite shuddered as she thought of his mouth on her hand and her wrist and the way he touched her face. Thankfully the meal had ended and, if she could endure the next hour, she would be free of him and his attentions for at least several days. 'Twas the reason she played this game with him now—let him have his way with her and then hopefully she could keep him away while she worked on a way to return to Henry.

She walked up the stairs silently. Edmee and his mother trailed her, whispering words that she neither could hear nor cared about. Soon she reached the third floor and walked into her chamber. Spying the door that opened into his room, she crossed to her dressing table and sat down. Edmee poured water that had been heating in the hearth into a bowl and brought it to her for washing.

The tension in the room grew as her mother-by-marriage remained at the door watching her. Finally, the lady ordered Edmee from the room and closed the door behind her.

"He is a good man, Marguerite."

"Of course, he is, my lady." She turned to face the older woman.

"If you give him but a small opportunity, he could bring you great happiness."

Marguerite forced a smile to her face and nodded. "Of course," she said again.

"But play him falsely and you risk great loss. He has been kind to you, making every effort to welcome you and to accept you in spite of…your past. Do not mistake his kindness for weakness or you will rue the day you underestimated him."

"Have I done something to offend you, my lady? I offer my apologies for my behavior during our journey. I confess that I was overwrought due to the hardness and length of it." She lowered her head and waited on Orrick's mother.

"I am not offended, my dear. I simply offer my advice as one woman to another who understands the difficulty of being the stranger in a new place."

Luckily, a knock at the door interrupted them. Marguerite rose and went to the door, ignoring the hard stare that followed her across the room.

"My lady, my lord Orrick is on his way from the hall."

She waved the servant in and faced Orrick's mother. "If you will excuse me, I would prepare for my lord's arrival."

Lady Constance came close to her and spoke so that the servant could not hear. "I know you are not a stupid woman, Marguerite. Heed my warning."

Shaken by the implied threat, she would not give the older woman the satisfaction of knowing how the words had affected her. Marguerite used the look of startled innocence she had perfected long ago and blinked several times. The sound of Orrick's approach prevented anything else from being said and Edmee closed the door after Lady Constance left.

Orrick's steps continued past her door and she could hear his servant speaking to him. Marguerite stood before the fire and allowed Edmee to unlace her ties and remove both her tunic and the gown beneath it. When the girl reached to lift her chemise, Marguerite stopped her and waved her out.

She had not stood naked before a man in many months and she hesitated to do so now. She slid her hands over her breasts and her stomach and wondered if the changes were apparent to anyone else. Would he know she had given birth? Was there some

way that a man could tell? 'Twas at times like this
that she found herself wishing that she had someone
to ask. Marguerite was so used to depending only on
herself, that it occurred rarely, but still…

The snap of the wood in the hearth dragged her
attention back and she realized that she was not
alone. Turning, she saw Orrick standing in the shadows of the doorway. She could hear his breathing
and swore she could feel his heat as much as that
thrown off by the hearth. She would play on his desire and get this over as quickly as possible. Quick
and over.

Her thin chemise allowed the light of the flames
to pass through it and Marguerite stood so that the
material became transparent. From his indrawn
breath, she knew she was exposed to him. Reaching
her arms up, she lifted her braids and tugged the ties
from them. Shaking her head, she allowed her hair
to unravel behind her. Orrick probably did not even
realize that he had taken several steps toward her. It
had never failed her in the past and it did not now.

He approached her stealthily, like a hunting cat
moving in on its prey. He pulled the loose robe he
wore off and stood naked before her. She could not
help but admire his muscular form and masculine
attributes. He fisted and opened his hands as he got
closer and she shook her head again, teasing him.
She knew she'd been successful when he took her in
his arms and held her so tightly that she thought she
could not breathe. Then he slid his hands into her
hair and wrapped it around his hands over and over
until she could not move.

His mouth was hot and wet and took hers. His tongue sparred with hers and he tasted of wine and lust. Although she stood trapped in his embrace, she was not idle. Leaning against him, she let him feel her body with his. She met his kiss and his tongue with her own and felt his hardness press against her belly. He was breathless when he lifted his mouth from hers and she closed her eyes so he could not see how unmoved she was.

Then, suddenly, he released her and stepped away. The air chilled her now that his heat was removed. Startled by his action, she watched as he looked over her from toe to head and then his gaze focused on her belly and breasts. His breathing was rough and labored and now she found hers matching it. Unable to stop it, her body tingled now under his gaze and moisture gathered in the place between her thighs.

When he had taken several paces back, he spoke. His voice was thick with his lust. "Your pardon, my lady. I allowed my ardor to overwhelm my good judgment."

She could think of nothing to say. Her body thrummed with a pulse she had not thought possible with anyone but Henry. Her plan to stay unaffected was going awry.

"I fear there is something I must ask you before we…" He could not say the word, but she knew what he meant. She nodded. "Are you breeding?"

Of all the things she thought he would ask, this was not one. She expected curiosity about her past with the king. She even expected him to ask of her physical experiences, but this?

"Breeding, my lord?" She met his gaze and saw that it was clear of lust now. He was still erect, but she knew that once focused on something other than the sex to come, he would lose it quickly. Damn! She did not want this drawn out overlong.

"A simple question, surely. Do you carry the king's child?"

"Why would you ask such a thing of me? And at this time?" Marguerite needed to get this back on its path. She sat at her table and began to brush her hair, hoping that he would react to that.

"The unseemly haste in which he accomplished our marriage. Your known past in his bed...or should I say him in yours? His established ability to beget children on his wife and others. All of these things went into my question."

When spoken like that, she felt dirty. And she had permitted no one to make her feel soiled. Her blood pounded in her veins as her anger rose. Marguerite stood and faced him. "And would you believe me if I answered nay?"

He did not answer quickly enough and she threw the brush in her hand at him. He swatted it away without difficulty and took a step toward her. "I think you fear that you cannot live up to what he shared with me. I think you fear I will be comparing you and discovering you less a man than he. I think..."

He was on her in a moment and she knew that she had said too much. He ripped the chemise from her and threw it to the floor. Pulling her into his arms, he touched her everywhere and plundered her mouth, more fiercely now than before. Before she knew what he planned, he walked them to the bed and fell into it without ever lifting his mouth from hers. Turning as they fell, she lay under him now, completely covered by his hard body.

"You are mine now, before God and the king, and I will not share you with anyone," he whispered hoarsely in her ear. "I will be the only man you think of in this bed."

He spread her legs with his knee between hers and she knew that it would be over soon. Orrick was too far into his lust and anger now to stop. His words were bold and exactly what she had expected once she put a name to his fears. She had learned early in her education in life that men hated to be compared to others, especially in bedplay.

Marguerite did nothing to encourage him, but neither did she resist him. He reached beneath her and lifted her hips toward him. But when she thought he would simply plunge inside her, he stopped and looked at her, truly looked at her. In an instant, he changed. Oh, he still wanted to take her, for she could see the lust in his gaze, but he let her hips fall back onto the bed and moved up so that their bodies met hip to hip and chest to chest.

The curly hair on his chest tickled her breasts and she felt the hardness of his thighs on her. He took her hands, entwined their fingers as he had at dinner and held them over her head. His kiss was searing, but so gentle that it scared her. She could accept lust. She could accept his forceful taking of her. But this new gentleness nearly undid her.

He rained kisses on her face and her mouth and then on her neck. Her body reacted, bucking against him and he moved closer and closer to her breasts. Marguerite could not control the moan that tore itself from her as he took her nipple into his mouth, his hot mouth, and tongued it until it pebbled. More sensitive than she remembered, her breasts swelled as he moved from one to the other.

And then, as her body reacted more to each touch of his mouth and his body against hers, he slowed down in his attentions. He would not release her hands and she arched against him, her body offering itself up to him. Finally, he let her hands go and she clutched at his shoulders. But instead of pushing him away, her traitorous hands held him close.

With a slow torturous method, he kissed his way down onto her belly and then her thighs. His cheeks, with the day's growth of beard on them, teased her as he pushed her open to his gaze. Realizing his intent, she grabbed for his head even as his mouth reached its goal.

And she was lost.

He did not stop until she keened out her release. As the sounds erupted from her and the wetness and heat inside spread, he crawled up her body and slid inside her. No force, no haste. Just a gentle push and he filled her completely. She felt every inch of him moving deep within her and yet it felt so different than anything before.

Confused and helpless against him, she opened her eyes and watched him above her. She could tell by the way he increased his movements and by the way his face tightened that he was ready to spill his seed. And with a groan he did. He continued to slide into her and then, spent, he let himself rest on her.

He did not move for several minutes and then he lifted himself out and off of her. He watched her silently for a moment and then began to climb from the bed. This time she tucked her hands under her so that they could not reach for him. She needed to regain control. He could not think he'd won. He could not think that he could simply take her when he wanted. The words, meant to wound, spilled out of her.

''Have you spent yourself for the night or will you want to bed me again as Henry always does?''

Her aim was true.

He staggered back away from her bed and left without a word, the door between their rooms slamming closed. 'Twould be some time before he gathered up his nerve to approach her again.

Marguerite crept from the bed on shaking legs and washed herself with the still-warm water in the basin. Her chemise was torn beyond use so she crawled into the bed naked, pulling the covers up to her shoulders. Her body felt strange, as though it was somehow different than it had been before. As she sought sleep, she thought on how her tactics had worked.

She could deal with his anger. When he nearly forced himself on her, her anger helped her to face him unafraid. It was his gentleness that she feared.

His gentleness would be her undoing.

She would need to guard herself against that or she would truly be lost.

Chapter Seven

Orrick was gone from the keep and the village the next morning when she awoke. Edmee told her that he traveled to the abbey and might be gone for several days.

Marguerite rose and washed and dressed with the help of her servant and then asked for a tray to be brought. She did not want to face his people this morn, especially not that rude Scot or her mother-by-marriage. What she wanted to do was walk outside.

The window seat was a comfortable place now that the morning sun shone down through the window and warmed the alcove and cushion. Peering out the window, she watched as the yard came alive with people. Servants carried on in their duties and the gates of Silloth were open to visitors. If people could come and go, then there was a way to send a message south. Deciding on her course of action, Marguerite told Edmee to find parchment and ink for her to use.

She surprised herself by finishing all of the food

on the tray. She'd expected to be tired this morning and not have an appetite at all. Ah, well, she had survived the night and submitted to Lord Orrick's attentions. Now, with him away from Silloth, she would have time to herself. Time to send a message to Henry and ask for his forgiveness once more.

Taking the quill and sharpening it, she composed the letter to him in her thoughts first. She detailed the horrors of the journey there and then the meanness of this keep and the surrounding lands. Marguerite revealed the lack of the amenities and comforts and entertainments that she was accustomed to in her life with him.

Dipping her quill into the ink once more, Marguerite began the more personal part of the letter, the part that told of how she had submitted to Lord Orrick's attentions and how it had broken her heart to be touched by any man other than Henry. She promised that, though her body had been taken against her will, her heart and love remained only his. Although she had clearly embellished some of her account, she felt in her soul that she did still belong to Henry. Then Orrick's heated words came back to her—*You are mine now… I will be the only man you think of in this bed.*

Her heart protested his claim, but she knew that when he softened his assault, he had commanded her body in a way that frightened her. She had not thought of Henry while Orrick took her. She had thought of nothing. She had only felt. A shudder wracked her body as she realized that her reaction had been worse than simply not thinking of Henry.

This man had pushed all thought, all control from her mind.

Putting the quill down on the table, she pressed her hands to her eyes and thought back to the time last year when she had first voiced her displeasure to Henry over her meaning to him. Oh, how she wished she had never demanded more of him. She wished she could go back and change it, change the complaints she gave and change how she told him of her pregnancy.

All she could do now was make him understand that she repented of her haughtiness and naive behavior. It took her a few hours but when she finished she was quite pleased with the results—two letters written to her uncle and a friend at court, each with a copy of the letter to Henry enclosed. She dare not try to have anything delivered directly to the king from here, so she sent them to two people she knew would support her in this matter.

Finished, she summoned Edmee and asked her to seek out the steward and have these letters taken to wherever the king was residing. A few minutes later, the steward and Lord Orrick's manservant arrived, red-faced and stammering. The steward went through a lengthy explanation about the difficulty of delivering such letters, but since he spoke English, she gave him a blank stare. Even if she wanted to, it was difficult to understand the English that these peasants spoke, due to their thick accents. 'Twas Lord Orrick's servant who realized the problem and he began to translate the steward's words into her language.

"My lady, Norwyn cannot send a messenger to

the king unless Lord Orrick gives his permission. And even then, my lord does not contact the king or his officials unless it is of the utmost importance.''

"And you question my intentions and my need to have these—'' she pointed at the folded and sealed letters ''—delivered to my kinfolk to assure them of my safe arrival here?''

"My l-lady,'' Gerard stammered again after repeating her words to Norwyn and hearing his response. "Norwyn does not question you on this. He but seeks to explain that he can do nothing without Lord Orrick's permission.''

She enjoyed their discomfort for a moment more then smiled at them. "Ah, then there is nothing to be concerned over, for Lord Orrick promised me that I could communicate with my family at any time and as often as I like.''

She waited for her words to get to the steward and smiled at him, daring him to contradict her or prohibit her from sending these letters. The two men looked at each other, clearly not believing her words, but neither was courageous enough to stand up to her.

"Then my son is even more generous in his care of you than I suspected.'' The Lady Constance entered the chamber and nodded to the steward, continuing in English, "If Lord Orrick has promised his wife this, Norwyn, then you must see to it.''

Marguerite held her breath as Lord Orrick's mother scrutinized her and the letters held by Norwyn. Lady Constance broke off her stare and waved the men from the chamber. "When Orrick returns, he can decide on the best way to send any more of Lady Marguerite's messages to *her family.''*

Norwyn and Gerard left and she waited for Lady Constance's true message. Had Orrick confided in her the events of the night before? Although the woman had helped her during the journey, Marguerite felt the anger, hostility and dislike pouring from her. She decided to make the first strike.

''My thanks for intervening with those servants. They had the boldness to question me about sending the letters.''

Marguerite walked to the window and sat down. Motioning to the chair before her dressing table, she invited Orrick's mother to sit, as well. The older woman refused with a shake of her head.

''I have been serving as my son's chatelaine since he gained his titles, but it is your right to do so now. If you would like, I will work with you until you have a grasp of how things are done here at Silloth. As you can see, Norwyn is still new to his duties and needs guidance.''

Surprised by the words and the offer, Marguerite thought about it. If she remained married to Orrick, 'twould be her responsibility to oversee the running of the keep and to see to the welfare of the people. But she did not plan to be here long enough to make such a thing necessary.

''I would plead for your indulgence, my lady,'' she began. ''I am not yet recovered from the journey and would ask for a few more days before doing as you suggest.'' Marguerite met the woman's gaze evenly. ''And I would like to observe this place before I take on those duties expected of me by you, my husband and his people.''

She was not certain if Lady Constance believed her, but the woman nodded and rose to leave. Marguerite stood, as well, in spite of any personal feelings about her mother-by-marriage, for polite behavior had been ingrained in her from her earliest memories. And that behavior had helped her through many difficult and even awkward situations.

''The day is fair,'' Lady Constance replied, nodding toward the sunshine that still filled the room through the window. ''Take advantage of it then. I will send your servant to you, and your husband's, as well.''

She frowned at the words.

''Orrick ordered Gerard to teach your maid English. 'Twill be easier if he guides you through the keep and village since he speaks both your language and ours.''

''I thank you for your consideration, Lady Constance,'' she said, becoming uncomfortable with the kindnesses being offered.

Within a few minutes, she and her small entourage entered the yard and Orrick's servant gave a continuous description of the people they passed and the various buildings they saw as they walked the length of Silloth within the walls to the east of the keep. Marguerite ignored the chatter as Gerard gave the English word for many of the sights around them. She could see that Edmee enjoyed the man's attention as they moved through the yard.

Silloth appeared to be an organized and ordered

place, with its people being in good health and of a lively disposition. Many of the manors and keeps she'd visited in Normandy were not as well kept as this. Lord Orrick was obviously a man talented at maintaining and administering his properties.

Although Edmee and Gerard were still involved in conversation, Marguerite decided that she'd walked enough for this afternoon and announced her intent to return to her chambers. Feeling better, she dismissed Edmee and told her to stay.

"My lady, I will escort you back," the manservant said.

"Nay, Gerard. It is a straight path back to the keep and one I can see plainly. Continue with your lessons with Edmee."

Edmee smiled coyly at the man and blushed. Marguerite understood what was happening here and nodded to them both. Clearly, the differences in their language and origins did not stop the growing attraction between them.

She left them and circled the back of the keep instead of returning directly to it. There, in a smaller fenced-in yard, dozens of men and boys worked with weapons and with horses. Ah, the training yard. She could not see this side of the yard from her window. Walking closer, she watched as some of the more experienced among them worked with sword and shield. Unfortunately, Lord Orrick's Scottish friend was one of them.

The giant had stripped down to his trews and his long, red hair was tied back. He moved with a certain grace that belied his size and roughness of manners.

A skilled warrior, she realized he must be formidable
as an adversary in battle. Marguerite stood quietly
for a few minutes, watching as he took down three
opponents without even seeming winded. Then he
noticed her, for he saluted her with his sword, drawing attention to her presence.

Marguerite backed away a few steps as those
around turned and bowed or curtsied to her. She
waved their gazes back to the men and called out to
continue. Most turned away and watched as the Scot
prepared to face another challenger. Then the words
drifted to her, loud enough for her and many to hear.

"Aye, I would give all the coins I have to get her
into my bed," a man said to the one next to him. "I
bet you she'd be worth every bit of it."

His friend laughed. "Ah, but she's not for the likes
of you or me. She only wants a royal cock to pleasure
her…or at least a noble one." The men laughed
heartily and others nearby snickered in agreement.

She flinched at the ugliness and insult of their
words. So, this was what Orrick's people thought of
her? As she began to turn away, feeling the need to
escape the dirtiness she now felt, her gaze caught that
of the Scot.

Has he seen her reaction? Did he know she understood the words spoken about her? Those men
would only have spoken so if they believed she could
not understand their words. Anger filled her, making
her heart race and her breathing labored. She could
have them whipped for such insults.

In ordering it to be done, though, she would reveal
the lie she had given to Orrick and lessen the advan-

tage she had of knowing what was said about her when everyone thought themselves safe in their words. Before she could react, he did.

Reaching over the fence, he grabbed one man in each of his massive hands and dragged them into the yard where he was. Then, with an efficiency of movement and effort, he pummeled one then the other into the ground. When they lay bruised and bleeding and moaning in pain, he leaned over them and spoke to only them in a low voice. She could not hear the words, did not want to hear them, but knew they were about her.

Not waiting for him to finish and worried that it would be obvious to him that she understood, Marguerite turned and walked away. Although she tried not to appear affected, she knew her steps were hurried. Once in the keep, she returned to her room and sat in the alcove.

Did they not understand? She was not a whore for money. She was the beloved of the king. The wife of his heart. Not some harlot who lay on her back for coin or trinkets. She had been raised to be the consort of a king and there was no shame in that. None at all.

She walked to the table and poured some of the wine there into a cup, drinking it all without stopping. Looking around the chamber, she gazed at the bed, remembering Orrick's words last night.

Now, for the second time in as many days, she felt dirty. And she swore to herself that she would not. These people, these peasants, were of the lower class and did not understand the lives and hearts of royalty.

They did not understand the needs of a king for a woman like her, one who shared his dreams, his love and, yes, his bed. She could not allow them—by their crude words and assumptions—to ruin the beauty of the relationship she had with Henry. She did not answer to them for her past or for her presence here. Marguerite of Alencon answered only to the king.

In spite of the certainty of her beliefs, she did not leave the chamber again for three days.

Chapter Eight

Orrick sharpened the quill for the third time even though it did not need it. For the fourth time he re-examined the latest report on the profit of the salt lathes and the sheep tended by the brothers here. Then he stood, walked to the window in the abbot's office and stared out.

"That is the third time you have looked out the window, my lord. Are you expecting someone?"

Orrick exchanged glances with the monk who then waved his two assistants from the room. When they were gone, Godfrey invited Orrick to sit.

"I would share something with you, Orrick. Something about myself that, although your father knew, you may not."

Godfrey's comment intrigued him. Godfrey had overseen his training and education here when he thought he might join the community. And they had worked together in the years since, inheriting his father's titles, lands and responsibilities. "What is that, Godfrey?"

"When I was young, nigh to your own age, I was a knight and even a crusader. I traveled all over the continent and to the East with my liege lord. I even married."

"Truly? I did not know," he said, surprised that he had not been privy to this information sooner.

"But after my wife's death, I turned my life over to God's service."

"And you tell me this now because…?" Orrick asked.

The monk stared at him for a moment without speaking, as though he expected Orrick to answer his own question. When he did not, he was gifted with a loud sigh from the abbot.

"Because you returned home with a new wife less than a sennight ago, one who, from all reports, is young and beauteous. Because you have stayed here for at least two days more than you needed to be here," Godfrey answered. Then he leaned forward in his chair and lowered his voice. "Because I am more worldly than the previous abbot and more able and willing to discuss matters of…well, matters that involve husbands and wives."

Orrick closed his eyes and shook his head in disbelief at the offer made to him. What could he say to this monk, to this holy brother? He was not even certain how he felt about what had happened between him and Marguerite. No, now he was lying to himself about it. The problem was that he felt too much and did not know what to do next. 'Twas true that he was hiding out here and postponing a return home and the inevitable task of facing a woman whom he wanted to possess in every way possible and whom he wanted to strangle at the same time.

"I...thank you for your kind offer, Godfrey, but..." he began. He was halted by Godfrey before he could say anything else.

"Orrick, I consider us to be friends as well as overseers of the king and church's business interests here. Know that I am here and would keep your confidences, if you have a need to unburden yourself of some troubles."

"I will gather my men and leave for Silloth," he said, standing. "I have been gone too long."

What he needed to do was go home and face the situation with his wife, even if she did not believe she was or would be wife to him for long. As though Godfrey had witnessed the previous conversations between Orrick and Marguerite, he spoke.

"Remember, my lord, that although marrying sight unseen is common in your rank, it creates difficulties that need time to be worked out. Many men respond with force and even violence when faced with a recalcitrant wife, but I would urge you to a thoughtful deliberation before taking any action to correct or reprimand her." Godfrey rounded the table and clapped him on the shoulder. "Going home now is the best idea. 'Tis a better thing to face trouble straight on than to allow it to become a larger problem than what it is."

They walked together out to the courtyard of the abbey and Orrick called out orders to his men. Within an hour, he had received Godfrey's blessings, mounted his horse and began the journey north to

Silloth. Orrick sent a messenger ahead to inform his steward and his wife of his impending arrival by the evening meal. He kept his men to a steady pace on a path that took them toward the Solway Firth and then west on the road that led to Silloth.

His thoughts turned to Marguerite. How had she fared in his absence? He had no doubts that she was being treated well and that her needs were being seen to by Norwyn and even by his mother. The messenger who passed through asking permission to deliver her letters to her family said so. Did she accept her fate and her place as his wife now that they had consummated their vows?

Regret and desire, a frustrating mix, filled him as he remembered her standing before the hearth that night. Although he did not see it then—he could see nothing but her then—he now realized that she had teased and goaded and challenged and insulted and inflamed him into taking her.

Each time he managed to distance himself or regain control, she pushed him further. When soft words and touches did not work, she changed her tactic to blatant enticement. When that stopped being effective and he asked his questions, she answered his insults with her own. When he realized he was taking her with a force unknown to him before and gentled his approach and manner, she delivered a blow to his manhood and his pride that had him fighting the urge to wrap his hands around her neck and squeeze until she breathed no more.

He could see the pattern in her actions, but could not understand her reasons yet. If she was opposed to the marriage and believed it would not last, then consummation was the last thing she should have urged him to. It sealed their vows and made it nigh to impossible for someone of his rank to end a marriage. Oh, kings and queens could command the attention of bishops and even the pope to remedy a hastily made or improper union, but he was a minor lord and that would not happen.

During the hours on the road, he turned it over and over in his thoughts. What were her reasons? And even more puzzling to him, he wondered which Marguerite would greet him on his return. The sullen, melancholy one? The temptress? The angry woman? Or some different facet of her that he had not yet seen?

He only knew that he could not, would not, put up with dishonesty on her part. If she wanted him not in her bed, he would not force his way in. No matter how much he wanted to possess and taste and touch every place on her body. No matter how much more he had hoped for in a wife. No matter what.

Just before dark they approached Silloth Keep and rode through the gates. The time for confrontation and truth between them had arrived.

He waited for his horse to be taken and then entered the keep with his men. The sounds and smells coming from the hall told him that dinner was ready. He took in a deep breath and let it out. 'Twas good to be back in his own place. Pausing for a moment in the chamber outside the hall, he loosened the armor he wore and allowed one of his servants to slide the chain mail over his head and off. Using water from a bucket offered by another servant, he splashed his face and head and wiped himself as clean as he could.

Unwilling to make his people wait on their meal any longer, he strode into the hall, greeting villagers and servants as he made his way to the dais. He tried not to notice the woman sitting next to his chair, but he could not help himself. Even from this distance, Orrick could tell that she was pale. Her face held no expression, but she did meet his gaze and nodded to him as he moved closer.

Marguerite stood with the others at the head table as he climbed the steps and waited for him to reach his seat before sitting back down. His mother sat on his right and Gavin to hers. Their faces gave away nothing of how the past four days had gone. He let out a breath and called to begin serving the meal. After the somewhat meager meals at the abbey, he looked forward to a more filling repast. His cook did not disappoint him.

This was the fare he was used to—hearty stew, bread, cheese and some sweets to end it. He drank ale instead of wine because that suited him, as well. With his silver safely stored away, they all ate from wooden bowls. Orrick felt no need to put on a display every night for only his family, retainers and people.

He glanced at Marguerite as she sat quietly at his side, accepting food and ale from him with murmured thanks. She did not initiate conversation, but she answered any questions asked of her. She seemed to pick at her food, not eating much and drinking less.

Was she as nervous about facing him as he was about her? Or was there something else at play? Finally, when everyone had their share, he pushed back his chair and stood, holding out his hand to her. She hesitated, dabbing her mouth with a napkin, but then she took a breath and stood, now meeting his gaze with her own. Was it fear he saw in her eyes? Gavin stood, as well, and approached him. Orrick was watching Marguerite and observed the color drain from her already-pale cheeks.

"I would speak to you, Orrick," Gavin said.

"In the morn. I am tired and wish to retire now," he answered.

"In the morn, then." Gavin spoke to him but looked at his wife as he agreed.

Marguerite met Gavin's eyes for the merest of moments, but 'twas long enough that he spied it. He led her off the dais, down the corridor and up to their chambers. Orrick allowed her to enter her room first and then closed the door behind them. She continued to cross the chamber and stood next to the window. The silence grew until he asked the question that had bothered him all the way from the hall to this room.

"What is between you and Gavin?"

"There is nothing between us, my lord," she answered quietly.

"Gavin and I have been friends since we were boys. I fostered with his family and then, when the king took back Carlisle and this area, he was kept here as a hostage against further aggressions on his clan's part. He stays now as a friend and captain of my soldiers. We have no secrets between us and I value his counsel and his honesty over anyone's.''

Orrick walked closer and Marguerite stepped back until she could move no more. ''Well, my lady? Do you tell me or do I hear it from him in the morn?''

What could it be that she was so frightened? Gavin would never betray his trust—he knew that implicitly—but he did not trust Marguerite. Not yet. Suddenly she looked ill to him and he was tempted to go to her. But he waited for her explanation.

''I can speak your English,'' she said in halting and accented English. ''Your friend knows it and will tell you in the morn if I do not.''

Frowning, he shook his head. ''This was something you had to hide from me? Was it so important you had to lie to me over it?''

Marguerite shook her head. ''Not so important.''

Orrick felt his anger build. He knew it was about more than just her lying over speaking his language, but he could not tamp it down. He gritted his teeth and glared at her. ''Did you think to make us all look foolish as we tried to help you? All of my people have tried to make you welcome and all you can do is lie to us?''

''I do not wish to be here, my lord. Can you not understand that?'' Her voice was soft and pleading, however all Orrick could hear were her insults from the other night.

''You have taken every opportunity to make that clear to me and to my people. I will not accept your dishonesty, lady.''

He took the final steps across to her and grasped

her shoulders. Before he could tell her that he expected an apology in the hall in the morn, she did the most unexpected thing—dropping to her knees, she rolled herself into a tight ball, protecting her head with her arms. Blinking in surprise, he stepped back as she cried out to him.

"Please, my lord. Please do not hit my face. Not my face."

She curled up tighter, if such a thing were possible, and he thought he could hear her crying. He had never hit a woman in his life, never raised a hand to one, so her belief that he would do so shocked him to his core. Had Henry mistreated her in this way? Although the king's womanizing behavior was well-known, Orrick had never heard any rumors that Henry beat his women.

His touch on her shoulders made her whimper, so he let go and moved away. After a few minutes, she finally dropped her arms and looked at him. Her body shuddered and her breaths hitched as she continued to watch everything he did.

"Although it would be my right, I have no intention or desire to hit you."

Marguerite nodded. "I just want to go back. I do not belong here." Her words were soft. Not a challenge but a simple declaration. He did notice that she still spoke in English.

"It is not in my hands, Marguerite. We both follow the king's orders." He walked over and sat on her bed. This was his chance to ask what he really wanted to know. "If you hoped for an end to this marriage, why did you…why did you encourage a consummation? Our vows, though unwanted on your part, are now valid before the law and the church.''

Confusion filled her eyes as she seemed to search for words to explain her actions to him. ''I knew you wanted me. I wanted it over quickly. If I had to share my body with a man other than Henry, I simply wanted it over.''

Pity filled him. The saddest part for her was that he would never have laid a hand on her if she had not signaled her willingness that night. In her misguided haste, she had caused exactly what she feared and hated the most—possession by another man. Marguerite was her own worst enemy, bringing about her own downfall.

Did he tell her? Would she understand the foolishness of her behavior if he did not? Orrick stood and walked to the door that stood between their chambers. Facing her, he spoke softly, knowing it would not lessen the blow to come.

''The other thing I have never done and will never do is to take a woman by force. If you had but said the word, if you had objected in any way, I would never have taken you that night,'' he said. ''And I will not again.''

Orrick pulled the door closed behind him, not waiting for her reaction to the truth. The sound of her sobs echoed across her room, through the closed door and into his heart, like a dagger twisting itself deeply.

Orrick did not recognize the sound at first. Disoriented from just falling asleep, he pushed himself up on his elbows and listened again. The moans grew stronger and louder and he climbed from his bed and waited.

The noise came from Marguerite's chambers.

He walked to the door between their rooms and pushed it open a crack. The fire in the hearth was low, but he could see her in the bed. Still wearing her gown, she lay curled and moaning. Orrick approached quietly for he realized that she cried out in her sleep. He walked to the side closest to her and leaned over her, pushing her hair away from her face.

Tear-swollen eyes and pale cheeks. He did not like her color. Now that he thought on it, she had been pale at dinner, as well as during their...discussion.

"Marguerite?" he whispered. "Are you well?"

Her eyes fluttered open and met his. Confusion and pain filled them. "I am ill, my lord. I am not..." Her words drifted off even as her eyes closed.

He brushed his hand over her forehead—thank God no fever. 'Twould take too long to rouse Brother Wilfrid to see to her so Orrick decided to call on his mother. Running back to his room, he grabbed his robe and threw it on, tying it as he made his way down the hallway to his mother's chambers. Knocking on her door, he soon had her awake and accompanying him back to Marguerite.

Standing aside as she examined Marguerite, he waited for some word of her condition. He discovered that he was not a patient man. What could be the matter with her? Was she ill? Or was she...? He could not even think the word in his thoughts. Were his mother's suspicions correct? After a few more minutes, the lady Constance returned to where he stood.

"Is she…?" He could not say it.

"'Tis a woman's illness, Orrick. She is in pain."

"Did I do this? Did I cause this when…?" He stopped as he remembered to whom he spoke. He was not going to discuss his relations with his wife…with his mother.

His mother frowned at his questions and then shook her head. "You could not have caused this. 'Tis her monthly. Marguerite said she has difficult fluxes. I will get her a heated stone to help her pain, and some of my sleeping draught. 'Twill get her through the night."

Orrick let out a breath. For a moment he worried that his strenuous possession of her had injured her in some way. But instead, this answered his question—she did not carry the king's child. Still standing by the door, he waited for his mother's return. Marguerite was awake, but no words were spoken between them.

Soon after his mother returned, Marguerite was dressed only in her chemise and held a heated stone wrapped in cloth against her stomach. After drinking the mixture brought by his mother, Marguerite lay silently on her side facing the now-stoked fire. With nothing else to be done, Orrick went back to his room. She would feel better in the morning. Just as he moved to pull the door closed behind him, he noticed her shivering.

Something in her called out to him and he found

himself climbing into her bed and sliding next to her. Maybe it was pity. He knew not and did not wish to know. She protested with a weak moan, but he settled himself under the covers and held her close.

"Let me just warm you, Marguerite," he whispered. "I want nothing more than to hold you."

She seemed to accept his offer of comfort and soon he felt her relax in his arms and her breathing became slow and even. As he drifted off to sleep, he realized that he had seen a completely different side of his wife.

What would the morrow bring?

Chapter Nine

Marguerite opened her eyes and stretched her limbs to test her body. The pain of the night before was gone, and although her courses were still upon her and would last several more days, she knew the worst was over. As she lay on the bed, she decided that the morning sunlight streaming in through the window was truly the best part of this keep and this room.

The sun was too high for morning. From its position near the top of the opening, it must be close to sext. The day was half over! Pushing back the covers, Marguerite called out for Edmee. As she put her feet to the floor, she realized that so much had happened the night before between Orrick and her.

"My lady! How do you fare this day?" Edmee was cheerful as usual and brought her a cup of ale. "My lord ordered that you should be undisturbed until you were ready to rise." The servant helped her from the bed and brushed her hair once she was seated at the dressing table. "I can call for a tray for you, if you are hungry."

Marguerite found she did not have to say a word for Edmee carried on the conversation without her. Soon though, through the maid's efficient services, she stood washed and dressed with her hair braided and veiled. Food held no attraction to her so she finished the cup of ale.

"Lady Constance has asked that you join her in the solar if you feel well enough. Her ladies are working on a new tapestry for the hall and she thought you might help them."

"Where is Lord Orrick?" No sounds came from his chamber, but in the middle of the day, he would not likely be there.

"My lord is about his business. If you have need of him, I could send someone for him."

"Nay. I would not disturb his work."

Marguerite thought back to what she could remember of last night. By the end of the meal she was feeling the effects of the onset of her courses. The nausea and stomach pain increased, but she managed to stay upright in her chair while Orrick finished his meal.

The Scot had made things worse, approaching Orrick as he had and letting her know with a glance that he would spill the secret he knew she had. How would Orrick have reacted if the truth came out in the hall? He had not beaten her as she had expected and prepared for as they'd walked to their chambers.

He was an enigma to her. She insulted and rejected him and he simply walked away. She lied to him and to his people and he did not punish her.

What kind of man was he?

He was nothing like her father, who met her resistance and headstrong behavior with firm discipline and a liberally applied cane. Nor was he like Henry, whose temper could flare at any moment and cause retribution, exile or imprisonment to be rained down upon even his most loyal subject.

She realized as she made her way to the solar that Orrick did indeed have a punishment of his own—the look of pity in his eyes when he told her of her error in judgment was enough to tear her soul apart. The beating she'd expected would have been easier to bear than the expression on his face when he said he would never have touched her without her consent.

In her efforts to be aloof and to control him, she had lost. Instead of remaining faithful in heart and body to Henry and the vows of love they shared, she'd held Orrick up against the other men she knew and had misjudged his lust and drew his touch needlessly.

Marguerite reached the door of the solar and the servant standing outside opened it for her. The room was large, and light streamed into it from not one, but two windows. A number of women worked on the looms, some on the embroidering racks, some on smaller pieces in their laps. Lady Constance called to her and motioned to an empty seat.

She took it silently and examined the work they were doing. The quality was exceptional and when finished it would complement wherever it was hung. Her skills with a needle and thread were passable so she did not fear embarrassing herself. She accepted one from one of the ladies and began working on the area in front of her, checking with the sketches of the finished drawing from time to time.

The chatting between the women ebbed and flowed and it was during a lull that she noticed one woman off to the side with a babe on her lap. The soft sounds of sucking drew her attention and she could not look away. The woman cradled the babe's head and sang quietly as the child suckled at her breast, and for a moment Marguerite would swear that her own breasts tightened and tingled.

She had not nursed her own babe, not even briefly, for she was more concerned with losing the milk and getting back to court. A wet nurse had done the duty for her and, until this moment, she had given no thought to what she had not done for her child.

Lady Constance must have seen her watching the scene, for she spoke to her. "That is Lady Claire. Her daughter is called Alianor."

"How old is the babe?" she asked, the words escaping before she could stop them.

"She is almost six months old now, my lady."

The same age as... Marguerite stopped herself now. Pushing away the thoughts that threatened, she nodded and leaned back to the work before her.

"How do you fare, Lady Marguerite?" Orrick's mother asked.

"I am better today, my lady. I ask your pardon for disturbing your sleep last night."

"Men so often have no idea of how to deal with *our* complaints. Orrick did the right thing coming to me rather than Brother Wilfrid."

The women all laughed at her comment. "My thanks for the draught you brought," she replied. She was grateful for the assistance in the night—to Lady Constance for coming to her aid and to Orrick for…the comfort he offered, as well.

The loud burp from the babe drew all their attention for a moment, but Marguerite's gaze lingered once more on the mother and child. Now fed, the babe began dozing on the woman's shoulder. How did that feel? Had her… No! She must not allow herself to dwell on that.

"I know many women whose monthly courses are lessened after the birth of a baby," Lady Constance offered. From the lady's expression, it was a hint and an encouragement to the wife of her son rather than a general comment. "The pains and illness can be much easier to bear after childbirth."

The sudden attention was almost too much for her. Marguerite knew that an heir was the first responsibility of a wife and that most of those in the room expected it of her. Lady Constance and mayhap only her closest confidante knew of the true situation between Orrick and her.

Part of her wanted to strike out and disabuse them of their false expectations. But memories of Orrick's treatment of her held her tongue. They would all know the truth soon enough when Henry called her back. There was no reason to make it their concern now. And she had no wish to embarrass him before his people.

"So I have heard, as well, my lady," she answered. Lady Constance turned her attentions back to the tapestry and Marguerite knew she felt confident that her message had been received. Over the next few hours, the women talked to her of their husbands and their lives, and most spoke in Norman. A few spoke in English and Lady Constance herself translated the words.

"My lady," Marguerite said in English. "I have informed Lord Orrick that I can speak in your English."

Although the others looked surprised by her announcement, Lady Constance did not. The Scot must have confided in her or Orrick had. "I cannot speak it well and have difficulty understanding some of it. But I am able to understand the words if spoken slowly. And I would prefer to speak in my own language since you all know that."

"My son has always favored the English of his upbringing rather than that of his Norman one. He prefers that we speak in English to aid your learning of it."

The challenge had been made.

The rules were set.

Everyone in the room waited for her objections or her acquiescence in the matter. Unwilling to give in and unwilling to make a scene, she stood and told Lady Constance—in Norman—that she needed a bit of air. Motioning to Edmee, she walked from the solar and left the keep with her maid trailing behind her.

"So, how did you know?" Orrick asked as he and Gavin crossed the training yard to observe two men working with quarterstaffs.

"I simply watched her reaction to words spoken around her. Although she controlled herself most of the time, the lady slipped up a few times."

"But, Gavin, what made you suspect her of dishonesty? You know her not." Orrick called out directions to the men fighting and waited for Gavin's explanation.

"She has grown up in and around the king and his court. Subterfuge, deceit and dissembling are in their natures."

"Harsh words about my wife," he said, noticing the frown that crossed his friend's brow. "Am I never to trust her?"

"She must prove herself worthy of that trust before you give it, Orrick. Anything else will lead to nothing good."

He paused again to instruct the soldiers and then turned to face Gavin. "Has she no good qualities? Does her past color everything about her now?"

"Do you ask this to convince me or yourself?"

"Neither. I seek but to understand her. In each encounter, I see a different facet of her and do not know which is truly her." Orrick dragged his hand through his hair, pushing it out of his face. "I think there is good in her, but that she has been taught and rewarded for behaving in certain ways."

Gavin snorted. "I would say so. The king had his uses for her and she—"

Orrick waved him silent. "I refer not to her skills in bed." Actually he did not want to think about that. The image of Marguerite beneath him, naked and writing in passion, was too powerful. "Her father raised her as the pawn he needed to remain close to Henry. She was groomed for the position and believes it was her due."

"As are most noble and all royal women raised to be," Gavin answered. "'Tis the way of things in your world, whether English or Norman or French."

"And you Scots? Are your women not used in marriage the same way? And sometimes outside of marriage?" Gavin glared his answer and Orrick continued. "She is not so different than other women."

"Except that she is your wife. And she is more intelligent than any woman I have ever met. 'Twas a brilliant strategy to keep us believing she could not understand our words. It enabled her to learn much about us and yet she gave away nothing about herself."

"I have learned some small things about her. I do not claim complete understanding yet. But I will. Given time, I will learn the rest of her secrets."

Orrick nodded as the men finished their exercises and moved out of the way so others could try. The next two on the field looked as though they had already been at the receiving end of a lesson, for they both wore blackened and bruised eyes and several gashes on their faces.

"Are you certain you wish to know them, Orrick? And will she learn yours?"

"My secrets? I have no secrets, Gavin."

He paused and waited. They watched these two stumble across the yard and avoid hitting each other more than they attempted to hit. Something was wrong here.

"The widow Ardys? Although you are discreet and even your mother knows not of her, some do. What will your new wife think of the mistress you keep?"

Gavin's words startled him, for Ardys was not his mistress—he considered her a friend and a companion. They were even bedmates at times. But he did not keep a mistress. Before he could argue to point, Gavin was over the fence and running toward the two men. Orrick followed to discover what was going on.

The men, seeing Gavin's approach, ran to Orrick and dropped to their knees. Gavin called out for them to be gone, but they did not move.

"What goes on here? How did you get those welts?" Orrick pointed to their faces, but they looked at Gavin. "How?" Orrick demanded.

"I did it, my lord," Gavin answered.

Confused, Orrick looked to Gavin for an explanation. The men paled even more.

"Why?" Orrick put his fists on his hips and waited. Something serious must have happened for Gavin to beat these men. "When?"

A crowd began to gather and Gavin looked worried. "My lord, let us continue this inside."

"Gavin… I trust you to oversee my men when I am not here. Explain it to me now," Orrick ground out harshly. The bile in his stomach threatened to overflow, for if Gavin raised his hands against Orrick's own men, it was a serious matter.

"They insulted the Lady Marguerite the day you left for the abbey."

"What did they say?"

Orrick stood motionless waiting to hear. The blood pounded in his head. He could only imagine what rumors and tales were going around his village. If anyone had heard his mother's pronouncement the day of his betrothal, they knew the truth about Marguerite.

"My lord!" the man Thurlow called out. "We meant nothing by it. We was just talking. We meant no insult." He reached out for Orrick's tunic, pleading, "Please, my lord."

Orrick looked at Gavin and realized in that moment that whatever they'd said, it had been heard by Marguerite and anyone else in the yard at the time. And that their words had startled her into giving away her secret to Gavin, who must have observed her reaction and known she understood the insult.

"She heard them?" Gavin nodded. "She understood?" Again his friend confirmed his fear. "Summon François and tell him to bring two whips," he called out to one of the soldiers in the yard. "Tie them to the fence now," he ordered.

His anger increased as he waited for his orders to be carried out. Soon, the yard was surrounded by villagers who had already heard of the ruckus. Good, they should all know what would befall them if they spoke against Lady Marguerite.

In spite of her past, in spite of her current denial of its permanence, she was his wife and their lady. An insult to her was an insult to him. As much as he worked to rule his people without cruelty or abuse, there were times when physical punishment must be used, and it was his role as lord to mete it out. And he hated it each time. He would not shirk from it, though.

When all was in place, he gave one of the whips to Gavin and one to François, the captain of the keep's guards. Calling out in a loud voice, he informed them of the punishment he'd decided on.

"Fifteen lashes each for the insults given to the Lady Marguerite. Give the first ten now," he ordered.

Although the crowd whispered and murmured, he said nothing as his decree was carried out. He stood, stone-faced, with his arms crossed over his chest, and watched each stripe. The men pulled against their bonds and writhed in pain as each lash was delivered. At ten, Gavin and François paused and looked to him.

"As husband of the woman defamed and as lord of this manor, I will give the last five lashes to each so that they and you all know that she is my wife and I will protect her person and her honor."

He hated this, but he knew he spoke the truth. He had to defend her; she was his wife and her dishonor would be his. As lord, he could not allow this behavior to happen again. Losing respect for her, they would lose respect for him, and only his response to such a challenge would maintain the power he held as lord.

Orrick lifted the whip given him by Gavin and shook it to gain the feel of it in his hand. He turned away from the men and flicked it toward the empty yard, loosening up his arm to begin. Turning back to deliver the rest of the prescribed punishment, he was shocked to find Marguerite standing between him and the men.

Winded, she had reached the yard just as Gavin and the other soldier finished counting out ten lashes to each of the men who had said the cruel words about her that day in this very place. Marguerite found an opening in the crowd and climbed between the wooden slats of the fence to reach Orrick. He did not see her as he claimed his right as husband and lord to defend her honor, but she ran to stand between him and his targets.

Unsure of why she wanted to intervene, she was not prepared for the emotions that moved across his gaze when Orrick saw her there. Anger, surprise and a deep sadness were etched in his expression. But not pity. At least there was no pity as he gazed on her now.

"My lord, I would ask for leniency for these two," she called out as she moved closer to him. "'Tis your right as lord to punish as you see fit, but still I ask it."

With his free hand, he took hers and pulled her closer. Whispering so that only he could hear the words, she continued. "They but spoke the truth, my lord. They said nothing more than you have said or thought about me."

"You would defend them? You heard their words?"

She caught Gavin's gaze and nodded to Orrick. "Aye. I heard them."

"And still you ask for mercy for them?"

Marguerite did not comprehend the reason behind her request, but she knew that the results of Orrick's punishment would be more harmful than good. She knew that she had to stop him from making this worse. The men involved would hate her, not him. Their families and friends would hate her. And somehow worse, she knew that Orrick would not forgive her for forcing his hand to this or himself for carrying it out. Even though she had thought about demanding it at the time and even though she had not asked for it now, she could feel that this would hurt him.

And she did not want to hurt him.

She bowed her head to him. "Mercy, my lord."

He stood still for several minutes and then stepped around her, walking toward the two tied men. He lifted the whip and delivered one more stinging lash to each of them before dropping it to the ground.

Now he bowed to her. "As my lady requests— leniency is granted." She watched as he strode from the yard, his people clearing a path for him. Others watching ran to assist the men who groaned in pain as their backs bled.

There was no one for her. None of his people approached her or spoke to her or even looked at her as she walked slowly back to the keep.

She was completely alone.

Chapter Ten

The hall was more silent than she could have imagined while holding so many within it. The castlefolk who took their meals with the lord were present. The lord's retainers and their wives were present. The lord's family was present. Only the lord was missing.

Although she'd have liked nothing more than to retreat to her chambers, Marguerite sat in Orrick's chair at the table and gave the order to begin serving the food. Orrick, Norwyn had told her, would not be at dinner this night and, as lady of the keep, 'twas her responsibility to oversee the meal.

She did not want to be lady here. Truly, she wanted nothing so much as to be gone, but after Orrick's public defense of her earlier today, she had no choice but to sit at his table and represent him to his people.

The servants brought out steaming pots of another stew and ladled it into the wooden bowls at each place. The plain fare was the same as it had been every night here after her first one. Her stomach, never settled during this time of the month, rebelled at the sight and smell of the fish pottage placed before her. With both Orrick's mother and people glaring at her, she dipped her spoon in the concoction and brought it to her mouth. At that signal, those below began their own meal. It was the last thing she put in her mouth through the meal other than a few pieces of dry bread.

Passing bowls of the stew, sharing their bread and cheeses and jugs of ale brought an end to the silence, but the hall was not the jovial, loud place that it usually was. From time to time, Marguerite noticed their furtive glances at her. No one would meet her gaze so she attempted to speak to those near her at the table. It did no good, for they engaged in their own conversations and did not involve her in them.

Impolite though it was, she tried to listen to their words and to catch the meaning or directions of their discussions. Through their thick English, she detected that the men spoke of fighting and working and the weather. The women spoke of needlework and family concerns and the weather. Each time she thought to try to offer a comment, the topic changed and she struggled to follow.

Being ignored was something new to her. Growing up, she was her father's hope for an alliance with the royal family. Although her father's legitimate son and heir would control their lands, titles and wealth, she kept her family in the center of the social state of affairs at Henry's court. With Henry, she was the acknowledged lady of his heart and anyone who wanted to gain access to him went to her. Here, she was the outsider with no true power or influence, and certainly after today, with enemies she could not see.

When it appeared that everyone had had their fill, Marguerite motioned to Orrick's man, Gerard, and she waited for his approach.

"Do you think Lord Orrick is coming at all, Gerard?" she asked softly. Gerard's face flushed and his gaze moved to several at the table. She knew without looking who he looked to for guidance.

"Nay, my lady," he answered in English. "My lord was quite clear that he would not return for any part of the meal."

"And he went where?" she asked.

If his face could turn a brighter crimson, she would be surprised. He stammered and began to answer her three different times before letting out his breath. "I could not say, my lady."

Marguerite heard the true answer in his words— *we all know where he is but we will not reveal it to you.*

"Very well. If everyone is finished, I will retire." She stood, and those in the hall did, as well. "Have a tray ready for Lord Orrick upon his return, Norwyn."

The steward bowed at her command, but they both knew it was a barely hidden insult. To intimate that the steward had to be reminded of his duty said he was not carrying out his responsibilities. Marguerite did not understand why she felt the need to strike out, only that something inside her hurt at being the outsider.

She nodded to Edmee and walked off the dais and

up the stairs to her chambers. Pausing before Orrick's door, she heard nothing inside to reveal his presence. So, he had not simply retired early. As she entered her room, she realized that the Scot had not been at supper, either. She suspected that wherever one was, the other would be, as well. The door opened and Marguerite expected Edmee to help her undress, but Lady Constance spoke instead.

"You did not eat."

She was worn-out from the day and her flux and did not now want a confrontation with Orrick's mother. Neither did she want to explain her every action.

"My thanks for your concern, but it is unwarranted. I had enough." She busied herself rearranging the brush and hair combs on her table.

"You ate nothing this morn and nothing through the day. I sent Edmee to the cook for some broth that may sit better in your stomach than the food prepared for supper."

Marguerite was amazed. The lady knew and had taken steps to see to her welfare. Her own mother had died giving birth to her and the only attention of a personal nature she'd received from her father's household was what was necessary to prepare her for her future role. She turned to face Lady Constance. But she could not think of a thing to say.

An uncomfortable silence encircled them until Edmee's steps and voice could be heard. She was speaking to someone as she walked and, peering out the door into the corridor, Marguerite saw that that someone was Orrick's servant. When the man noticed her watching, he stepped aside and allowed Edmee into the room.

Edmee curtsied to both of them and placed the tray on the table. Before Marguerite could say so, Lady Constance waved the girl from the room. "Please eat while it's hot, Marguerite."

Her stomach growled before she could refuse, and since she was hungry, she pulled the stool over, sat and ate the steaming broth. Tiny bits of carrot and barley floated in it, but it was not as thick and overpowering as the fish stew had been at dinner. Orrick's mother walked to the window and stood quietly. Dipping small pieces of bread into it, the broth both filled yet settled Marguerite's stomach and she finished it quickly. Drinking a small amount of ale, she looked over at Lady Constance's stiff back.

"I must speak to you about what occurred today."

"Lady Constance, I am tired and not feeling well and would like to retire. Candidly, I wish not to speak of it at all, but if you feel we must, could it be on the morrow?"

Marguerite walked to the bed and sat on it. Truly, she wanted to climb under its many layers of blankets and furs and stay there for days. Tugging off the veil that covered her hair, she waited for the lady's response. It shocked her when it came.

"'Tis my fault that those men insulted you."

Their gazes met and Marguerite read the guilt there.

"When my son announced his betrothal to you, I spoke unwisely and in front of others. If I had kept my counsel or spoken to Orrick privately, no one would have known of your past.''

Stunned, she felt tears burning in her throat and eyes. Never had anyone apologized for speaking behind her back. She'd heard all the insults—king's whore, bitch of Alencon and many others—but no one ever acknowledged using them to her. Now, this proud woman did. What could she say?

''I have spoken to Orrick about it and have made it clear to those women who serve me that I was wrong. If you think there is something else I can do to prevent any more damage, tell me.''

Marguerite had never felt this unsure of herself or of how to proceed. She nodded and looked away. ''What did Lord Orrick say?''

''He only acknowledged my womanly weakness to misuse gossip and asked me to apologize to you.'' The lady drew closer. ''He was concerned that you would blame yourself for what he did to the men involved.''

Confused, Marguerite shook her head. ''But Orrick is lord here and no one can question him. He can punish as he see fits, no matter the person or cause. He is…a peculiar man.''

''True. But his upbringing was different. His father insisted that the prior at the abbey train him even as he learned from his father. He is a deliberate, thoughtful man, one who is slow to anger, but does not waver from doing what is necessary.''

''Where is he? Where is Lord Orrick now?''

Lady Constance hesitated in her reply. What were they all hiding? ''I believe him to be on the roof of the keep. At times, he enjoys watching the sun set from there.''

Suddenly not tired, Marguerite stood and walked past Lady Constance. She needed to find Orrick. To speak to him. To see if the actions he'd taken on her behalf had…had hurt him. Climbing the stairs that led to the rooftop, she was not even sure of what she would say or what she wanted to know from him. Reaching the top of the steps, she pushed open the heavy door and stepped out.

The winds that cut across the roof from the ocean whipped her hair and gown and she fought to gather her hair with a tie. A guard approached and asked her why she was there.

''I seek Lord Orrick.''

The guard nodded his head in the direction of the west wall and Marguerite saw him then. Facing the rapidly setting sun, he stood as the winds blew his hair and cloak wildly around his shoulders. She could not tell if his eyes were opened or closed, but he appeared as still as a statue. She walked to his side and just stood next to him.

The darkness pressed forward from the east and the remaining rays of sunlight threw themselves into it. Sharp shadows and piercing threads of light alternated against the sky. The day, which had been a pleasant one, now became a colder evening as the sun set. Marguerite shivered, having forgotten her cloak.

''Here now, step closer and share mine,'' Orrick said, holding his cloak open to her. She waited only a moment to accept his offer. "What brings you here?"

Marguerite was enveloped by his warmth. He placed her before him, facing the sun as he was, and wrapped his arms and heavy cloak around her. Her head, peeking out of the embrace, felt the heat of his chest and neck. He leaned his chin down on her.

"Did you come to watch the sun go down? You nearly missed it but I think the last few rays as it surrenders to the night are the best."

Marguerite watched as the light splashed widely over the keep and then disappeared bit by bit until they stood in the afterglow. Darker, but not quite full night yet. He held her still but did not speak. Finally she could wait no more.

"Why did you whip those men today? Gavin saw to them and there was no reason to…"

"Defend your honor? You are my wife—'tis my place to do so."

Turning to face him, she tried to step away. His arms loosened their hold but did not release her completely. "But you know the truth. You know they spoke of my life and that I do not wish to be your wife."

A frown crossed his face and she wondered what he was thinking. She had told him honestly that she did not wish to be here, did not wish to marry him and did not consider this marriage to be anything but a temporary farce. The foundations of her arguments were beginning to shake a bit since their physical intimacy; however, Marguerite was certain that Henry would find a way around that. With the onset of her flux, at least she was relieved that there would be no result of that intimacy to make the situation more difficult to undo.

"Am I such an ogre that you could not find some happiness as my wife?" His tone spoke of amusement—the glint in his eyes gave away how serious this question of his was.

"I love Henry."

"So you have said. Many times."

"Do you not believe me? Do you think he will abandon all that we have together?" she asked. A part of her wanted him to give her the answer she needed to hear.

"I believe that first love is a thorny issue, filled with anticipation and hopes and expectations that are usually dashed by realities of life. It is most difficult to accept the end of the first love someone bears for another. And when that first love is not returned, it is the most difficult to forget."

"Do you tease me? Think you that my feelings for the king should be played for your amusement?" Angry, she tried to step farther away, but Orrick held her firmly in his grasp.

"I do not make light of your feelings. I would only suggest that your opposition to this marriage, our marriage, is based on feelings that are colored by your belief in the love you have for Henry. And I suggest that those feelings are not completely reliable when it comes to the king."

Unable and unwilling to face that possibility, she chose another subject. "Your mother apologized to me," she blurted out.

"Ah. Is that what drove you here to find me? Did she make it worse with her good-hearted attempt to make it better?"

Lord Orrick untied the cloak and placed it fully around her shoulders. Now she could face him.

"Nay, my lord. Her words seemed genuine." Marguerite shook her head.

"They were. I ask that you not embarrass her by speaking of this further. She is a proud woman who recognized the wrongness in her actions. If you have it in your heart to let the matter be settled now, I would ask you to do just that."

His sincere request sent shivers of fright through her. She did not want him beholden to her for anything. 'Twould make it easier when she left if there were no soft feelings between them. Even as she wished not to agree, she gathered his cloak tighter around her and nodded. And against her mind's decision not to speak of such things, she did now.

"I wanted to tell you my reasons for intervening today," she said, changing their topic to something no less personal to her.

He lifted his face and turned away from her. Eyes closed, he stood as the winds buffeted them. She did not speak, for his actions seemed to say he did not want to hear her words. Marguerite gathered the folds of his cloak around her against the winds. As she inhaled, she took in the scent that was Lord Orrick. Male. Leather. Metal.

She breathed in again for some hint of the other traits she knew but the cloth did not reveal his innate kindness or his loyalty or his… What foolishness was this? She shook her head and smiled at the whimsical thoughts.

"Lady, I do not need to know your reasons," he said, turning back to her. "Your actions gave me the opportunity to show mercy. There is no need to know more than that."

"And showing mercy is important to you, my lord?"

She wanted to know why he did what no other lord would have. Why did he not relish his place as the one who would mete out the punishment he declared? Her own father showed no compunction for imposing strict discipline in his households and for wielding the whip or cane as he saw fit. Once she witnessed him nearly beat a servant to death for ruining his favorite tunic.

He laughed roughly and smiled at her. "Is it not the Christian duty of any lord to show mercy to those in his care?"

Did he know how much he showed his difference by his choice of words? In his care? This place, these people, were in his control and he rightfully could determine their conditions and treatment. She frowned at him.

"I fear my upbringing and training was thoroughly swayed by the good brothers at the abbey. For a time, before my brothers died, they believed I would join their ranks. Their influence differs from that of my more temporal mentors and trainers."

"You had brothers?" She had been raised separately from her half brother and half sister but, to her knowledge, her father had no other children.

"And a sister." The laughter left his face and voice. "I fear it was their loss that causes my mother to cling the way she does to me. Their deaths changed her," he said softly.

Something inside her shouted a warning. She did not want to know this. She would not be here much longer and she wanted none of this personal knowledge of this man or his family, present or past. Marguerite shook loose from the soft feelings growing within her heart and peeled his cloak from her shoulders. Holding it out to him, she waited for him to take it.

"My lord, I seek my chambers now. 'Tis been a long and tiring day for me."

The urge and need to write to Henry grew within her and Marguerite began to choose the words she would use even as she turned from him. She'd taken only a few steps when he called to her.

"Lady? Before you go, I would ask something of you."

Marguerite took a deep breath and let it out before facing him. Not sure of his request, she tried to calm the thoughts that swirled through her. When she thought herself in control of her uncertainty, she turned back to him.

"My lord?"

"Actually, I have two requests of you. First," he said stepping closer, "Brother Wilfrid was not trained at the abbey as many others are and so his knowledge of Latin is not as strong as it could be."

"Why do you not have him removed then?" she asked.

"He has much to offer my people with his healing skills and so I hesitate to get rid of him." She thought he was making merry of her, but he continued before she could say it. "I know that you can read and write Latin and so I would like you to work with him to translate his scrolls to the English he speaks more easily."

"Surely your clerk can do that, my lord?" Marguerite could not understand why she did not want to agree, but fear caught in her chest. "Is not that something he should do?"

"Lady, Wilfrid has served as clerk, as well, in his years here." Lord Orrick took her hand and held it in his. "The good brother is getting old and Abbot Godfrey cannot assign a replacement here now. I need someone, on a temporary basis, to assist Wilfrid in reading the scrolls that come to him from the abbey. Surely, someone as well-educated as you could see to this with little effort?"

She knew he mimicked her words purposely to goad her into agreeing. It would appear to be a simple request and it was certainly within her abilities to carry out. To refuse after his kindnesses to her would make her appear mean-spirited and spiteful. And to her surprise, she did not want him to think of her that way.

"I am willing to try, my lord. So long as he is willing to work with a woman?"

"It should be no problem in that regard. Wilfrid has been exposed to my mother for years." His voice was lighter now. He teased her.

"Will he condemn me?"

Marguerite did not think before she asked the question that truly haunted her. So many of the religious associated with Henry's court made her uncomfortable with their view of educated women. Especially women who used their minds and bodies to attain what they could not otherwise get. One of Henry's prelates had a habit of speaking to her outside the king's presence to harass and condemn her. *Brazen, godless whore of Babylon* was his favorite greeting, uttered too quietly for anyone but her to hear and with a hatred and vehemence that shook her to the core every time he said it. Even now, a shudder passed through her as she remembered the sound of the words.

"Nay," he answered, shaking his head. "He is a gentle soul who will appreciate the assistance he receives."

The kindness in his tone scared her again and the urge to run to safety filled her. She nodded and turned again. "I will seek him out on the morrow, my lord," she said as she walked away from him.

"There is still the matter of my second request, Marguerite." His voice was louder now.

"My lord?" She faced him and waited.

"I would have you speak in my language to my people. While you are here, of course."

She only realized as he changed from Norman to his English that they had been speaking in hers. The amusement was back in his tone. She neither nodded nor gave her agreement to him, but she only turned and walked toward the door.

"My lady?" he called, loud enough to draw the

guard's attention. The guard stepped back away only after Lord Orrick signaled him to do so.

"Another request, my lord?" Crossing her arms over her chest, she grew impatient. "You spoke of only two."

"This is more of an order." Lord Orrick closed the gap between them and looked down on her from his towering view, forcing her to lean her head back to meet his gaze. His mouth was close enough to hers to touch their lips, but he did not.

"I would have you call me by my given name when we are alone."

His deep voice poured over her and she felt a heat grow within her. He could be extremely attractive at times. The feelings coursing through her body alarmed her. She did not want to be drawn to this man; she wanted to be gone from here and never see him or his people or his village again.

Her voice caught in her throat and so, rather than let him hear the trembling in it, she nodded at him and backed away. When there was sufficient distance between them, she turned and walked toward the door. Later when she realized that she'd run, she would blame it on the cold winds and not the dangerous man who called to her.

Chapter Eleven

Orrick strode down the steps after Marguerite had run away and went to his workroom on the main floor of the keep. Gavin waited there for him and they planned an evening visit to the village, but Orrick's encounter with his wife and the insights that encounter revealed put a twist in his plans. Opening the door without warning, he found his friend face-down on the table, snoring.

Taking hold of the jug and sliding it from Gavin's grasp, Orrick poured a cup of wine for himself and sat down on the nearest stool. This was a strange ending to a strange day. Debating on whether or not to wake Gavin, Orrick decided not to—he was not certain he wanted to face all the questions that Gavin would raise to him in the privacy of this place. And Orrick knew he had more questions now than when he'd left the yard after seeing to the punishment of the two men.

Had Marguerite even realized the pain that now cracked through the icy veneer she usually affected?

Although none of those involved had confessed the exact words spoken, he could imagine what they were. Many had spoken them openly around and to him at Henry's court. When he'd first met her, he believed the cold exterior she wore covered a colder heart, but watching her struggles over these past few weeks, he was no longer so sure.

And her intervention today demonstrated more of an interest or concern than he truly thought her capable of. He did not know who the target of her concerns was. However, he believed her presence on the roof was more hopeful than not.

How would she feel when she discovered that he lied to her?

He had not wanted to show mercy to those men today. Instead, the fury inside of him demanded their blood, and nearly their lives, for what they did to her. In spite of his father's late efforts to eradicate the ''softness of preparation'' he'd received at the abbey, he'd not succeeded in removing it. Orrick found his decisions were often tempered with the good brothers' words and teachings. But all the layers of self-control were destroyed when he knew Marguerite had heard hateful words from his people.

And her accusation that he thought of her in no different a way than his people did, cut him to the heart. He knew in that moment that his punishment and anger at the men was really just misdirected anger at himself for his own actions toward her.

Oh, she had added her own insults to their encounters and even goaded him to bad behavior. But he was older and more experienced in dealing with matters of discipline than she and he should have controlled the urge to strike out or strike back at her or his people for his own shortcomings.

Even though she did not know it yet, there was, for the first time in her life, a chance for her to make a new life, one not filled with the dangers and falseness and intrigues of court. One where she could grow and be the woman she was capable of.

Of course the fact that she did not want such a life was not lost on him. Her presence before him tonight and the weakened argument about her love for Henry told him she was beginning to question the reasons for her life and her decisions.

Orrick was not certain when he'd made the choice to keep her or the one to try to tempt her so that she wanted to stay, but his request for her to work with Brother Wilfrid was the first step in his plan. From his observations and from what he knew of her life, Marguerite had only ever been taught that she was a means to an end for her father. Not that it wasn't a noblewoman's place to marry advantageously and to bring or keep property and titles into the family. Not that women were supposed to choose their own destinies and ignore the wishes and advice of their fathers or husbands.

But Orrick had watched the other women and marriages and knew that they could gain much in that union. Women could use their skills and talents to make their lives and the lives of their husbands and families happy and content. That was the kind of marriage he wanted, and now he knew that he wanted it with Marguerite.

Her past be damned.

Orrick understood that Henry would never call her back. He knew that another already shared the king's bed and had taken her place as his mistress. There was no place for her to go back to now, for her father in Normandy and her uncle here in England stood firmly and visibly in support of the king's decision and there would be no one to plead her case for return to court. She knew none of this and, since his mother had indeed learned her lesson about sharing gossip, no one at Silloth would ever speak of it to her.

Shifting on his stool, he wondered what it would take to make Marguerite realize her past was just that. He feared that the spirit within her, the fire that had given her the strength and passion to attain the king's attention and to survive in the surreal life at court, would be extinguished when she learned the truth. He smiled grimly. 'Twould be a sad waste.

An idea filled his thoughts and he laughed at the challenges and rewards it presented to him. It was, however, a way to make her life here better. Would it balance the crushing blow that Henry's abandonment would cause? He hoped so.

Standing, Orrick approached his sleeping friend and shook him awake. Even before his eyes opened, Gavin's hand moved to his side, searching for the sword he usually wore. A normal reaction for the warrior he was.

"I need you to choose three men for a journey. They must be able to travel quickly and far and be able to keep their mouths shut."

If Gavin thought his request was a strange one for the middle of the night, he gave no sign. Then Orrick took the jug and poured them both another cup from it. Motioning his friend back to his seat, Orrick smiled.

"I have a plan...."

Chapter Twelve

"And this one is…?" she asked, holding up the small green glass vial.

"Feverfew," Brother Wilfrid replied. "'Tis used to lower fevers and to treat pains in the—" Marguerite looked at the old man and saw the glint in his good eye "—head," he finished, and they both laughed. One of the first things she'd learned about Wilfrid was that he loved to use vulgar language. Oh, nothing too offensive to her, but "pain in the arse" was his favorite and he used it often to describe most of those who lived in Silloth.

Except Lord Orrick. Brother Wilfrid never uttered an unkind word about the lord of Silloth. That was the second thing she'd learned about him—he was completely faithful to serving God and Lord Orrick. So, when Marguerite joined him under the guise of learning his skills with healing herbs, he agreed quickly to see to her lack of knowledge on the subject.

She knew the real reason she was helping him so

she allowed the misunderstanding to continue. And, true to Orrick's description of him, he offered her kindness and his knowledge all mixed with a few good English curses. After the first few hours with him, Marguerite found that she hungered for the time when she used her mind in his workroom.

"I thought you had yarrow for treating fevers?" She squinted at the lines of script she'd written on the parchment before her until she found what she searched for. "Here it is, yarrow is for healing wounds, stanching bleeding and for fevers."

"Sometimes, one or the other is not available to me, so I keep small quantities of both on hand."

'Twas a sound practice. She nodded and picked up the next jar in front of her. Lifting the lid, she sniffed it carefully as the herbalist had shown her. Marguerite had been too eager that first day and found herself lying on the floor looking up into the concerned face of the good brother when the fumes of a potent concoction overwhelmed her. She did not make the same mistake again.

Looking at the dried leaves, she tried to remember which ones they were. Betony? Bindweed? Lady's Mantle? Not sure, she held the container up to the monk.

"Adder's Tongue. For healing wounds and for skin irritations."

Marguerite paused to look more closely at the leaves before sealing the jar tightly and placing it on the shelf above the worktable. It had taken them nearly a fortnight to organize the herbs and concoctions and ointments, but only a half-dozen remained.

At the least, Brother Wilfrid's replacement would find a well-ordered supply of the needed herbs and medicaments and a written inventory of all that the room held. Although she was certain that the new herbalist and lord's clerk would read and write in Latin, Marguerite had done as Orrick requested and translated all the records into English as they'd worked to gather them.

By the time a servant brought their noon meal, the final six were catalogued and stored. Her fingertips were blackened from the ink and her hair was barely controlled in the braid that fell into her lap as she worked. Marguerite rose from her seat and stretched her arms over her head, rolling her shoulders to loosen the tightness there from holding the quill so tightly while writing. Careful not to touch the front of her gown, she scooped some of the soap Wilfrid kept on hand into her palm and worked it into her fingers.

"Stained for life, my lady?" Intent on her efforts to remove the ink, she startled at the voice. Looking up, she watched as Lord Orrick stepped closer and filled the doorway.

"I fear so, my lord. My father's servants would bemoan the condition to which I've allowed them to suffer."

She examined them closely and realized the truth of her words—Berthilde would have had her soaking in some bitter-smelling bath until the ink was removed, even if it meant her skin went with the stains. Realizing the mistruth in her words, she shook her head. "This would never have happened in my father's house, for once I mastered the skill of writing, I was not permitted to do it, for fear 'twould do just this.'' Marguerite held her discolored hands out to him.

Lord Orrick watched her movements as she massaged the soap into the beds of her nails and over her palms. Dipping into the bowl of warmed water, she rinsed them and dried with a towel kept for that purpose. The stains were now shared with the cloth.

''I think there are worse things in this world than well-used hands,'' he said. ''Not using the skills within them is a terrible waste.''

He took one of her hands and lifted it closer to his face. Turning it over and back, he rubbed his thumb over her palm and her fingers and up to her wrist. The soft tickling sensation turned into a tingling that crept up her palm into her arm and through her as he continued a methodical massage. She shivered when he leaned down and touched his lips to the inside of her wrist. Unable or unwilling to move, she was not certain which held her in place as she watched him repeat the same action on her other hand.

Would he stop?

Where else would he place his lips?

Smooth and warm, she could almost remember the feel of them on her neck and on her breasts. Another shudder went through her as she felt the heated memory of his kiss and caress on her skin that night. 'Twas only Brother Wilfrid's loud and unsubtle cough that broke into the reverie that enveloped both of them. She jumped back a step from Orrick, finally reclaiming her hands from his grasp.

"What service can I provide for you this day, my lord?" Wilfrid asked, standing in Orrick's presence.

"I came to steal my...the lady from you, Brother. She complained that this place was never without storms and rain and now that the clouds have loosed their hold, I would show her my lands."

Not sure why, Marguerite shook her head, refusing his invitation. "My lord, I fear that our work is not done here."

"Brother? What say you? Can you spare your assistant for a short time if I promise to return her to you when you finish with your midafternoon prayers?" Orrick smiled at the monk and waited. She already knew that Wilfrid would deny Orrick nothing, and the fact of spending nearly three hours with him moved closer to happening.

"My lady, if the weather is clearing I should make a visit to the village. I know you wish not to accompany me to that duty, so this is the perfect time for Lord Orrick's request."

Orrick frowned at the monk's words but did not ask for more elaboration of it. Now her fate was sealed with no gracious or practical escape.

"May I get my cloak, my lord?" Mayhap if she could get out of the workroom alone, she could distract him with some other task. Edmee's appearance, with Marguerite's cloak in hand, told her there was no way to avoid this. "You have arranged all the details, then?"

"Even some food and a mount suited to you."

Orrick took the cloak from her servant and placed it on her shoulders. He held out his arm to her and she laid her hand on it, allowing him to guide her from the workroom, through the main floor of the keep and out into the yard. A boy from the stables stood holding a horse for her to mount, and with Orrick's hand-up, she did.

Taking the reins and wrapping them around her palms, she arranged her skirts and waited for Orrick to mount. He stood talking to one of his soldiers and then swung up onto his larger horse. She followed him out through the gate, around the southern edge of the curtain wall and past part of the village.

He was correct—the rain had given way to a sunshine that warmed the lands here. Instead of the enduring gray that made the stones of Silloth Keep appear dull and despairing, the sunlight caught on the walls and made them sparkle. Like the onyx beads in her jewel case, the bright light brought out aspects not usually seen and the whole castle gleamed.

Their path turned downhill and Marguerite realized that they headed for the ocean. The steep path took all her concentration and it was not until they reached the flat beach that she looked back to see how far they had descended. It nearly took her breath away! They were more than a hundred feet below the keep now, on the side that faced the ocean and the winds.

Looking up even higher, she could see the top of the keep where she had stood that evening with Orrick to watch the sun set. Now, so far beneath it, she marveled at the design and construction of the castle.

So close to the edge of the cliff, Silloth appeared to be a huge weapon thrust up into the sky from its base in the sea.

"Henry granted my father permission to turn the wooden keep to a stone one over fifteen years ago. The designer of it chose to use the natural outcropping of rock and cliffs." Orrick leaned closer to her and pointed to the landscape above them and to the north. "From the sea, it cannot be distinguished from the cliffs due to its position and color."

"So, enemies approaching from the ocean cannot see that there is a defending castle here?"

"Just so, my lady. A wise strategy?"

"'Twould appear so. Do the tides rise to that mark on the cliff?" Marguerite pointed to a place where the sea had worn smooth the surface of the rocks.

"Aye. And since the water moves in from both west and north, the beach is not a haven for those on the attack."

She watched the waves break onto the beach. The tide was decreasing now from what she could tell, the water rushing out to the ocean more than it stayed on the beach. It was as she observed the pattern of the moving water that she realized there were no guards with them. Or servants. Were they so safe here?

"Has Silloth been attacked in the past?"

"Many times over the centuries. This is a valuable position on the coast so it has been coveted by the Romans, the Britons, Vikings, Scots and the English. All through history it has changed hands as the powers that control the land change."

Orrick touched the sides of his horse and Marguerite followed him to a small, rocky outcropping closer to the water's edge. Once there, he dismounted and helped her to the ground. He untied the sack containing the food and a wineskin from behind his saddle and hobbled both horses to keep them from running away. Holding out his hand again to her, he led her to sit on one of the larger rocks. The surface was flat and now well-heated from the sun.

Marguerite grew nervous as he sat next to her. Looking around for the guards, Orrick must have seen her expression.

"What do you fear, lady?" He lifted her chin so that their gazes met. "Your nervousness is obvious to me."

"Where are the guards?" She licked her dry lips. "Is it safe to be here?"

"I had the beach searched before I brought you here," he said, his eyes glittering with that frequently present glimmer of amusement. "My men are just over the ridge to the south and up on the battlements of the keep. No one can approach here without being seen by them."

"Can we be seen?" Marguerite looked back and forth. Being alone with him brought other concerns to mind, but she pushed them away.

"If I give the signal, my men will come forward. If I do not, they will not. I assure you, lady, we are alone."

Exactly what she feared. Through careful forethought she had managed to avoid him for more than a fortnight. Though they shared the evening meal and saw each other throughout the day, she had not been alone with him since that night on the battlements on the keep. Marguerite swallowed and glanced back at him.

She knew he wanted her. He could not completely mask the look of desire in his eyes. He had thought to kiss her on the keep's roof that night, just as he was doing now. And with no one around them, no one could intervene. The worst of it was that Marguerite found herself wanting him to kiss her.

Just when her body wanted to lean in to his, she forced herself away. Surprised to see that he had not moved closer, she took in a deep breath and tried to ease the quickening pace of her heart. "To what purpose did you bring me here, my lord?"

"My lord? I thought you understood my recent order?" That damned glimmer was back in his green eyes.

"We have not been alone since your order was given, my lord…Orrick."

"That is better. My purpose today was a simple one, Marguerite. You have been working constantly with Wilfrid over these past weeks and I thought you could use some time out of doors."

"I walk every day," she began to argue.

"From the keep to the chapel and back. But to my knowledge you never leave the yard or go to the village. You are not a prisoner in Silloth Keep, so why is that?"

Orrick reached into the sack and brought out a chunk of cheese. Tearing off a piece, he offered it to her. Biting into his own, he seemed to watch her every move, almost daring her to lie. She tried to swallow the cheese, but it stuck in her throat. Orrick was there immediately with the wineskin.

"I have no need to go to the village."

She wished that he would not press her about this. He did not like it when she said she wanted to leave. He did not like it when she expressed her faith in Henry. So why did he make her answer these questions? When he began to ask something, she lifted her hand to his chest to stop him.

"My lord. Orrick. I pray thee, do not ask if you wish not to hear my answer."

Marguerite watched as his gaze moved down to her hand and, in horror, she realized what she had done and how discolored her hands were. Pulling away, she allowed the sleeves of her gown to cover them. Years of indoctrination made her embarrassed over their condition.

A lady's hands should be white and soft-skinned. Dirty hands are the sign of a peasant. Her gown should be clean and her hair always groomed and under a veil.

"Why do you hide your hands?" Orrick gently grasped her wrists and brought her hands out from the sleeves.

"The woman my father appointed to teach me the correct ways of appearance and behavior would be horrified to see what I have allowed to happen. I would be punished if I had shown myself in my father's hall as I do here."

He lifted her hands between them and waited for her to look on them. Seeing the ink stains once more, she realized that her recent disregard for her appearance shamed her and her father.

"Hands marked by honest work are not an embarrassment."

"But they are, my—Orrick. 'Tis grooming and appearance and bearing that separates the noble-born from the peasants."

"Mayhap in the land of your childhood, Marguerite. Mayhap at the king's court. But not here in Silloth. Here, the work you do for the good of all matters more than how you look accomplishing it. Here, who you are matters more than what you wear."

She frowned at him. His thinking was so peculiar. How could he believe these notions? At court, she…

"I am sounding like a monk once again," he said in explanation. "And being a barbarian from the godforsaken outskirts of civilization, I do not comprehend the overwhelming importance of clean hands and ornately arranged hair."

Orrick stood and turned away from her, facing into the winds that skipped over the ocean. When he did not face her, she slid off the rocks and walked to his side. Why could he not understand?

"Orrick," she said, placing her hand on his arm. "Please hear me. I mean no insult to you by my words or by being ill at ease over my hands. This is who I am."

"No, Marguerite, this is not who you are. It is who they made you think you must be."

"It is the only way I know to be, Orrick. It is not pretense. It is me."

He grasped her by the shoulders and stared down

at her, his eyes piercing her with their intensity. "And you would return to that? To a place and to people who value you for your appearance over your contributions? To those who offer you disguise and affectation instead of honest feelings?"

"I..." Marguerite choked on the words she tried to force out. She wanted to scream out "Yes," but something would not free the assertion from within her. Her place was not here. She did not want to live here. Pulling free of his hold, she stumbled back.

"Have any of your family or those you called friend answered your call for help? Have they interceded on your behalf with Henry?" he asked, stepping forward. His voice quieted until she could almost not hear it above the crashing of the waves. "Will they endanger their own standing to speak for you? Those are the traits of true friends."

She could not answer him, for her thoughts and feelings were jumbled inside of her. Unable to speak, she did the only thing she could. Marguerite lifted her skirts and ran.

Chapter Thirteen

In spite of the way his words sounded, he was no holy brother. When the sun shone down on her hair in its enchanting disarray, when her blue eyes glittered like jewels and when her lips parted ever so slightly, he wanted to bury his hardness in her. His body constantly reminded him of the earthy sin of lust whenever he saw his wife…or heard her…or thought about her. Even now, he ached for her.

Whistling out his signal, Orrick waited for his men to return and follow Marguerite before stripping off his clothes and diving into the cold water. Battling against the temperature of the water and the ocean currents were usually enough to stave off his physical reaction to Marguerite. Today he doubted it would be successful.

With steady strokes, he swam a distance offshore and then parallel to the edge of the water. Pausing for a moment, he whistled again, letting the one soldier remaining on the beach and the guards on the keep see his position. He may be irrational swimming in the wild ocean, but he was not foolish enough to do it when none could see him. Content that he was under surveillance, he went back to his ritual.

When he felt as though his arms and legs were like stones pulling him down, he pushed his way to shore and walked to the rocks where he'd brought Marguerite. The guard standing between the cliff and the water returned to his post farther down the beach and Orrick gathered up his clothes. Finding the sack of food, he took out the remaining cooked meat, bread and cheese and ate every bit. He waited for the wind and warmth of the sun to dry him off. Drinking deeply from the wineskin, he wondered if he'd pushed her too hard today.

As he suspected and Wilfrid confirmed, she was an intelligent woman with a gift in languages and the decidedly unfemale ability to reason and debate important and worldly issues. Wilfrid had laughed as he told Orrick of some of the discussions that occurred while sorting and organizing his workroom. The old man was more rested and in better spirits since Marguerite started her work there and Orrick felt vindicated even if he had put them together under false pretenses.

Orrick wondered what Marguerite would think if she knew that her father had educated her the same way and in the same subjects and skills that the queen had been educated in. Wilfrid remarked more than once that Marguerite's wisdom and knowledge and canny sense of politics rivaled Eleanor of Aquitaine's. Unfortunately for Marguerite's father, her young and inexperienced heart got in the way of his plans and fouled up his strategy of replacing the old queen with a new, younger version of the same woman.

Orrick recognized that, if given enough time, she would put all the pieces together. He knew that she would realize that she was not returning to court. He prayed that she would accept her gifts and use them for the welfare of their people. And he hoped that she would open her heart to the love he wanted to share with her.

He stuffed the remnants of the food back into the sack. After tugging his stockings back on and pulling his tunic and over-tunic over his head, Orrick allowed himself to laugh at the last thought. His efforts to avoid feeling anything for her were lackluster at best.

From their first encounter, she had entranced him. Anger, pity, admiration, exasperation, fondness, challenge and an almost overwhelming desire were only some of the emotions she engendered in him. He was not certain why he had been granted the ability to see so much about her, especially the fears she would not even admit to herself and the needs she could not acknowledge.

It had been his gift even from his childhood. He could see straight to the heart of someone. It made him the peacemaker between his brothers then and it made it so much more difficult as lord now. To crush someone or punish them simply because he had the right to do so was impossible when he could discern their motives and intentions. To strike out in anger was usually not something he did, except, it seemed, when it involved Marguerite's feelings.

This ability made it possible for him to accept her declarations of love for the king and her insistence that she would not stay here. He could discern that she had suffered deep wounds to her soul that made it impossible, for now, to accept what he offered.

So, he would bide his time and prod her to the decisions that no one else but she could make. He only hoped that he would be part of the future she chose for herself when her heart healed.

His wife reacted as he knew she would—she withdrew to her room, feverishly writing more letters to those at court who could plead her case with the king. She took her meals in her chambers and would not speak to anyone who went to inquire after her.

Everyone in the keep seemed to be affected by the change in mood between the lord and lady. Wilfrid looked askance at him when Orrick told him not to expect Marguerite's presence in his workroom for a few days. Edmee, enjoying her free time in the pursuit of things other than household tasks, was called back to attend to Marguerite's needs. Gavin was beaten to a pulp on a daily basis as Orrick found another way to wear himself out.

And to his amazement, everyone tried in their own way to entreat her from her rooms. Including himself. When Edmee mentioned Marguerite's continued concern over the ink stains on her hands, Brother Wilfrid provided concoctions meant to remove them. When Edmee told Lady Constance that she was unable to dress her lady's hair, his mother sent her own maid to see to the task. Even he tried to do something to cheer her—he had a new tunic and gown made to replace the one that she had damaged during her hours in Wilfrid's workroom and a sturdy apron made for her use there.

Orrick recognized that she was trying to confirm herself by falling back to the ways she'd been trained. Whenever threatened, she first retreated and then came out changed a bit. To his surprise, she arrived in the hall for the evening meal just two days after seeking the refuge of her rooms.

He stood at her approach, as did everyone in the hall. Guiding her to her chair, Orrick marveled at her appearance. She was breathtaking in her beauty. Her hair was twisted and tied in some elaborate style with a veil and circlet of gold over it. The dress she wore was the one he had given her, but the necklace of expensive jewels around her neck was not.

Orrick fought the urge to laugh out at her obvious tactics. He might have been insulted by the band of gold and rubies and emeralds had he not known that she was trying to protect herself from his advances. So, he was accomplishing something!

The meal was served and Orrick waited to see how she responded during it. Once more, the polite, accomplished woman was presented, the one who answered questions and shared his food, but kept her distance. Halfway through the main courses, he realized she spoke in English. Did she know what she did?

All through the meal, he observed her touching the

necklace. He did not believe she did it consciously, but several times her hand reached up to touch the stones or the gold and moved them to lie in a certain way. Orrick wondered what the significance of this particular bauble was to her. Finally the meal was over and he rose to escort her back to her room.

"My lord, with your permission I would like to visit Brother Wilfrid before I retire."

It was not the usual thing to do, but Orrick saw no harm in it. If she wished to speak to the monk, he had no objections. "If you wish," he answered. "I will escort you there."

She nodded and placed her hand on his. Walking down from the dais, he led her through the corridors to the workroom off the kitchen and storage rooms near the back entrance of the keep.

When they were but a few steps away from their destination, he paused to ask her, "Do you intend to tell him you will not be returning to help him?"

As she looked at him, a frown crossed her brow. "Why would you think that, my lord?"

He was about to correct her, for he loved the sound of his name on her lips, when two kitchen maids walked past them.

"Your distress over the condition of your hands. If working with quill and ink will mark your hands, we should find some other way for you to assist him."

"I confess, my lord, that the sight of my black fingers did disturb me at first, but I have thought on your words and decided to continue working with

Wilfrid. At least until his replacement arrives from the abbey.''

Orrick felt a pang of guilt at his deception. No replacement would come for he had not requested one.

''Besides, Wilfrid sent me the most wonderful cleanser that removes most of the ink,'' she said, lifting her hands to his inspection. Although a few shadows remained, most of the stains were gone. ''And the apron you gave me will protect my gown from damage in his workroom. My thanks for it…and the gowns.''

Her voice deepened to an attractive husky whisper that sent chills through him. She turned to go into the room, but he held her back for a moment, pulling her to face him. Nodding at the necklace she wore, he spoke. ''I cannot compete with the gifts you have received from the king, but I meant it with all the best intentions. I did not mean to hurt your feelings about your attention to the womanly details of dress and appearance and wished to compensate you for the loss of the gown you've been wearing to work with Wilfrid.''

Marguerite lifted her face to meet his eyes. ''And I accept your gift in the way it was intended.''

Orrick could resist her no longer. Without touching any other part of her, he joined their mouths in a heated kiss. Stepping closer, he lifted his mouth from hers and then took hers again, moving his tongue inside to taste her. When she offered no resistance, he moved his hand to the back of her head and brought her closer. Orrick felt her hands clutch at his arms and felt her opening to him so he wrapped his arms around her and held her.

Drawing back enough to look at her, he saw that her eyes were closed. He kissed her over and over until they were breathless with deep, wet, hot kisses. Kisses filled with the desire he felt for her. Kisses filled with the hopes and dreams he allowed himself to think about when she was near. With her body between him and the door of the workroom, he pressed against her and let her feel what his desire for her did to him. She was no virgin. She knew the desire she roused in him. All she had to do was say yes and he would join with her.

Suddenly he realized that he was trying to seduce his wife against the door in a hallway. Orrick stepped back and Marguerite followed him. Lifting her hands from him, Orrick tried to rearrange her veil before it tumbled from her head. The damn thing did fall off when the door to the workroom was pulled open from the inside and they both lost their balance and stumbled into the chamber.

"My lord. My lady. Come in and be welcome," Brother Wilfrid said. "I did not hear you knock at first, but you must know that my door is always open to you."

Orrick caught Marguerite's gaze and they both laughed at the situation and at what must have made the noise that Wilfrid interpreted as a knock on his door. She gained her footing and replaced her headpiece without his further assistance. He knew the time was at hand for him to retreat so he nodded to them both and stepped into the corridor.

"And my lady?" He waited until she faced him. "My door is always open to you."

She blushed at his words. Good. That meant she understood his invitation. With another nod to the monk, he left.

Every night for the next fortnight, he left the door between their chambers ajar. Even when her monthly time arrived again and she needed the sleeping draught from his mother, he kept it open, hoping she would seek simple comfort with him. But she did not.

They ate meals together, saw each other throughout the days, but their encounters were polite and brief. She never left the keep and yard and never visited the village. She continued to work with Wilfrid, spent some hours in his mother's solar with her and the women working on the new tapestry for the hall and in all respects save one was an appropriate wife.

Although he knew that his mother had offered and encouraged Marguerite to take her rightful place as lady of Silloth, Marguerite stood back and did not become involved in the running of the keep or the village. The harvest approached and 'twas his mother and Norwyn who oversaw the preparations to bring in the crops, salt fish and meat, and stock up on food and supplies for the coming winter.

Orrick waited for his men to return from Normandy. He hoped that the information they brought back would help him break this impasse with Marguerite. But after a month with no word from them, his optimism began to fail.

The sea became too cold and too rough for his daily swims and Gavin refused to meet him in the yard, so he had no outlet for the tension that grew within him. Ardys made it clear that, married or not, he was still welcome in her bed, but Orrick's feelings for the attractive widow had changed with his marriage. The woman he wanted slept only a few yards from him each night and she would not take the step to bridge that short distance.

So, when he no longer believed his efforts to make her part of his life were successful, he relented and sought out the widow's company in the village. After Marguerite retired for the night, he and Gavin made their way there.

Chapter Fourteen

Marguerite startled awake in the middle of the night. She could not ignore the incessant knocking coming from Orrick's room. Sliding from her bed, she tugged on a robe and went to the door between their chambers. 'Twas open as was his custom since he made his invitation and intention clear to her. Pushing it farther, the knocking was louder.

She spoke his name as she walked in, but no one was in the room. His bed was empty and the coverings were not disturbed. He had not been to bed yet? Looking around, she saw there was no sign of his recent presence in the room. As the knocking continued, she pulled the door open to face the surprised expressions of Norwyn and three of Orrick's men. They looked as though they had traveled long and hard to get here and their disappointment at not finding their lord was clear.

"Is Lord Orrick within, my lady?" Norwyn asked even as he peered around her into the chamber. "It is important that these men speak to him."

"He is not here, Norwyn," she said, stepping out of his way. He seemed to distrust her answer so she opened the door farther to let him see. "And I know not where he is."

The men looked at each other and then at her. Orrick answered not to her or to anyone else here. They bowed to her and were about to leave when Lady Constance arrived. Norwyn whispered to her and the lady answered the same way. With a cursory glance at her, Norwyn and the men followed Orrick's mother down the hall.

Ardys.

In the village.

She nearly missed the words for they were spoken so softly and not meant for her to hear. Who was Ardys? Where could Orrick be? If not in his chambers, where was he? Mayhap somewhere else in the keep? Mayhap with the Scot?

Marguerite berated herself for her concern. Orrick could be anywhere and 'twas none of her business. She had worked hard to hold herself separate from all those who made Silloth their home, and to become involved now would be the wrong thing to do.

"Lady Constance, is there some problem?" she finally asked since the hushed whispering had not stopped.

"Nay, Marguerite. These men were told to report directly and immediately to Orrick on their return and are trying to do that."

"No one knows where Lord Orrick is?" she asked.

"I am here," Orrick answered from behind the small group.

Walking from the stairway, she could see him tense when he recognized the men waiting for him. Marguerite watched as he exchanged looks with them. Something was very wrong.

"My lord? Is all well?"

He met her gaze for a moment before nodding to the men to leave. The apprehension in him was palpable, very unlike the Orrick she had come to know. "I am sorry that your rest was disturbed, lady. I will take my business to the hall."

She had been dismissed. His curt words of apology did nothing to ease it. Now as she watched, he whispered something to his mother who, from the expression on her face, did not like the answer she received, either. Turning away, his mother walked away in the direction of her rooms. Then, they faced each other in the empty hallway.

The moment lasted forever for her. There was something in his voice, something in his gaze and in his stance that screamed of danger to her. She could not figure out if the danger was from him or aimed at him. He had not answered her original question. "Is all well, Orrick?"

She was certain that the flickering of the torch in the sconce on the wall behind him made it look as though he shook his head when in truth he nodded. Without another word, he turned and walked down the corridor, his steps echoing behind him as he went.

Marguerite closed his door and walked back to her

chamber. She dropped her robe at the side of her bed and climbed back in. After this incident, she was certain she would not sleep the rest of the night. She lay silently listening to the sounds of the night and thinking about the strange situation with Orrick. When the dawn's light crept over the edge of the window in her room, she was still awake and feeling like a doomed criminal about to face their fate.

Orrick followed the small group down into the hall and then into the room that he and Norwyn used to oversee his estates. He ignored the surprised look on Norwyn's face when he ordered the steward out of the room. He took a seat at the table and motioned for the men to sit, as well. The knots in his gut tightened and he knew it was the grave expressions and demeanor of the men that caused it. This did not bode well for his plan to make Marguerite want to stay in Silloth.

"My lord, we would not have disturbed you if this was not important," Philippe began.

"So you had no success, then?"

Philippe glanced at the others and then swallowed hard. "Yes and no, my lord."

"Stop this, Philippe. I sent you to locate some female relative of Lady Marguerite's and to bring her back here to live. Did you or did you not?" Again, the men exchanged glances and none looked willing to speak of their mission. What in bloody hell was going on? "It is the middle of the night. I see no woman in your company. Tell me the rest of it.

Now." He forced the words out through his clench-ed jaws.

Philippe stuttered initially but finally spoke. "My lord, we discovered that the lady has a younger sis-ter."

"A sister? No cousin?" Orrick did not think that Marguerite's father would allow a daughter of his to move here without a beneficial marriage...beneficial to his coffers of course.

"A sister, my lord, who is planning on taking her vows soon," the soldier said. And then, licking his dry lips, he continued. "And a daughter."

Orrick could not comprehend at first. A daughter? Marguerite? Holy Mother of God! Marguerite had given birth to the king's bastard.

"A daughter?" He hoped for some different ex-planation, but the one that was obvious explained so many things about her behavior and her unrelenting belief that Henry would not give her up to another man.

"About a half-year ago, my lord," Philippe an-swered. "The lady left court about six months before that and word was given that she and the king had a...falling-out." The soldier looked completely un-comfortable discussing such personal matters with his lord, but he went on. "When the king convened his court at Woodstock to see to the knighting of Prince Geoffrey, the lady was called back and every-one expected...well, my lord, they expected that all had been forgiven."

Orrick closed his eyes as he heard this news. So Marguerite had given the king a child and then expected her reward. Most likely Henry had led her to believe that she would achieve that for which she had been trained and prepared all her life—a union with him. Unfortunately for her, the king's need for Queen Eleanor's lands, titles and wealth was undiminished and so a marriage for Marguerite was arranged to a barbarian lord of the north.

The room filled with silence as he contemplated only a few of the ramifications of this news. If Marguerite's child was elsewhere, could she ever be happy here? Had Henry made some arrangements for the upbringing of the child or had he threatened Marguerite if she did not comply with his plan? Orrick rubbed his eyes with his palms and let out his breath.

"Is there more?" He would hear it all now.

"We have letters from the lady's sister. She did not know of your marriage, my lord." Philippe reached into his tunic and took out two separate parchment packages. Orrick hesitated accepting them.

"Do you know what is contained in these?"

"Nay, my lord. They were sealed as you see them when we received them."

"Did you tell her your purpose? Does she know that you learned of the babe?" He took the letters and looked at them. One was addressed to him, the other to Marguerite.

"Nay, my lord. We were discreet as you ordered. We found out about the babe from a servant at the convent. The girl is being raised there."

"Raised there? By whom?"

"The convent is run by the Gilbertines and there

is a lay community. The babe lives with her nurse there. Lady Dominique, or should I say, Sister Dominique, oversees her care.''

Arrangements like that had the mark of royal interference. The Gilbertines were an English order and had but two convents outside England—one in Ireland and one in Normandy. The one in Caen had been opened under the direct patronage of the king.

Orrick noticed that the men were exhausted. From their appearance, they had hurried back to Silloth with this news for him without regard to their comfort. He stood and went to the door. Clutching the letters in his hand, he turned to the men.

"Speak of this to no one. Not your lovers—" he looked at Philippe "—and not your wives," he said, making the other two meet his gaze. "If you have questions about anything you heard or learned while carrying out my orders, come to me. Not to Norwyn. Not to Gavin. To me." He waited until they each acknowledged this order and then opened the door. His steward still waited outside.

"Norwyn, they need food and drink."

"Aye, my lord," Norwyn said, never questioning the time of night or the difficulty there might be in carrying out his orders.

"And two days of rest before going back to their duties here."

"Aye, my lord." Norwyn nodded and led the men toward the kitchen.

When they had gone, Orrick closed the door and collapsed back into the chair. Still shocked by the news, he could not even think about it. He laid the

letters on the table and looked at the ornate script.
Did the one to Marguerite contain only sisterly greetings? Or was there more than that? What words did
his contain? Part of him feared opening it, for each
time he learned something new about Marguerite or
her past, it created more problems for him.

Hours later, as the keep came to life outside the
chamber, Orrick still sat with both letters before him.
If he destroyed them both, Marguerite would never
know. Any news within would remain unknown to
her. Since none of those people she sent messages to
ever responded, there would be nothing to tell her
that her sister knew of their marriage. Nothing to tell
her that he knew about her daughter. Nothing to tell
her that he knew more of her secrets.

In the end, he remembered his demand of her for
honesty between them. Even though she had not
complied completely with it, he could not give her
less than he expected from her. Now knowing the
basis for her reluctance or inability to be candid with
him, he understood more. And, in spite of his knowledge of this unbreakable bond between her and
Henry, he wanted her to stay with him…and be his
wife in truth. Steeling himself for the worst and hoping for the best, he broke the wax seal on the letter
addressed to him and opened it.

Brother Wilfrid sent word that he was spending
the morning in the village, so Marguerite did not
leave her room. Orrick had not returned to his chambers yet and she feared whatever matters those men
had with him. Mayhap it had nothing at all to do

with her, but the peculiar behavior of coming to the lord's chambers in the middle of the night and of Orrick's strange appearance in the corridor with no explanation of his absence unnerved her.

Edmee brought a tray as she requested, however Marguerite found herself unable to eat a bite of food. She had finally decided on a walk to ease the anxiety within her, when Orrick entered from his chambers. She jumped to her feet to face him.

"My lady, please pardon this intrusion," he said, walking across the room. "I thought to find you with Brother Wilfrid, but I was informed he went to the village."

My lady? He usually called her by name, for he was more comfortable with that than she. Something was different in his eyes as he looked upon her.

"Is this about your men last night?" she blurted out, unable to keep her concerns to herself. She entwined her fingers and tried to steady her hands.

"Actually, it is. Please sit." He pointed at the alcove seat and she sat, or dropped, into it. "I had thought that part of your resistance to remaining here was that you knew no one here," he began without meeting her gaze. "When you would reveal nothing of your family or your life, I sent my men to Normandy to seek the truth."

The room grew both dim and hot around her. He sought the truth? She must continue breathing. She could not faint. Forcing the breaths in and out of her body, Marguerite tried to stay calm. Clutching her hands even more tightly, she swallowed and managed to speak.

"The truth, my lord? And what did your men find on their quest for the truth?" She tried to look deep within herself for the courage that usually allowed her to appear serene and composed. She feared that that skill had deserted her.

"I did not know you have a sister."

"A s-sister?" she stammered. "I have a sister." She needed to pull her thoughts together. She did not want to reveal more than he already knew. "A younger sister, my lord. Dominique."

"I thought your mother died giving birth to you."

She could feel his scrutiny as she gathered her words. She might be able to get through this if she did not meet his eyes again. "She did. Dominique and I share the same father, but have different mothers." Marguerite smoothed her gown over her legs. "My mother was a cousin to the king of France and Dominique's is cousin to the count of Toulouse." She fell back to the old ways, the haughty behavior that she had perfected before coming here. "You probably discovered that she has entered the convent in Caen and intends to take her vows. Or mayhap she has by now."

In trying to hold any doubts about her course in life at bay, she had not thought of her sister in weeks and weeks. She tried to remember how long her training as a novice was and could not.

"Nay, she has not taken her final vows yet."

Surprised, she did look at him now and found his stare unnerving. He managed to undermine the practice of many years with his straightforward behavior. "My thanks for that news, for I have not seen her in…'' No! She could not think about that time. ''…for some months.''

Orrick walked closer to her and held out a small package of parchment. ''She asked that this be delivered to you.''

A letter from Dominique? Had he read it? She saw the wax seal and knew that he had not. But, in order to take the letter from him, she had to unclasp her hands and reveal how badly they were trembling. Hoping he would misinterpret her shaking as excitement over hearing news of her sister, she reached for it.

''I had hoped that on hearing my request, she could recommend some cousin or friend who might come here and be companion to you. Her letter to me revealed an absence of suitable relatives for that purpose.''

She put the letter in her lap and held it. His benevolence continually surprised her. And reminded of her darkest deception, she knew that she did not deserve the consideration with which he treated her. Tears burned in her throat and threatened to flow freely.

He stroked her cheek with the back of his hand. She was tempted to pull away and tempted to turn in to his caress, but instead sat motionless trying to control the emotions that pushed relentlessly forward.

''I would have you happy here, Marguerite,'' he said in that voice that touched something deep within her and sent chills through her.

"News of my sister has made me happy, my lord."

"Then I hope that the contents of the letter brings you more joy." He dropped his hand and stepped back. "I will give you some privacy so that you may read it at your leisure."

She watched him walk to the door before calling out to him. "My lord?" He stopped without facing her. "Orrick. Pray thee accept my thanks for this and for what you did."

Orrick nodded and left without another word. She turned the letter over and over, wondering if glad tidings would be found. She slid back against the seat and broke the seal on the parchment.

More than an hour later, Marguerite knew the truth and any measure of happiness she'd gained with knowledge of her sister's well-being or by Orrick's intentions was destroyed by the words written in the letter.

Chapter Fifteen

Waspish.

She'd turned waspish since the day he'd given her the letter from her sister. Instead of making things better between them, everything was worse. Her temper drove him from the keep. In spite of the colder weather and growing winds, he rode along the water's edge inspecting the keep's wall. Anything to stay away from Marguerite.

She scolded not only her maid, but any servant who crossed her path. And she did it in Norman. His mother complained to him. Norwyn complained. Even Gavin complained. The only person she was civil to was Brother Wilfrid. So, her time spent in his workroom was a respite to everyone else and Orrick encouraged her to visit there more often.

He needed a wife now. He could not continue in this limbo of having one in name only who did nothing to aid him in overseeing his lands and people. There was too much to be done and his wife should have been working along with him.

Instead, she remained aloof or hostile.

Orrick knew that something in the letter had caused this—he recognized the pattern within her behavior, and although he attempted to talk to her about it, she refused. The only thing different in her reaction was that this time she spent no time writing letters to those at Henry's court.

What could her sister have said to bring on such a change? Did she worry that he knew about her daughter? Mayhap he should reveal his knowledge to her and soothe any fears she had?

He reined in his mount and slid off to walk. He was a fair man and he'd tried in every way over the months since their marriage to make her welcome here. He accommodated her behavior because he knew the reasons for it, but he knew his self-control was slipping. Orrick was tired of the uneven life he lived now, never knowing if she would adapt or not. He could not continue with upheaval after upheaval.

Gavin urged him to beat her into submission. Brother Wilfrid, sensing his anger, counseled temperance and forbearance. He thought his mother suggested that he throw Marguerite over the cliff, but he was certain he must have misheard her words.

Orrick feared he was at the end of his wits. All it would take was one more incident and he would have it out with her. Self-control be damned. This had to be resolved. Her behavior worsened and so he decided to speak to her directly and end this ridiculous situation.

Orrick stood outside her chamber door choosing the words he would speak when he heard her voice within. Listening for a moment, he realized that Marguerite was ranting to her maid. Although Edmee spoke in English as he'd requested, Marguerite again spoke in her Norman dialect. This, after he made it clear that he wanted her to begin using the local tongue. She knew English. Her possible unfamiliarity with it was the reason he'd asked her to work with Brother Wilfrid in translating the abbey's messages and records into English. True to her talents, she mastered it in a short time.

This was now simply a continued refusal on her part to become part of his household. A continued refusal to be his wife. His anger grew as he heard her insult his keep, his people and their behavior and his mother's "provincial" ideas and manners. His hands fisted as the blood pounded in his ears. When she called her chambers a pigsty, he lost control.

Orrick forced the door open, letting it slam against the wall behind it. He stalked across the chamber until he stood close to Marguerite, close enough to make her take a step back and away from him.

Did she know what she had done? Did she even care that he was past controlling his anger and his disappointment?

"A pigsty, lady? Think you this a pigsty?" He stepped even closer, towering over her and enjoying the look of uncertainty in her eyes. She was trapped between him and the window alcove. "Let me disabuse you of your mistake."

He lifted her by the hips and threw her over his shoulder, leaving her maid to gape at his actions.

Marguerite screamed as he wrapped his arm around her thighs and strode out of the room.

"Let me go!" she screeched, wiggling against his hold. "Put me down!"

"Nay, lady. 'Tis time for you to learn the cost of your careless words and your abominable behavior."

He was not oblivious to the reaction of all the servants and villagers he passed—he just did not care at this point. Until she learned the lesson he was about to begin to teach her, there would be no peace between them. Even worse and more important to him, there would be no marriage between them. As difficult and embarrassing as this would be, 'twas time for both of them to either take the step forward or end the farce that existed now.

By the time he left the keep, crossed the yard and carried her through the gate, Marguerite's struggles had calmed a bit. She probably realized they were being watched and followed and the part of her that could put on that icy facade must be taking over. She was silent when they arrived at his chosen destination.

He stopped before the muddy enclosure in the middle of the village. The smell alone would have alerted her to his intentions, but the squealing and rooting of the pigs made it clear where they were.

She must have had an inkling of what he planned to do, for her struggles began anew. Without putting her on her feet, he shifted her into his arms and climbed over the low fence around the pigsty. He chose not to go too far in, but looked for a clear spot. Finding it, he dumped his wife into the mud.

"You obviously did not know what a pigsty was, lady. Consider yourself informed of what one is. And what it is not."

He stepped out and left her squirming and screeching in the mud. Her maid stood just outside the enclosure clearly as shocked at his behavior as everyone else and obviously unsure about what to do. At this point, he cared not.

Orrick turned and walked away, leaving all of those who followed him to watch as Marguerite struggled against her own anger, the sticky mud and her gown as it dragged her down to the ground several times. A sinking feeling tugged at his gut as he heard the laughter growing behind him. Mayhap exposing her to this public embarrassment was not the best way he could have handled this, but he had ignored too many instances of her bad behavior since she'd arrived and it needed to stop.

By rights he could have beaten her into submission. By rights he could have her confined as a prisoner. By rights there were any number of ways to force her compliance. He was certain he could have gained that with a small measure of the brutal treatment he suspected she'd suffered at her father's direction or at his hand. But that was not his way.

And he did not want compliance. He wanted acceptance and cooperation and, damn his softheartedness, he wanted her to choose him over Henry.

As he retraced his steps through the village to the keep, he heard Norwyn ordering everyone back to their duties. He did not—would not—look back, but was surprised to see Ardys and the boy standing near her cottage ahead. The look of disappointment on her face struck at him. He stopped and would have spoken to her had she not frowned and shaken her head.

Marguerite caught up with him then and passed him without stopping. Of all the reactions he'd seen from her in the past and expected now, he was not prepared for the look of pure misery in her face. The pain of her embarrassment tore at him and he tried to reach for her to assist her. She sidestepped to avoid his touch and continued up the path to the keep without ever looking at him.

Orrick decided it was time to end this. He would gain Godfrey's support and write to Henry for release from this debacle. No one deserved this much unhappiness from a marriage—not he and certainly not Marguerite.

Not able to face any more humiliation, Marguerite did not speak to or look at any of Silloth's people as she made her way back to the keep and the privacy of her chambers. The initial amusement of the villagers at seeing her thrown into the pigsty passed quickly and she sensed that everyone observing the scene was aware that some line had been crossed.

She stood by the window staring out as Edmee wordlessly prepared a bath for her. Orrick had not returned from the village yet and she wondered if the red-haired woman at the top of the hill was the cause. There was some connection between she and Orrick for Marguerite had witnessed the exchange of glances at her approach.

Was this Ardys, the woman whose name had been whispered in the corridor?

The woman who was most likely Orrick's leman.

He had not approached her since that night those months ago, and Marguerite realized that he must be taking his pleasures on the other woman. She spied a young, blond-haired, green-eyed boy at the woman's side whom she now suspected was Orrick's by-blow.

Now she knew where he went when his chamber was empty so many nights. Could she bear this additional humiliation? Her mother had both caused and suffered through it, but could she? On the heels of Dominique's letter, she thought not.

Edmee approached and began to unlace her tunic and gown. Marguerite stood silently and endured it. Without word or objection, she followed her maid's directions and found herself seated in the tub of steaming water. The door closed and Marguerite was finally alone.

It did not take long for the sorrow and despair to overwhelm her. Her father had manipulated and used her. Henry had betrayed and abandoned her. Orrick, who had tried to make her see the truth, had tired of her and humiliated her before his people.

What choices were there for a woman whose life was a complete sham? What paths opened for a woman who had made her way by giving up her body, her heart and even her child for the empty promises of powerful men? What would happen to her now that even Orrick, the kindest of men, did not want her?

Chapter Sixteen

The steaming water soothed her and cleaned her, but after dressing, Marguerite felt a restlessness she could not explain. The day was bright with sunshine and she wanted to walk, but did not wish to face the people of Silloth.

The beach. She could walk on the beach. It was windy and colder than the last time she'd been there with Orrick so she took her cloak with her. Since most of those who worked in the keep were at their midday meal, she left the keep and walked to the gate without encountering any servants. The guard hesitated when she approached, but did not stop her from going out into the village.

Marguerite walked along the wall of the keep until she reached the trail that led to the beach. After reaching the bottom of the steep path, she was not certain if it was easier on foot or on horseback. Breathing heavily, she paused to regain her breath. Walking near the water's edge would be less difficult than fighting with the loose sand, but she did not want to feel the icy bite of the ocean now.

She decided that she could walk closer to the water and yet avoid getting wet, so she made her way to that point. Turning back, she looked up at the dark-stoned keep of Silloth. The tide was in, blocking the northern beaches, so she headed south in the brighter sun. A few minutes later, she met the guards who were routinely stationed there. When she tried to pass them without comment, they whistled and signaled the guards on the top of the keep.

The system was fascinating. The various pitches and numbers of whistles meant something different. Marguerite watched as they held this long-distance conversation over her head. One of the guards waved her on and the other began to follow her, although he allowed some space between them. She was about to reject their protection, but thought better of it.

Enjoying the breezes, she tugged her veil and bar-bette from her head and allowed her hair, still damp from her bath, to dry in the air. Walking briskly, she allowed the winds to buffet her along. Soon, she was far enough down the shore that the guard left behind was a speck in the distance.

Her life felt as aimless to her as this foray down the beach did—it had no destination, no path and no schedule. Her sister's words in the letter tore asunder all that she believed about her love for Henry and his for her. She, who prided herself on being intel-ligent, was a fool for all that she had missed going on around her.

She could blame it on her father's machinations.

He pushed and prodded and forced and focused her in one direction without pause or hesitation. But she had wanted it, wanted Henry. And all that it meant to be his mistress. The jewels. The power. The importance.

Any doubt on her part that this was not a noble goal had left her years ago. Any qualms or embarrassment had faded away as the sheer size and quantity of her rewards increased. More servants, more gowns, more attention. The saddest part was the level of self-deception she had accomplished in her life.

Her hair whipped around her and was nearly dry. Marguerite spied a large rock and walked to it. The surface was smooth and warm, so she sat to let the winds have at her. Closing her eyes and turning her face into them, she tried to figure out where she had made the first mistake.

She remembered when she was eight years old and her father first told her of his plans to make her a queen. Up to that point her tutors had praised her for her skills and talents in reading and writing and languages, but after that, nothing was enough, nothing was acceptable, no effort sufficient in their eyes. Isolated in one of her father's estates in southern Anjou, her every move was scrutinized and criticized until the perfection her father sought in her was accomplished.

Her beloved nurse was replaced for being too soft with her and Berthilde appeared one day to oversee her education and lessons in deportment and appearance. In the beginning, any refusal on her part was met with swift and severe punishments—beatings, starving and other methods were used to ensure her compliance. After a time, her natural temper was beaten down and she acquiesced in all things her father demanded.

The ironic part was that if he'd shown her any love or affection, she would have done his bidding without resistance. Instead, she was constantly reminded of the gratitude she owed him for taking a worthless, bastard daughter and turning her into a woman who would be queen. Eventually, she believed and accepted all that he told her. His dreams were now hers.

Nothing escaped her father's attention to details. He had even made certain that in spite of her virginal state, she knew how to please a man in bedplay. Comte Ranulf of Alencon left nothing to chance in his strategy to present the king with the perfect replacement for Queen Eleanor.

For eight years she prepared. Her father made it quite clear to her that failure was not a possibility. He had given her everything to make certain she could fulfill his expectations. And when finally brought to court to be presented to Henry, she was the woman her father had forged through years of training and preparation—educated, refined, beautiful, ruthless and determined to take the place owed to her and to her father for his unswerving loyalty to the Plantagenet king.

So, where was her mistake? How could a child have stopped Ranulf in his pursuit of his desires? How did someone say no to a king?

Marguerite turned a bit to follow the sun as it moved in the sky. Gathering her hair and wrapping it around her fist, she made a loose arrangement with it that fit back into the netting of the barbette. Peering down the beach, she saw that the guard was still standing watch. Leaning back, she lay on the rock and tried to think on her error in judgment.

Once she'd arrived at court, Ranulf teased Henry with glimpses of her. She was the bait and the king was the prize. Her father made certain that everything accomplished about her was shown to its best—her skills at reading, her talent on the psaltery and recorder, her dancing were all displayed to the king and his court. And while noblemen from the Plantagenet provinces were bidding for her hand in marriage, Henry and her father were coming to terms of their own for the king's possession of her.

And possess her he did, for once he came to her bed, he did not leave it. He was obsessed with her for months and months and took her everywhere he traveled on the continent. He was a hot-blooded man who never tired of bedplay and rarely slept for long. Their nights went on and on until she usually collapsed from the exhaustion of pleasing his wild appetite.

Marguerite shifted on the rock. If she were being honest with herself, she enjoyed that part of it, for it was in that moment of joining that he was truly hers and no one else's. It was the only time she knew she had his full attention and love.

Or did she? Was that her mistake—believing that what he gave her was love? For believing that Henry ever belonged to anyone, let alone her?

No, she realized as she drifted off to sleep. Her

mistake had been the craving for more as everything she desired was given to her. Once she had Henry, she felt safe from her father. The temper last seen as a child came out in bursts. The need for Henry's affection and attention grew and, with it, jealousy. She grew overwhelmed with the increasing tension at court and it was then that she stepped over the boundary.

She could not imagine Henry not taking steps to make their child legitimate. She knew once she told him of her pregnancy, all things would fall into place for her. Never had she thought about the fallacies that lay as a foundation for all she did.

Now, she had lost it all—her position, her power and, even worse, her child for a man who could not be faithful to her. She'd given up her daughter in the hopes of returning to the king's side and instead he'd thrown her away. For all her intelligence, she was a stupid, foolish woman.

That was her last thought as the warmth of the sun lulled her to sleep.

"She's gone where?" Orrick asked. Gavin had brought him word of Marguerite's departure from the keep while he was still at the blacksmith's workplace. "Did anyone think to stop her?"

"She is being followed, Orrick. She is safe."

"If she's on my lands, she'd better be safe." He left the smithy with Gavin at his heels and went to his horse. "Which direction did she go in?"

"Orrick, she has been in the sight of the guards at all times. Calm yourself, man."

"Damn it, Gavin. I asked what direction she went in."

"South. She walked to the water's edge and went south."

Orrick mounted and pushed his horse to a gallop. Frustrated at having to slow for the steep path and on the sandy surface of the beach, he followed the shore away from Silloth Keep. Marguerite had not left the keep and yard on her own since she arrived in Silloth. Why now? To what purpose and to what destination?

It seemed to take forever for him to cover the distance that she had walked, but a short time later he spied his soldier standing midway between the surf and the end of the beach. As he passed him, the guard pointed to an outcropping of rocks higher on the beach.

She did not move. Was she ill? Surely she would have called for help if she needed it? He slowed his horse and jumped from it to her side. In sleep, the frown she'd worn on her brow for weeks was gone. Her breathing was slow and even. He watched her for a few minutes and realized how young she was to have experienced all that she had—the good and the bad. Clouds covered the sun and Marguerite shivered as the warmth decreased. He knew he must wake her.

"Marguerite," he said as he touched her shoulder. "Are you well?"

Her eyes fluttered open and then her gaze focused and she blinked at him. Looking around, she seemed to remember where she was, but his presence probably puzzled her.

"I am well...Orrick," she said as he helped her sit up. "I did not realize I was so tired when I sat down here."

He nodded and dropped his hand to his side. Certainly she did not want his touch now. Not after what he had done to humiliate her earlier in the day. Before he could speak, the sound of many horses galloping erupted and they were surrounded by a troop of his soldiers led by Gavin. Marguerite slid off the rock and stood at his side, still half-asleep. As she swayed, she grabbed on to his arm.

"My lord. My lady," Gavin said, nodding to them. "Are you well?"

"Gavin, you can go back to the keep. Marguerite is safe."

"Are you certain, my lord?" he asked with his smart-arse grin on his face. "The way you charged out of the keep to find the lady, well...we all thought Silloth was under attack."

The swine would pay for this impertinence. Orrick swore under his breath that he would crush Gavin into the ground in a pile of blood and bones when next they met in the practice yard.

"You may return to the keep, Gavin. I will escort the lady back when she is ready to return."

With a final smirk, Gavin led the men away and left a fresh horse behind for his use. He waited until they were a good distance down the beach before facing her. Once more she surprised him.

"How far do your lands extend?" She looked to the south as she asked.

"About two days walking to the south. Silloth Keep and village and the lands attached to it are my largest estate." She sat back down and looked up at him, her eyes unreadable and blank. "Were you trying to walk off my lands, lady?"

"And where would I go?" she asked quietly. He was not certain if she wanted an answer or not, but he decided that this place and time were a good one to discuss his conclusion with her.

"You could go to the convent where your sister lives. You could go to one of your dower properties. You could even go to my mother's dower property when she goes there to live."

"So," she sighed, "you are putting me aside, then?"

"Is that not what you have been asking me to do?" She nodded slowly in reply, her gaze still empty. "I will ask Abbot Godfrey to petition the bishop for an annulment. Until it is granted, you may choose where you would like to live."

His heart was heavy as he spoke the words that would change their lives. "I will also petition the king for his support."

"You will?"

"I am certain that with the letters you've been writing to him, he will assure the end of this arrangement and take you back to his...side." The words burned his throat and the bile rose in his gut as he admitted them.

"You know of my letters?" she asked. At his nod,

she touched his hand as she spoke. "You did not deserve this, Orrick. A wife who is not a wife. A king who does not keep his faith with a vassal so loyal as you." She sighed again and looked away, her gaze staring out over the ocean. "I will go wherever you wish to put me. At least you can have some happiness and comfort with your leman if I am gone from the keep. I can be ready to leave by morning."

He could not believe her words. "Leman?"

"The woman Ardys. Is she not your leman and her boy your son?" She squinted up at him.

He took her by the shoulders and turned her to face him. "Marguerite, whatever Ardys may have been to me in the past, she has not shared my bed since our marriage. She is but a friend. And the boy is not my son. She is a widow and cares for her brother's child."

The frown was back between her brows. Did she not believe him? "I do not spread my seed in women not my wife. I have no by-blows like…" He stopped himself just before admitting that he knew about her daughter with Henry.

"Like Henry? He has sired at least ten children by five women in addition to the eight given him by the queen." She looked through him as she admitted it. "Mayhap you knew that already? I think that I was the only one in his kingdom that did not."

He thought back to her words when they met just before their marriage ceremony. She had completely believed in Henry and now she knew the truth.

"How did you learn of this? Did my mother tell you?"

"Nay!" she cried out. "Do not blame your mother for this. My sister's letter told me that and so much more."

"And you still wish to return to the king knowing that?" How could she place so little value on herself?

"The king does not want me back, Orrick. He has washed his hands of me." Her voice was hollow as she spoke. But through the emotionless tone, he could feel the pain emanating from within her. "I was simply one in a line of available bodies in his bed. He used me, and then when I left court and my father feared losing his influence, he was given my sister."

"Your sister?" He shook his head. He did not know this.

"She was not as well trained as I nor so ready as I to accept the honor of being the king's whore." Orrick winced at her words. "She escaped and begged the bishop to admit her to the convent. That is how she ended up there."

"Marguerite," he began, not knowing what to say.

"Did you know of the woman he called his 'lovely English rose'?" Her gaze was sharper now. He nodded. Everyone in England had heard about the king's affair with Rosamunde Clifford. Even Eleanor in her captivity knew of fair Rosamunde. "He used to call me his lovely lily of Alencon."

She broke free from his hold and took a few steps away. He searched his heart for something to say, something that would ease the terrible betrayal she had suffered. But he could find nothing that would not sound contrived or false.

"You did try to warn me. I just was not ready to listen." She turned and gave him a sad smile. "'Twas too late even the day of our wedding, but I could not believe you. I was still living my father's truths."

"Was it not unkind for your sister to reveal these things to you when no good can come of knowing them?"

"Dominique is not a cruel person, Orrick. She thought to give me reasons to rejoice in our marriage. She did not know that I did not choose this. She thought that I had somehow managed to escape our father's plans and wanted me to know that I had made the right decision." Tears streamed down Marguerite's face now. "She did not know that you do not want me, either."

"Marguerite, I want you."

"Oh, yes, that way." She nodded at him. "I know of your desire to bed me."

"No," he said, shaking his head. "Well, yes, that way, too. But I have wanted you as my wife since I met you in that little chamber at Woodstock."

"But I insulted you and rejected you. Why would you even consider me for your wife?" She reached up and wiped the tears from her cheeks.

He lifted his hand and completed the task. "Because I need more in a wife than a bedmate. I need a wife who can oversee my lands and my people. I need a wife to whom I can talk about many subjects. I need a wife who can hold her own with my Scots friend and the brothers at Abbeytown. I want a wife who can think and speak for herself and can be my helpmate.''

''You see more in me than I think is there, Orrick.''

He lifted her hand to his mouth and kissed her palm. ''I have been told that before.''

''I cannot promise that my past will disappear. Or that I can fulfill the needs you have in a wife.''

''Marguerite, you can make the choice,'' he said. She visibly startled at his words. ''I will not force you to stay. My offer to send you to your sister stands.'' He looked away before saying the rest for it was painful for him to admit this truth. ''I know you do not love me as you love Henry, but I would make a good husband if you stay.''

He knew that if she agreed now to stay it would be because of the terrible secrets she had shared with him and out of a sense of beholding. He did not want that. She began to give him an answer, but he held his finger to her lips stopping her.

''If you stay, it must be your choice. I am no longer willing to have a wife who is not a wife. If you stay, your life will not be as it was in Alencon or at the court. Overseeing Silloth and my other estates is a tremendous amount of work and even my wife will do her part. My mother is gaining in years and cannot do as she did in her younger days. The lady of Silloth will have many responsibilities to fill her days.''

Orrick stepped back and held out his hand to her.

"Take some time to make your decision. Come to me when you have made it."

She nodded in reply and he trotted over to his horse. Mounting, he held out his hand to her and helped her up behind him. She pressed up against his back and wrapped her arms around his waist and he touched the horse's sides to spur it on. If anyone in the village or the yard thought it strange to see the lord and lady return together after such a tumultuous day, they did not comment on it. Riding through the gate, Orrick offered up a prayer that he would be her choice.

Chapter Seventeen

"When will you stop acting like a dim-witted, lovesick fool and tell the woman what everyone else in this keep knows?"

Gavin had caught him off guard and Orrick reeled back away from the open window that overlooked the keep's walled-in gardens. Marguerite worked there below with Wilfrid, gathering herbs and clearing away weeds. He grabbed his friend's tunic and dragged him far enough away so that their voices would not carry out to the garden.

"Damn you, Gavin! Have you no care for my privacy?" Orrick tossed the Scot to the ground.

Jumping to his feet and dusting himself off, Gavin laughed. "She is your wife. Just take her to your bed."

"With that approach to women, I wonder not how you have escaped the bonds of marriage." Orrick waved him closer. "I hope you meet your match when your uncle summons you home to a bride."

Gavin shuddered. "Do not be wishing such a thing

on me just because you must suffer it. Besides, my 'approach to women,' as you call it, seems to yield many willing women in my bed. When it is time, any bride I marry will be a compliant, obedient lass, not like the willful, prickly one you married.''

His friend shuddered again, and now it was Orrick's turn to laugh. '''Twould not surprise me if you have as many challenges in your marriage as I have now. God's luck be with you in that. So, did you come only to torment me or did you have some news?'' Orrick walked toward the hall with Gavin in tow.

''Although I would like nothing better than to witness it, François has offered to lead your escort to Abbeytown. He said all is ready for your departure in the morning.''

Orrick still had not told Marguerite that she was accompanying him to the abbey on the morrow. Except for her brief escape to the beach over a week ago, she had not left the walls of Silloth. And in spite of his words giving her the choice of staying here, with him, or leaving, he had no intention of leaving her decision to chance or whim. And with this visit to the abbey, he was boldly bribing her.

''You have not told her yet, have you?''

''Not told her what?'' he asked, not wanting to give his friend something more to harass him about.

Gavin smacked him on the shoulder and laughed. '''Twould appear that you have not told her she is traveling with you to the abbey and you've not told her that you love her.''

''Do not tread there, friend,'' he warned. ''She

will know of the journey before dinner. The other is not something I plan to reveal to her.''

''Orrick, as I said before, everyone in Silloth knows how you feel about the lady, except her. Your mooning gaze follows her every step. You are never far from her side. Just tell her she is yours and tell her she is staying and be done with this torment.''

Now he laughed. If it were as easy as that. ''I cannot compete with the love she bears for Henry.'' He offered his fear to his friend. ''He is her first love and in spite of knowing now of his betrayal, she loves him still.''

Gavin frowned at him and stopped. Leaning against the wall of the corridor and crossing his arms, Gavin shook his head.

''Did she tell you that she still loves him? She is far too intelligent for that. If she knows what you told to me, she cannot yet have tender feelings for him.''

''She is a woman,'' he said. He had not revealed the other bond that would always keep Marguerite's heart bound to the king's. Even though she knew about Henry's other offspring, sharing a daughter with the king would always allow Henry a foothold in her heart.

''But not a fool. Not now when she knows the deception and lies,'' Gavin said, shaking his head. ''She is too smart for that.''

''When did you become her supporter? You did not trust her.''

''I have always admired pluck in a woman, Orrick. And I would not wish a bride for you like that one you last considered…what was her name? She came from near your mother's dower keep in Ravenglass.''

Eloise, daughter of Lord Rupert of Furness. Orrick fought to contain his shudder. Lucky for him, meeting the prospective bride was part of his demand to his father for agreeing to the betrothal. The overwhelming ferocity of her religious practices unnerved him. He did not want a wife who, at their first introduction, sank to her knees praying that she would be spared from the abomination of carnal knowledge in their marriage.

Now Gavin joined him in shuddering as they both remembered the vivid scene of wailing women and Lord Rupert's reaction to his daughter's behavior that happened here at Silloth just before Orrick's father died. The debacle had so upset his mother that she did not pursue another match for him. ''The Almighty must have the sense of humor of a Scot,'' he said laughing.

''Is this an insult or a compliment, Orrick?''

''I am not certain, but it seems strange that He sends brides my way that are so extreme in their differences. Lady Eloise who would have died happily a virgin within our marriage for one reason and Lady Marguerite who seems quite happy to avoid my bed for another. A strange sense of humor indeed.''

''What will you do, Orrick? If Henry gave her to you, I cannot believe he will support an end to your marriage.''

They arrived at the hall. Orrick slowed and lowered his voice to Gavin. ''I had truly hoped that once she adjusted to the reality of our marriage she would settle to it. I never did want her to learn the truths of Henry's other women or to crush her spirit with the existence of those others he sired even as she thought she owned his heart. Now—'' he let out a breath ''—I cannot find it within me to force her to stay here or to stay married against her will.''

'''Tis already accomplished, Orrick. You are married. She must understand that fact?''

''Of course she does. She knows I am completely within my rights as her husband to keep her here, or to lock her away or to punish her in any way I deem needed. She is, as my friend constantly reminds me, a very intelligent person.''

''So, you plan to give her up?''

''Hell, no,'' Orrick said, slapping Gavin on the shoulder. ''I plan to make her want to stay married to me.''

''You will sink that low?''

''Oh, aye. To whatever I need to keep her here. I know her weaknesses now and will play to them until she surrenders to me.''

''Deception? Intrigue?'' Gavin asked, rubbing his hands together and no doubt readying himself for a good battle.

''Nay, Gavin. She's had her fill of that. I will tempt her with honesty, openness and books.''

''Books? Orrick, the lack of a woman's touch and taste has made you daft!''

''Books, my friend. Her education was extensive and I know exactly where there are books rare and special enough to make her hands itch to hold them.''

''Books?'' Gavin said, his face screwed up in disbelief and distaste. "I think my plan of taking her to your bed and pleasuring her until she agrees to stay is a better one. Even beating her into submission would make more sense than tempting her with books. Daft Englishmen and their bedeviled ways!"

"Worry not, friend. There will be time for the pleasuring or beating once I draw her in. Plenty of time." Orrick laughed and Gavin shook his head.

"You still have too much monk in you, Orrick," Gavin said poking him on the shoulder. "Far too much time spent learning and not enough time spent tupping or fighting."

"So my father lamented before his death."

"If you have nothing pressing right now, we could remedy the fighting part?"

Gavin's appetite for a good fight never waned even in these past few weeks when Orrick had beaten him soundly and consistently. The invitation was a good sign; his fighting partner was ready to face him. With swords or fists, it mattered not for them, so Orrick informed Norwyn of his intentions and they walked out to the yard. He would seek out Marguerite and tell her the plans to travel to Abbeytown after he finished beating the arrogance out of his friend. Too much monk? Not likely...

"May I make you known to my wife, Lady Marguerite?"

He felt her hand shaking where it lay on his, but she kept the smile on her face as she curtsied to Godfrey. The abbot took her hand and drew her close.

"Come, my lady. I have some wine I keep just for special visitors. Sit and rest from your journey."

She looked back to him and then followed Godfrey into his office. She had not asked him, but she probably worried over the same matter as she had when meeting Wilfrid for the first time. The clergy made her nervous. Uncertain if Godfrey planned this to be a private interview or not, Orrick waited at the door and watched her.

Was it a sin to want her so much? He watched as Godfrey drew her into conversation about Silloth and her impressions of the area and he wanted her. When the abbot handed her a goblet of wine and she touched it to her mouth, he ached to hold her. Regardless of his assertions to Gavin, all he thought of was the pleasure they could have if only she would come to him.

"My lord?" Godfrey called out. Orrick had been so deep in lusting for his wife that he'd missed the monk's call. "Please join us."

Orrick stepped inside and walked to the hearth, just far enough away so that he could watch her face. Some of the nervousness was gone, but she kept looking to him as though his presence protected her.

"Tell me of your journey from Normandy," Godfrey said. "I was born in the province of Aquitaine, but spent much of my life in Normandy. 'Tis so long since I have been to the land of my birth—" he smiled "—but I will never forget the blessed sunshine and warmth of those lands." The monk spoke in Norman to her.

"My lord Orrick wishes me to speak in English,

good abbot," she replied, smiling at him. "I would oblige him if you do not mind?"

When spoken like that, it made him feel mean-spirited. He had meant it to help her gain an ease with the language she would need to speak, not as a punishment.

"Or we could speak Latin and he would not know what we were saying about him?" Godfrey switched to the ancient tongue of Rome, one that had always given him fits when learning to read, write or speak it.

A look of devilment settled on her features, her eyes brighter than they had been in weeks, and she laughed at Godfrey. "Or Greek? I like the sound of Latin, but I am more proficient at Greek."

He watched as the monk and his wife continued to talk between themselves. Orrick knew that if he asked, she would stop conversing in the old language, but it made his heart glad to see her enjoying something as simple as talking. He'd never seen Marguerite this animated, and a pang of jealousy tore through him. Is this how she was at court? When she was sure of herself and in the center of attention?

He had nothing to compare with but the day of their wedding and he realized that even then Marguerite was different—she was confident that she knew Henry's heart and mind and she gleamed with an icy veneer that nothing could penetrate. Today, there was personality, but without the facade she wore a few months ago.

After a few minutes, Godfrey nodded to him and then stood before Marguerite. "'Tis such a joy to hear it spoken, my lady. My thanks to you for indulging an old man. And pardon, my lord, for taking so much of your wife's time from you.''

''I do not mind at all, Godfrey. I can see that meeting you has pleased her, as well.''

''I must demand your time now, my lord, for we have much to review from this past month. My lady, because we do not have women religious here in our community, I am sorry to tell you that you will have to restrict your movements and that of your maid to this building, the church and the courtyard between.''

''I understand, Abbot. Lord Orrick, will we stay here tonight or begin our journey back to Silloth?''

''I have a small house outside the walls of the abbey, lady. We will spend the night there before traveling.'' He attempted to read something in her eyes or on her face, but it was blank.

''My lady, if you go to the fourth door down this corridor,'' Godfrey said, pointing to the left as they reached his door, ''tell the brother on duty there that I sent you.''

Orrick fought to keep the smile from his face. He knew what lay behind that door and would love to see her face when she beheld it. She nodded to Godfrey and now he could tell that she thought she went to some room to rest or eat. With Edmee following close behind, Marguerite curtsied to them and left the room.

''Did you tell her?''

''I thought to let her enjoy the surprise.''

''Think you that it will please her?'' Godfrey asked in a whisper.

"Oh, aye. If I know anything about her, she will be overwhelmed."

"Come then, Orrick. Let her take pleasure in the treasures of that chamber and we will complete our business."

"You forewarned Brother David of her arrival?"

"Aye. Although if she reacts as I suspect she will, David may need help."

Orrick laughed and followed Godfrey in the other direction. He knew that once she opened the door there, she would not leave willingly.

Little specks of dust danced in the air around and over her as she spun around and around in the chamber. Growing dizzy, she thought she'd forgotten to breathe. The monk stood to one side with a knowing grin on his face and she knew that Orrick had planned this.

Shelves lined the room from ceiling to floor and were filled with manuscripts of all sizes and description. Light pierced the darkness through windows at the top of the room and cast fingertiplike sunbeams into the nooks and crannies of the collection.

Marguerite tried to discern titles from the center of the room but she was too far from the books. Taking a few cautious steps closer, she gasped as she realized the treasures within this chamber.

"That cannot be," she murmured to no one as she recognized books she'd only heard about but had never dreamed she'd see in her lifetime. *The Iliad* in Greek, *The Song of Roland,* many copies of the Bible and other religious manuscripts. As she walked slowly around the perimeter of the room, she saw books written in the Carolingian language of her ancestors as well as by the famous writers and orators of Rome. Vergil's *Aeneid* was there, and some others in Italian and Latin. Even some eastern languages she was not familiar with. Could that be? A tome by Dioscorides, the great physician and herbalist? The urge to touch them was overpowering.

"My lady, if you tell me which you would like to examine, I will take it down for you," Brother David said.

"Truly? I may read one?" Her hand did move on its own then to touch the first book she'd seen. Homer's *Iliad*.

"Abbot Godfrey said you may read any that you wish."

She gasped as the monk stepped past her and lifted the large book from its place. She moved out of his way and followed him as he placed it on a table. He motioned for her to sit and she did so quickly, not wanting to miss this opportunity. During her education, she had read tracts from manuscripts and selections from the great philosophers and writers, but she had never seen a complete collection like this one. 'Twas far too costly even for her wealthy father's coffers.

The pages were covered with beautifully-formed words and colorful illustrations ringed the edges, telling in pictures what the words said. Achilles' last stand against the warriors of Troy. The Trojan war that decimated Troy and cost so many Greek and

Trojan lives. Helen, the most beautiful woman of all time.

She looked around the room once more, not daring to believe that she was in the center of so many exquisite pieces of literature. Brother David stood next to her and then she realized that Edmee still stood at the door.

"Come, Edmee," she said, waving her maid to her side. "Let me read some of this to you."

"You read Greek, my lady?" the monk asked.

"Aye, Brother, I do. Can you?"

"Nay. I have a fair talent in Latin, but not Greek," he said with a shameful tone. "Although the abbot hopes I will learn, I do not think there is enough time in the rest of my life to gain the skills needed."

"Do you read French or Norman or only English?"

"Language has always been my downfall, lady. Now, I can do wonders with columns of numbers, but letters all jumble together for me."

She laughed. She knew her skills were unusual and even more unusual for a woman, but 'twas the best part of all she endured in training to be the consort of a king. Her father had once quipped that her education rivaled even that of the queen and she took pride now in what she had mastered, for whatever the reason.

"Would it bother you if I read some of this out loud? I have not practiced my Greek in years and now I have two opportunities in one hour."

"No, my lady. My task was to be at your service today so it will be as you wish."

Tears filled her eyes for she knew that Orrick had arranged this for her. How did he pick out the most important things among so many little details? He never revealed this to her when convincing her to accompany him here for his business—he simply touted the chance to explore the lands away from Silloth and to see what she had missed on the journey north. After months in only keep and yard, she felt ready to look over the lands that he owned or managed with the abbey.

Edmee sat at her side and the monk took a seat in a high-backed chair next to the table and Marguerite opened to the first page and began reading the tale in English, both to practice her skills and so that the brother would understand.

Two hours later, when Orrick came seeking her, her companions were asleep but she read on.

Chapter Eighteen

"How did you know?"

"Know what, lady?"

"My weakness."

He took a step closer and leaned down to her. "'Tis always a sound strategy to know your opponent's strengths and weaknesses."

"And am I your opponent?" she asked, not turning her head or meeting his gaze. The room suddenly felt much smaller as though the shelves had moved in toward them and the ceiling had shrunk from its original height.

"I thought so when first we met," he said, his deep voice sending chills down her neck where his breath tickled the skin. "But I learned quickly that you presented yourself with your own worst challenges."

Now she did turn to him, sliding on the bench to put some room between them. How did he have such a canny sense about people? "What do you mean?"

"Your first days here you were in the defensive

position, among strangers without knowledge of what forces were against you, no idea of your allies or enemies. Pretending not to know our language was an intelligent move on your part.''

It was odd to hear her behavior explained in such terms, but she conceded that he did describe her first days clearly.

''But then you made a critical error and went on the offensive. Do you comprehend what I mean?''

The night she seduced him. Her first downfall with him. She nodded and waited for his words, feeling the heat of a blush enter her cheeks. Memories of him and his touch still haunted her from that night.

'''Twas on my journey back from here that I realized that you were your own worst enemy.''

''I do not think I like that description.''

''I would think not, but is it accurate?''

Marguerite fell silent thinking on his words. Damn him, he was right! Forced to admit it, she met his eyes and found that glint of humor in their green depths.

''Mayhap…'' That was all she was willing to offer in the way of an admission.

''You were familiar with court intrigues and not prepared for those who would be direct and not stab you in the back. My people know only their existence here and have never been exposed to the kind of life you have lived. Even when they insulted you, they did it within your hearing.''

His men. She swallowed as she thought on his punishment of them for their insults. He reached out and lifted a stray curl from her face.

"I do not think your actions are so straightforward now, my lord," she accused. "I think you have alternate intentions than simply coming here to complete your business with the abbot. Intentions that concern me."

He stood and pulled her up to stand. Although she feared looking up into his face, he guided her chin with his hand. She found herself clutching his tunic to steady herself.

"In the spirit of this holy establishment, I will freely confess my intentions toward you. I want you as my wife and I will do whatever is necessary to make you stay. By fair means or foul...."

Part of her thrilled to his nearness, to the unspoken promise within his words. In spite of everything he knew about her, in spite of everything that had happened between them, he still pursued her as though she had personal worth. As though she mattered. That thought gave her pause. She had always mattered to some man for the wealth or power she brought. 'Twas never really her.

Had she yet learned not to trust the promises of men in search of all she brought with her? Orrick had been clear about his desire to bed her. He gained new titles and land with their marriage. Were these attempts to lure her into a true marriage simply his efforts to keep all that he now possessed? Did it demonstrate his unwillingness to part with the wealth rather than with her?

"Why do you want me? For the land? For the wealth promised by Henry if you took me as wife? So, you are like the ones who came before?"

Hurt filled his eyes, but he did not relinquish his hold on her or her gaze. "'Twould be the easiest explanation of my actions, would it not? Is that what you believe?"

"I cannot, I do not, trust my instincts any longer, my lord. They have failed me so consistently that I no longer consider them reliable."

"What would you trust, then? Would the words of a holy brother be enough to convince you? Mayhap you will read the wording of the marriage contracts and see the truth?" He clenched his jaws.

He began to pull away from her, but something inside made her stop him. Grasping at him, she held him close. "Tell me your truth, Orrick. Tell me your intentions and reasons. Make me believe." 'Twas a desperate plea from a woman needing a reason to believe that she mattered. She could hear it in her own voice.

"Upon our marriage, I took control of several profitable estates that bordered my lands. Although I have power over those lands, the profits go to you to be used as you see fit. You can keep the gold or donate it, as you wish. Abbot Godfrey is the administrator of your wealth. So you see, part of the reason behind this journey is so that you might consult with him on the disposition of your wealth."

She gasped. This was unheard of. A woman with her own fortune? Gold to spend as she wished?

"If an annulment ends this marriage, I keep control of the lands and the income is split evenly between us."

"I do not understand," she said. "To what purpose is the contract worded so? How did you agree to something like that?'' Her voice grew louder and Brother David let out a snore and shifted in his chair, before settling back to sleep. ''Did the abbot not counsel you against signing such a document?'' she whispered. When he smiled, she realized she was aggrieved on his behalf for her gains.

''When the king orders you to something, 'tis wiser not to refuse him. I believe he was more interested in protecting you than 'twould appear at first by his actions.''

It felt as though her legs were gone and it was only his embrace that kept her standing. This news was shocking, both in its details and in its plan. An annulment would give him gold yet he did not want it? And staying married benefited her, not only in the life he offered, but also directly by putting gold into her hands. Yet he encouraged that. Why?

She decided that it was time to press for the rest of it—he had never answered her original question. The facts he presented had only raised more questions.

''Why, Orrick? Why do you want me?''

He took a breath in and let it out. ''Do you remember when you accused me of teasing you over the importance of first love? You thought I made light of those special feelings you bear for Henry.''

She shook her head. Thoughts of love for Henry seemed so very far away at this moment, but she remembered Orrick's words spoken to her on the roof of the Silloth Keep.

"I know the pain of an unrequited first love, Marguerite."

"Some woman has turned away from your soft feelings toward her? Surely not Ardys?"

He touched his hand to her cheek and then brought his lips down on hers. After a single kiss, he drew back and smiled sadly at her.

"In spite of knowing your heart and your body have been given to someone else, I have fallen in love with you, Marguerite. You are the first woman I have loved and I know the pain you feel over your loss of Henry, for I live every day with the disappointment of not having your love."

Her throat tightened and she could not say a word. Tears filled her eyes and threatened to spill over.

"Here now, I did not mean to ruin this occasion for you. I hope you liked the surprise I arranged?" He released her and took a few steps from her side. "There is still at least another hour of daylight. Why do you not take advantage of it while I finish more work with Godfrey? Then we will make our way to the house for an evening meal."

She sensed he was running from her and from his admission to her, but she was so overwhelmed, she could do nothing to stop him. Marguerite nodded and Orrick walked quickly from the room.

The more she learned about him, the more of an enigma he became. Every time she thought to be gaining some understanding about him—even about herself—he turned it inside out. The man to whom she gave her all tossed her aside and the man who she continued to vex and who stood to gain more from her leaving wanted her to stay.

It made no sense. None at all.

Brother David roused just then from his nap and he stretched and stood. "Your pardon, my lady. Your voice was so soothing that I confess to being lulled to sleep. Would you like to continue?"

Pushing away the confusion in her heart and in her thoughts, she decided not to waste the time that Orrick had given her. "Mayhap I could see that collection of remedies from the physician Dioscorides? *De Matera Medica*. There on the third shelf."

She pointed to the large red leather-bound book she'd seen earlier. She thought there might be something of interest to Brother Wilfrid in it so she spent the rest of the time in the chamber leafing through the many herbal concoctions and medical facts reportedly spoken and written by the esteemed healer from ancient times.

Unfortunately, her thoughts continued to return over and over to the words wrung from Orrick—*In spite of knowing your heart and your body have been given to someone else, I have fallen in love with you....*

"I was despairing of you finding an appropriate match, my lord."

Orrick did not turn from staring out the window. He'd begun to think that telling Marguerite of the true feelings he held for her wasn't the good idea it had seemed to be. Gavin had urged him to disclose his love and he'd followed his friend's advice.

When Marguerite had pressed him for the reason behind his actions, actions that presented a loss to him in the things that mattered most to noblemen, he'd told her the truth. Even though she had made it clear that she was deeply unhappy here, he'd revealed his love and told her he would press his case to keep her. Now that pledge seemed foolhardy at best as his confidence that he could convince her to stay waned.

"Your lady mother, as well," Godfrey continued.

That caught his attention. "You've spoken to my mother about my marriage?"

"Written to, not spoken to." The monk nodded and smiled.

"Then you know of her opposition to Marguerite," Orrick said, now turning to face the abbot.

"I did not sense opposition, Orrick. I sensed concern over the king's choice at first, but I do not believe she disapproves of your wife."

Startled by the revelation that Godfrey communicated with his mother, and seemingly on some regular schedule, Orrick crossed the room to stand before Godfrey. "Of course she does!"

"Lady Constance agrees with me that Marguerite is a good match for you. You two share many traits in common and that can be the basis of a sound marriage."

"I do not know how you can say that, Godfrey. Marguerite refuses to take her place as my wife and my mother has…"

He stopped and thought on his mother's opposition. She had only openly complained about Marguerite during that time when Marguerite's behavior was driving everyone mad. Lady Constance had requested that Marguerite take her rightful place as lady of Silloth and had tried to make her welcome. Mayhap she did not oppose this marriage?

"You are both intelligent, well-read, good spirited people. She has a wonderful mind for a woman, Orrick, and would be of great help to you in all aspects of running your estates."

"If she wanted to stay."

"What do you mean? 'Tis obvious to anyone watching you that you love each other. What reason could there be for her to leave?"

It hurt to admit failure, but if not to your confessor, then to whom could you? "She has a child by the king."

Godfrey looked startled as he should at news of this seriousness. "I do not understand. A child?"

"'Tis a natural consequence of physical relations between a man and a woman," he said dryly. He could hear the bitterness in his voice. "Now she will always be bound to him. As a result, she does not wish to continue in this marriage."

"Orrick, marriage is a serious institution and obligation. She cannot simply decide not to be married."

"As you said, Godfrey, she is intelligent. She knows that an annulment is the only way, and I have promised to gain your support for it."

The abbot leaned his head into his hands and Orrick thought he could hear him swearing under his breath. "You would risk your immortal soul by lying?"

"I promised her I would ask for your backing in this, Godfrey. She does not want to remain here as my wife."

The monk slammed his hands down on the table and looked at him, glaring at him in a most unreligious manner. "In order to gain my support for this, you must be able to answer my questions truthfully and on pain of eternal damnation if you lie."

"And your questions?" If it would bring her happiness, he would consider it.

"Do you wish to end this marriage?"

Orrick winced. No.

"Is there some link of affinity or consanguinity that is prohibited by God's laws?"

Orrick clenched his jaws. No.

"Did you agree to this marriage under false pretenses or at a time when you could not legally give your consent?"

Orrick turned away at that one since he and Godfrey had discussed the "pretenses" of the marriage in advance. In depth.

"One last question."

Orrick tensed, knowing what was coming.

"Have you consummated this marriage?"

"Damn it, Godfrey! I do not want an annulment. I admit it to you." Orrick paced the length of the chamber. "I have offered her all that I have and it is not enough." Orrick sat on a stool and held his head in his hands. He felt the monk's hand on his shoulder and he looked up.

"I tell you that the woman who sat here a few hours ago loves you, Orrick. She is most likely battling with her feelings even as you are. I would counsel you to give this more time," Godfrey urged. "Tell her I will take the matter under consideration. That should delay her enough to give her the time she needs to realize what is in her heart."

"You may have the honor of telling her that, friend. I also told her about the provisions in the contract for her income. I am certain you will want to make arrangements with her for the profits the estates have made."

Godfrey frowned and then smiled. Orrick worried more about the smile. "I will go and speak to her now."

Brother David replaced the priceless book on the shelf as she watched. The room grew darker as the sun moved toward setting, and candles would be needed to read any longer. Since the monks would be called to prayer and their meager evening meal, Marguerite prepared to leave. She had already sent Edmee out to meet with their party.

"My lady? Might I have a word with you before you leave?" The abbot stood at the door. She nodded and he motioned to the corridor. "Walk with me?"

'Twould be discourteous to refuse his request, and she was curious. She walked at his side back past his office and then farther down the other side of the building.

"Orrick thought that collection might please you."

"It did, Abbot. I have only heard of such books as the ones you have."

"There are many that you could borrow for a time. Not the rare ones, but some of those that we have copies of would be available to you."

"Truly?"

"Lord Orrick's sponsorship supports this abbey and its work. Allowing his wife access to our collection is the least we can do to show our appreciation."

"Good abbot, if I did not know better, I would say that sounds like bribery."

"'Tis bribery, my lady. Pure and simple."

She laughed out loud at his candor. "I suspect you serve as my lord's confessor as well as his friend and mentor."

"I do, my lady. I must admit, however, that it is such a joyous difference to find a woman who appreciates the written word." The abbot paused before a door. "You will, I believe, find this interesting, as well."

He opened the door and Marguerite beheld the largest scriptorium she'd ever seen. Dozens of raised writing tables filled the chamber. Some monks continued to work by the light of precious beeswax candles spread throughout the room. The silence that permeated such a large room with so many people within it amazed her.

"Our brothers supply a number of monasteries and abbeys and churches in the north of England with prayer books and Bibles. And we accept private commissions, as well."

Her presence at the door did not seem to disturb

the monks and she marveled at their abilities as well as their concentration to the task of reproducing the manuscripts in their collection.

"I would like to donate one-fourth of my income to help fund your work here, Abbot."

"That would be a generous gift to us, my lady."

"I would like one-fourth sent to my sister's community, as well."

"God will bless you for your charity, my lady."

She turned to face him now for the rest of it. It only seemed right to her that Orrick share in the income that his administration produced. "I would like Lord Orrick to receive one-fourth, as well."

"He would rather have the benefits of your education and your skills than your gold."

Marguerite blinked in surprise, shocked by this monk's honesty. "Will the gold compensate him if I cannot give him what he wishes for?"

"My lady, even this old man can see the love you bear for each other and the pride that keeps you from sharing it."

"Is that what you think? Pride keeps us apart?"

She knew now from whom Orrick had learned his ability to assess others so well. She did not argue his words about love since she had begun to suspect that the feelings she held in her heart for Orrick were love. 'Twas very different from the feelings she bore for Henry though, so she was not certain enough to tell Orrick yet.

The abbot began walking from the chamber and Marguerite followed him. He left the building and stepped into the courtyard. "Lady, I know of your relationship with the king and I think we both understand that it could not have continued. Although you may have given your heart in good faith, his is known to be fickle and changeable.''

Could she ask this holy man advice? Other religious men had turned her away, insulted and snubbed her. But Godfrey was as different from them as Orrick was from the nobles she knew at court. As if he heard her concerns voiced, he took her hand in his and patted it.

''My lady, my history is unlike most clergy here. I have lived in the secular world and even lived in the holy estate of marriage before taking my vows. There is little you could say that would surprise or shock me. Feel at ease and do not worry that I could not comprehend your troubles.''

Deciding that she did indeed need his insight, she nodded. Her hands trembled and so she held them tightly together. Marguerite hesitated to even think it.

''If I was so very wrong about my love for the king, how do I know if I am making the same mistake again? I mean that I lived in ignorance of Henry's ways and saw only what he showed me.'' She had changed in these past few weeks. Once she'd seen Henry's perfidy for what it was, 'twas difficult to trust anyone again. Or consider loving someone else. ''How do I know that is not happening all over again?''

''Now that all you know is gone, you must learn anew.''

''But how do I do that?''

"Be pragmatic, lady. Apply what you learned from reading the philosophers and scientists. Accept what you can prove or what can be demonstrated. Examine the evidence before you and decide which path to take."

"Good brother, that sounds much too rigid to be applied to matters of the heart," Marguerite argued.

"Do not worry. Lord Orrick's character will withstand any test you perform. But, lady, I ask you not to trifle with him." The abbot leaned toward her and smiled. "He is a good man and I suspect you would be happy with him. Orrick is much like a son to me, but he would be better off without you if you play him as Henry played you."

The words were meant to startle her and they did. "I will consider your words, Abbot."

"'Tis all I ask of you."

But Marguerite knew it was so much more that he asked than simple reflection on his words. Was she ready to take the next step?

Chapter Nineteen

Orrick's house outside the abbey walls sat next to a small stream in the middle of an orchard. Not big, it consisted of two small bedchambers and one larger room used as both kitchen and hall. A small barn nearby served as stable and a place for his men to sleep. Marguerite and her maid were given one of the chambers and Orrick took the other.

'Twas not the way he wanted it to be, but he had promised Godfrey to give Marguerite time. From the grave expression she wore when they met in the courtyard of the abbey, he wondered if he would live long enough for her to have enough time to make her decision.

Dinner was accomplished quietly for they both seemed caught up in their own thoughts. After making a final check on his men, Orrick sought his bed. The night went on and on and he could not find the solace of sleep. A noise outside his door alerted him to someone moving through the house. Pulling a tunic over his head, he slid from the bed and, with sword in hand, he opened the door.

"Marguerite? What are you doing wandering at this time of night?" He lowered his sword and watched as she stood unmoving outside his chamber.

"I would speak to you."

The shadows in the room played over her face and he could not read any expression there. Stepping back from the door, he bid her to enter. He lit a candle and placed it on the table next to the bed and waited for her to say what she came to say. Standing near the small window, he waited on her.

Her hair was loose, the first time he'd seen it so for a very long time. It flowed over her shoulders and outlined her womanly curves, and the desire within him that lay near the surface threatened to erupt. She wore only a dressing robe over her chemise and bare toes peeked out from under those.

Marguerite started and stopped and started and stopped again. Each time the words came out in a nonsensical mix. Finally she took a deep breath and he knew the time of decision was here.

"I fear giving myself to you, Orrick. Each time I think I have made up my mind, the terror keeps the words from being spoken and my pledge from being made."

With those words, he wanted to run to her and take her in his arms, but he knew she was not convinced yet that it would work between them. "Do you fear that I will hurt you?"

"Oh, not in a physical way. There have been many times when you could have struck me down for what

I said or did and you did not. Nay, I do not fear you that way.''

He sat on the bed now, thinking he might be less intimidating if he did not tower over her in the small room. ''Then pray tell me what you fear.''

''I fear being wrong again, Orrick, and being played the fool.''

''I think you have some idea of the man I am and that you would not be treated that way. I have professed my love to you. Do you think I am capable of such duplicity?''

He almost smiled at her hesitation, and part of him wanted to point out that she felt safe enough with him to think over his question.

''Nay, I think not.'' She shook her head. ''But I was wrong before.''

''You were with the wrong man,'' he said confidently.

''He is the king,'' she replied as though that explained why he should behave badly.

''In the matter of your love for him, Marguerite, he was just a man.'' She tangled her fingers in the edge of her robe and would not meet his eyes now. ''There is something else worrying you. Tell me.'' He stood and took her hands in his, rubbing them as he sought to ease her fear.

''I fear you will set me aside,'' she said softly. ''When you realize that you have gotten the lesser part of the bargain, you will push me away and my life will be destroyed again. I will be destroyed again.''

''I will not. If you give yourself to me, I will protect you and cherish you as my own. I have sworn it once before church and king and I will swear it to you here and now. I will not let you go.''

He would scream it out to anyone listening if she wanted. She nodded as though accepting his word and took her hands from him. Turning away from him, she spoke the words so softly he thought he might be mistaken.

''I would be your wife, Orrick. In all ways.'' She slipped the robe from her shoulders and faced him now.

Tremors of desire pierced him at the thought of what she offered. However much he wanted her, and he did want her, she needed to understand the seriousness and completeness of the step they took.

''If you give yourself to me now, Marguerite, there will be no others between us. It will be as though we begin our marriage this night and go forward from here. If you are not willing to make that commitment, do not do this.''

''I have made my choice, Orrick. I will stand by it.''

He held his hand out to her and this time, she did not hesitate in accepting it. Orrick drew her to him and wrapped his arms around her. She reacted as he'd allowed himself to dream she would, by sliding her hands around him and pulling him even closer. When he could feel every part of her against him, he whispered her name and she looked up at him.

His mouth came down on hers and he gifted her with kisses that took her breath away. She opened to him and he tasted her mouth and her tongue and kissed every part of her face before coming back to her lips. Marguerite felt the proof of his desire against her belly, and this time it inflamed her own for him.

Everything within her tightened as his mouth moved lower onto her neck and, as he teased her with tender bites on the skin there, she could feel the heat growing between them. The moisture between her thighs increased and she wanted him to fill her emptiness and make them as one. The layers of clothing they wore bothered her now, so she released her grip on him and stepped back to get rid of her chemise.

He smiled at her efforts and helped tug the shift over her head. Then they removed his tunic and each stood naked before the other. The sight of his wide shoulders, narrow waist and hips and long legs enticed her to wickedness. Without moving closer, she placed her hand on his chest and let it slide down, exploring the hard muscles there and on his belly and down farther past his hips to his thighs. His indrawn breath told her of the success of her touch.

Her body reacted, as well, and the urge to press against him grew stronger until she took the step that closed the gap between them. Now it was her chance to gasp as their bodies met and the heat of his embrace melted any hesitation she had. Marguerite felt her breasts swell against him as the hair on his chest teased the sensitive tips.

Gathering her close, Orrick kissed her again and she felt his hand moving down her skin as hers had on him. Shudders of pleasure shook her as he found the wetness between her legs and teased even more of it from her. Spreading her with his hand, his fingers moved over the slick folds there until her legs trembled and threatened to give out.

He paused and guided her to the side of the bed. When she thought he would pull her onto it, instead he sat on the edge and brought her to stand astride his legs exposing her heat to his touch once more. When she thought she would scream with the pleasure of his caresses, he slid back onto the bed and lifted her into his lap. With her knees around his hips now, she was more accessible to him and he played her body with a fervor that threatened to drive her mad.

Marguerite marveled that he did not demand that she see to his satisfaction first. He gave and gave, stroking and tasting and touching and teasing her until, inflamed beyond her expectations, her peak was upon her. Wave after wave of throbbing pleasure surged through her, moving from inside her core to her skin, making her burn with his every touch.

Just as she thought she was done, he turned her over and filled her emptiness with his hardness. As he plunged into her, she felt the aching grow until another peak and another overwhelmed her. He claimed her then, calling out her name and, after only a few thrusts, marking her with his seed.

She was his now.

It took some time before she could breathe again. He remained within her, not as hard as before, but still there. She clenched the muscles she had there to feel him deep inside and he laughed.

"I feel you, love," he said in a husky whisper. "Do you wish for more?"

Orrick did not wait for an answer but slipped his hand between their still-joined bodies and touched the engorged bud between her legs. He rubbed it until she could bear no more and screamed out her release again. 'Twas his turn to laugh for he kept his hand there and touched her over and over until her body could respond no more.

As she found herself sinking into the sleep that followed physical satisfaction, she thought it sad that men could reach their release only once when women could enjoy it over and over again.

Just as the first rays of the morning sun pierced the darkness, she woke. Her body felt relaxed and complete as it had not in such a long time. This time had been so different than the first time when she had pushed him into taking her body.

This time she had given her love to him, as well.

He had not asked it of her. No words of love were spoken on her part, for she was not certain how to broach such a thing with him. It felt premature somehow to make such a declaration and she did not want him to think her false. So she tried to open herself to him and to accept his body even as she accepted his love.

He rolled over and lay on his back now and she watched him as he slept at her side. His handsome features were even more so when asleep and relaxed. His lips that had given her such pleasure were opened slightly and his hair lay in disarray around his head. Her hand itched to feel the curly hair on his chest, so she did.

Gently she stroked down, following its path past his waist and onto his belly and then around his manhood. She barely touched him, but that part of him reacted, growing larger and harder in nothing more than a moment or two. Orrick stretched beneath her touch and growled in a masculine voice that tempted her yet again.

"Taunting the beastie, are you, my lady?"

As an answer, Marguerite wrapped her hand around his hardness and caressed it. "Aye, my lord. 'Twould seem that way."

When he would have pressed her back against the bed, she pushed back and climbed over him. Sitting astride his hips, she brought her hair over her shoulders so that it fell over him as a curtain. Orrick tried to lift her hips to settle her on him, but she decided that this time she would see to his satisfaction.

Sliding back, she leaned closer to his flesh and breathed on it. When it pulsed in her grasp, she laughed. "I feel you, too," she said. Then she touched the tip of her tongue on the smooth skin and watched him react.

"I think 'tis time to tame the beastie, my lord."

"If you dare," he growled as he entangled his hands in her hair and held her there. "Only if you dare."

She dared.

And lived to tell.

No one said a word, but all seemed to know. Marguerite found herself blushing, *blushing,* at his every glance and every touch. And touch her he did as they broke their fast, as he assisted her from her horse, as they sat waiting in the abbot's office. His hand traced from the line of her shoulder, onto her neck and around to her hairline. She shivered with both the memories of his touch in the night and with the anticipation of what would be in the nights to come.

He had complained this morn when Edmee gathered her hair into a tight roll and hid it beneath a heavy snood and veil. Even as she explained that it was out of respect for the abbot and good brothers that she covered her hair so, he attempted to unravel her maid's work. Now he threatened it once more and she tried to push his hand away. 'Twas only the abbot's arrival that sent him jumping back away from her like a guilty youth.

"'Twould seem that you have reached an accord then?" Brother Godfrey asked as he placed a package on the table and sat down.

Orrick looked to her before answering. She nodded. "Aye, Godfrey, my lady and I are at peace."

"My heart is glad for you both." The monk smiled. "You leave to return to Silloth?"

"If that is what I hope, we will leave as soon as my wife sees it," Orrick said, nodding to the package that Brother Godfrey had brought in with him.

"As you commissioned, Orrick," the abbot said, handing it to him. "And done just in time, it would seem."

She could not imagine what was in it, but Orrick now held it out to her. A bubble of excitement filled her. He had commissioned something for her? If his words were true, she thought she knew the contents. Her hands trembled as she untied the cord around it and opened the layers of waterproof canvas.

It was! It was a Book of Hours, and as she opened it and saw her name inscribed inside, tears filled her eyes.

"I thought this to be a bribe, but now I would be pleased if you would consider this a morning gift."

"A bribe?" she asked, her voice shaking as she held back the tears. "A morning gift?"

"I asked Godfrey to see to this when I visited here after our wedding. I thought that such a gift might soften your heart to me."

"It might have," she offered, laughing and crying at the same time.

The book was exquisite with its illuminations and pages trimmed in gold. Each page contained prayers and a meditation for its owner and this one was personalized with her patron saint's day decorated in gold leaf. Again, his kindness overwhelmed her and the tears fell in earnest.

"Here now," he said as he offered his sleeve to her to stave off the flow. "It is newly made and the ink will wash away if you cry like that." His voice was gruff but it did not fool her now.

Trying to regain her control, she asked her other question. "What is a morning gift?"

"'Tis an old custom among the Welsh and others to give a gift to the bride on the morning after the wedding night. The gift's extravagance is the way the husband proclaims his satisfaction with the marriage.''

She could only imagine the cost of this book. "So, my lord. Are you pleased?''

"Oh, aye,'' Orrick whispered to her. In spite of the abbot's presence he leaned down and touched his lips to hers. "Very pleased.''

"And if a bride is pleased with her husband, how does she show him?'' His desire called to hers and she could not help but tease him back.

"She could always—''

"Ahem,'' Brother Godfrey interrupted loudly. "I am quite certain that you will find a way, my lady. Once you are back in Silloth, that is.''

He busied himself wrapping the coverings back around the book and tying it securely. Orrick laughed and gave her another quick kiss before moving away.

"My lord. My lady. I am glad that you are happy now in your marriage, but I do need to offer some advice to you both.''

"Of course, Abbot,'' she said. His words had given her solace and guidance before so she welcomed them now.

"Take you joy in each other, but remember that there is more to marriage than the simple passion between husband and wife. There will be hurdles and obstructions in your path and you must work together to make it past them.''

His words were more serious than she expected and she shivered as though an icy finger had touched the back of her neck. Shrugging it off, she thanked him for his counsel. At Orrick's approach, she stood and accepted the book from him. After a blessing from the abbot, they joined Orrick's men and Edmee in the courtyard and began their journey back to Silloth.

Chapter Twenty

"What think you of my decision?" Orrick asked in a whisper.

"I would suggest, my lord, that you lessen the fine and increase the work he must give to you in repayment of his misdeed. The winter approaches and there is much to be done."

Orrick smiled at her words, for Marguerite demonstrated an uncanny ability to come up with more innovative punishments than the ones he usually assigned to his villeins and servants. This was the second time she sat with him at his manor court and even Norwyn bowed to her abilities. Norwyn usually handled this, but at least three or four times a year, it was Orrick's custom to sit in judgment of his villeins and servants and to accept their payments to him as their lord.

"Four pence and ten days' work before midwinter's day," he called out.

"Aye, my lord," the man answered.

Bowing, the man went over to Norwyn to arrange

the payment of his fine and Orrick pushed away from the table. After several hours of hearing complaints, he wanted to escape. With Marguerite. Norwyn finally called out an end to the procedures and everyone stood as Orrick escorted Marguerite from the dais.

Without giving her a chance to object, he led her down the corridor and up the stairs to his chambers. Waving off a few who followed them calling out questions, he did not stop. Once in his room, he closed the door and spun her around to face him.

"Orrick! 'Tis the middle of the morning!" She laughed as he pulled the snood and veil from her head and loosened her hair until it fell around her.

"I have some important matters to discuss with you, my lady," he said, now attacking the laces of her sleeves. Tied too tightly, he moved to the ones at the side of her tunic.

"I do not think you have important matters to *discuss* at all, my lord," she answered, and she kissed his cheeks and forehead as he leaned to his task. "I think this is a thinly disguised ploy."

He would have words with Edmee after this about how she dressed her lady, for undressing her was taking too much time. Thwarted in an orderly approach, he pulled out his dagger and slit all the laces that held her clothes together. She screeched as she grabbed at the tunic and the gown and the sleeves, which left her chemise unattended. After sparing a half-second for regret, he once more took the dagger and sliced down the front of the chemise, opening her to his view and touch.

Finally he could slide his hands up to cup her breasts as he had wanted to do the entire time in the hall this morn. He'd been away for five long days, arriving home this morn, and he did not want to wait until night to show her how much he missed her. Now she gasped at his touch, but did not resist his efforts. Marguerite covered his hands with hers and guided them down. With a knowing smile, he caressed her where she most wanted him to.

"I think you simply wish to tup me, my lord," she said on a sigh as he made her gasp again and again. She clutched at his arms and let her head drop back against the door.

Orrick leaned down and took one of her enticing nipples into his mouth, teasing it to hardness with his tongue and teeth. "And do you have any objections to that, my lady?"

His bold wife reached down now and slipped her hands inside his tunic, grasping his manhood. "None at all, my lord."

He tried to control himself. Truly he did. At first. Once she touched him, he tugged his tunic up, pressed her back and took her where they stood. He would have stopped if there had been any hesitation in her reaction, but there was none. Marguerite made him crazy.

Finally, after more than a few minutes of eager thrusts and touches, with her arms around his shoulders, her hot mouth on his and her legs around his hips, she keened out her release and he let his seed spill within her. It was some time before their

breathing slowed and he lowered her legs to the floor
so she could stand.

"I told you that you should have accompanied me
to Abbeytown," he said as a way of explaining his
lustful behavior.

Marguerite gathered the edges of her chemise, tunic and gown and pushed her hair out of her face.
She looked as though she'd been caught outside as
the sea winds blew fiercely. She looked wondrous to
him. He ached to hold her, but the quick tupping did
not give him that chance.

"As your wife, it is my place to stay here and
oversee your lands when you travel."

She walked into her chambers and dropped the
layers of now-loosened and hanging clothes in a heap
on the floor. Holding out the sliced laces to him, he
refused to regret what he'd done.

"Tell your maid not to tie them so tightly next
time." Orrick crossed his arms over his chest.

"The girl is so moonstruck over Gerard that 'tis a
miracle she can accomplish anything." Searching
through her clothes chest, she lifted up another chemise and pulled it over her head. "Does he feel the
same for her, Orrick? I would not see her hurt."

"Have you seen either of them since we rode
through the gates this morn?" Hopefully his man
showed more finesse with the maid than his lord had
shown with his lady.

She glared at him through the open door. "I wish
for more for her than just that. She was always kind
to me even when I was abominable and I would see
her happily settled."

Orrick smiled. "Gerard asked for permission to marry her as we rode through the gates. I told him to speak to you."

Her smile lit his soul. "'Tis well, then."

She moved around her chambers and then sat in the window seat, pushing new laces through the holes made for them in her tunic and sleeves. The changes in her these past weeks were extraordinary. When she first arrived, she would never had seen to her own needs in this way.

"Speaking of settling in, how do Richard's sons fare?" The castellan from his mother's Ravenglass Keep had sent his sons to foster at Silloth. Their arrival just prior to his recent departure had forced him to expose the lies he'd told both Wilfrid and Marguerite about their work together.

She glared at him for a moment and then her expression softened. "They are well. Thriving already under Wilfrid's supervision." As if she sensed his fear, she shook her head. "I do forgive you, Orrick. Worry not over the past."

Although she still spent time with the monk each day, Marguerite's time was now divided seeing to many more tasks. Under his mother's tutelage and using her own intellect and instincts, Marguerite was taking over the responsibilities of lady of his estates. He'd promised her a spring visit to the southernmost of his properties so that she could see the extent of his—their—lands.

He rearranged his own clothing and waited for her to finish seeing to hers. He would meet with Norwyn and his assistants for an accounting on the comple-

tion of the harvests in the village's outlying fields.
The weather had held steady and the crops of wheat
and barley and rye were, from earlier reports, larger
than expected. Together with those of his other vil-
lages, his people stood in good stead for the coming
winter.

"Where is my mother?"

"She spends most of her mornings in the solar.
Her women are nearly done the new tapestry. I suggested that she make a matching one for her own
hall."

She rose and put her gown back on, tying it down
the front. The tunic went on next and she could reach
the laces under her arm. The sleeves presented a
problem so he went to help her.

"They are not her women, Marguerite. As lady of
Silloth, they are yours." Something kept her from
spending time among the women his mother gathered
in the solar each day. "Only two will go to live with
her when she leaves in the spring." At her glance,
he continued, "Lady Anne who is her cousin and
Lady Clare whose husband will take command of the
soldiers at Ravenglass Keep."

If he had not been watching, he would have missed
the pain that flashed across her face. He did not think
it was Lady Clare that she would miss. Lady Clare's
babe usually spent some hours in the solar each day.
A girl. About eight months old now.

The same age as the child Marguerite left behind
at the convent in Normandy.

Did she miss the babe? Did she even think of her
and what could have been? Did she want another?

They never spoke of children, but he needed heirs and expected to get them on her. Their frequent relations would, pray God, prove fruitful soon and she would bear his child. Would she trust him enough then to reveal her final secret? Orrick realized that that was the only dark spot within the happiness they had now. She still did not trust him.

"My mother reminded me of two cousins in my father's family who might be of a mind to come and live here. So that you may have your own companions when she leaves." He held out his hand to her. "What say you?"

"I would say that I have the most considerate husband in the land." She replaced the veil over her now-braided hair and took his hand.

"You might not consider me kind if you knew the ways I plan to keep you from your sleep this night." He wanted to remove the sadness that now lay deep in her eyes. Her wanted her to smile at him once more.

She did gift him with one, but it did not match in brilliance the earlier one. "Come, my lord. There are many hours before we can retire, and if we begin our tasks, mayhap the day will speed to its end."

He was about to open the door to the corridor when she paused and looked at him. Lifting her hand to his cheek, she cupped it softly in her palm.

"I do love you, Orrick. Truly."

Orrick turned her hand over and kissed the place where her palm met her wrist, a favorite of hers. "And I you, Marguerite."

As they left and headed back into the busy activ-

ities of the keep, he realized that it was the first time
she had declared it in words to him. Her body told
him in so many ways. Her attention to her new responsibilities showed him. Her attitude toward him
and his people spoke of it. But this was the first that
the words had passed her lips.

They reached the hall when Norwyn called to him.
She nodded and went her own way, with the now-
bedraggled Edmee dogging her steps. He paused and
watched her walk away.

Could there be love without trust?

The thought bothered him throughout the day and
into several more until the answer was forced upon
him by the arrival of Henry's messenger.

"My lord," one of Norwyn's troop of assistants
called out as Orrick rode through the gate. "There is
an urgent message from the abbot awaiting your attention in the hall."

"You just returned from him a few days ago,"
Gavin said from his place beside Orrick. "What
could be so important that he sends a messenger
now?"

"I suppose I must go and discover the cause of
Godfrey's upset."

He led the small company of men with him to the
stables and dismounted. Gavin was at his side on the
steps leading into the keep, when the keep's guards
sounded their horn. Orrick turned to see what had
caused the call. Four men on horseback rode through
the gate without stopping. One rode with a banner
instantly recognizable to any nobleman in England

or on the continent—the two golden rampant lions faced one another on a field of red.

The coat of arms of the House of Plantagenet.

Henry Plantagenet.

Gavin cursed in several different languages as they watched their approach. "What could this be?"

"I know not, but I have a feeling in my gut it cannot be good." He turned to Gavin. "Would you go and keep Marguerite from the hall? She is most likely with Wilfrid now in his workroom. I must meet these men in the hall there and I would hear this news first."

"Is that necessary, Orrick? She is your wife."

Something was not right about this. "Go now and keep her from the hall." His tone told Gavin it was an order and no longer a request.

Gavin did not reply, but his angry snort told Orrick clearly what he thought of excluding Marguerite from receiving the king's messenger. He strode off just as the group dismounted in front of the steps. With impeccable timing, Norwyn came to his side to greet the party.

Orrick accepted their greetings and invited them into the hall where Norwyn had already ordered refreshments for them. The leader of the party nodded to him and Orrick escorted him into the smaller room just off the main hall where they could have some measure of privacy.

"My lord," the man began. "I am Gilbert and I bear greetings and messages from the king to his loyal vassal the lord of Silloth and his wife, the Lady Marguerite."

'Twas not good. He had no choice but to be hospitable and accept the messages and whatever news they contained. The tightening in his gut warned him as it always did. He motioned for the man to sit, but he shook his head. Orrick understood—he would remain standing until his duty was carried out, then seek his ease.

"And your message?" He sat in the large chair kept in this room for him.

"I would present it to both you, my lord, and the lady."

"I will accept whatever message you bring to my wife," he said, emphasizing the word *wife*. Everyone knew of a husband's right to represent his wife in all matters.

"My orders come from the king, my lord. I would ask—"

His words were interrupted by some clamor outside the chamber. After a moment of voices growing louder, there was a knock and a defeated-looking Gavin opened it to admit a flushed-face Marguerite.

"My lord, I understand that there are visitors to Silloth," she said as she walked to his side. She had not glanced at the courier yet, but she did as she stopped before him. The expression on her face told him that she, too, recognized the coat of arms the man wore on his tunic and on his cloak.

"My lady, I bring you greetings from the king." With a flourishing wave of his hand, Henry's envoy bowed deeply to her before speaking.

"The king?" At first she lost all color and Orrick

thought she might faint. Then he saw her clench her fists as she waited for his words.

"I have a letter for each of you and a command to attend to the king in Carlisle on Sunday next. The king's presence will grace the dedication ceremony of the new charter house at the cathedral there and His Grace requests your presence, as well."

The messenger reached inside his pouch and took out several packages. Handing a thin one to Marguerite, he held out two more to Orrick. Waves of nausea passed over him as he accepted the parchments that he knew would change his life. Uncertainty of how it would change made his hand shake in spite of his best efforts not to show his discomfort.

"The king wishes Lord Orrick to attend him?" Marguerite looked from the letter she held back to the man.

"My lady, the king specifically requests your presence and sends this as a token of his esteem."

Orrick would always remember praying that she would not take the box the messenger lifted from his pouch. He prayed with all his might that she would not reach out. That she would not accept the gift and what it meant to them. He swore his heart seized when a smile broke out on her face and she held out her hand.

"The king wants me to attend him?"

The joy in her eyes nearly struck him down. He heard nothing else said in the chamber for her words had destroyed everything he had hoped for these past months. She still loved the king.

Still clutching his messages, he stood and pushed

past both of them. In the corridor he called out to
Norwyn to see to their needs. He could not breathe.
He could not bear to look on her. Giving the parchments to his steward, Orrick only knew he needed to
be away from here, away from her.

Chapter Twenty-One

She waited for two days to explain, but he avoided her. 'Twas like in the days when she first arrived—she could hear the disapproval in the voices of the people of Silloth and see and feel it in the hard stares that followed her every step.

Orrick did not return to his chambers and, for the first time since giving herself to him, she slept alone. If truth be told, sleep did not enter into it, for all she did was toss and turn through the long, dark nights. All she could see when she closed her eyes was the stricken expression in his eyes as she'd reached out to the messenger.

Over and over, the scene repeated itself until she wanted to cry. And she did. But none of this would end unless she could explain to Orrick what had happened in that chamber.

A summons from the king was a command and not a request, and Marguerite knew preparations must be made if they were to arrive in Carlisle in time. On the third day, she decided to begin those arrangements. When Norwyn answered her orders with a benign sort of ignorance, she went to the only person in the keep who could do anything. She sought out Lady Constance.

She found Orrick's mother in her chambers. From the expression the lady wore when she realized who knocked at her door, Marguerite was not certain she would allow her entrance.

"My lady, please," she said, pushing against the door. "I must speak to you."

Once in the room, she waited for Lady Constance to excuse her servants before saying anything more. When they were the only ones left, she faced the older woman.

"You know that the king has summoned us to Carlisle." Every living person in Silloth knew about it. Nothing ever stayed a secret within this keep or village. Marguerite held out the letter she'd received from Henry.

Lady Constance said nothing as she took the letter and read it. "This is not what I expected."

"What do you mean? 'Tis simply a letter requiring my presence on Sunday next. I assume Orrick's letter was the same." Orrick's mother did not respond. Then Marguerite remembered that he received a thin and a thick packet from the courier.

"Lady, he must attend the king! If he refuses without good reasons, the king's reaction will be terrible to behold. I have seen this before and Orrick must realize he has—we have—no choice in this matter."

"My son must have his own reasons for ignoring the king's call," Lady Constance said quietly, but her voice betrayed her lack of faith in her own answer.

Marguerite moved closer and touched her hand. "Please, lady, speak to your son since he will not speak to me. Make him understand...."

"I believe he understands more than you think."

She gasped as she realized what the woman meant, what Orrick suspected. "The king summoned both of us."

"The gift was only for you."

"And I will give it back to him when I see him. I want nothing from the king. Surely Orrick knows this."

Lady Constance did not answer, which made it too clear to Marguerite. They all believed that the king wanted her back. And, for one brief instant, when the messenger said his words, she had believed it, as well.

Apparently the difference was that, in spite of his call and his gift, she knew she did not want the king back. Orrick's lack of faith in her cut her to her core, but there was no time to waste feeling sorry for herself.

"I must speak to him. Please tell me where he is." She grabbed his mother's hand and begged. "Please."

"Why should I take your side in this? All you have done is bring sadness and shame to my son's heart and to his honor."

The words stabbed at Marguerite's heart and she could only imagine what Orrick thought if his mother dared to voice these.

"Henry will not tolerate being disobeyed. He will destroy Orrick and the people of Silloth and all of your lands will suffer for my lord's disobedience." She knelt before the older woman. "I know the king. We must answer this summons," she said, pointing at the letter. "And if I must give myself to him once again to save Orrick and his people, it is a price I am willing to pay."

Lady Constance paled and Marguerite climbed to her feet. "The preparations must be made and I will go alone if he will not. Norwyn will not obey my word. If you love your son as I do, you must make him cooperate with me."

The older woman trembled and Marguerite decided she must find Orrick without her. Picking up the letter from where it fell, she turned and walked to the door.

"I will speak to him."

Marguerite nodded and left without another word.

By the time the people ate their evening meal, baggage was packed, horses and supplies allocated and men assigned to escort her to Carlisle. The journey would take nigh to a week, first through Abbeytown then onto Thursby and to Carlisle. She had still not seen or heard Orrick, but his mother must have been successful in convincing him.

Unwilling to face the hostility in the hall, she had a tray delivered to her. She tried to settle her spirits by reading, but even the beautiful book taunted her in her unhappiness. She hoped she would not have to pay the price she'd named to Orrick's mother, but as she examined her conscience she knew she would be willing to do it to save Orrick from the king's wrath.

And then what? Where would she go? Orrick would never take her back. The king would only do this to punish her for loving someone else. As she had warned Orrick, her life would be destroyed. Even her now loyal servant Edmee had deserted her by accepting Orrick's offer of a place to live.

Marguerite did not know what drew her attention to the window, but she would have recognized his form anywhere. Orrick stood below in the yard speaking to some of his men. As she pressed her face against the expensive glass and whispered his name, he looked up as though he had heard her. Their gazes met for several moments until he turned away and finished talking to the guards. Without looking back, he climbed onto his horse and rode through the gate and headed into the village.

He went to Ardys.

Shaking, she slid down onto the cushions. She knew that she owed him an explanation for her reaction to the messenger's words, but he was not blameless. If he trusted her and loved her as he professed to, he would have waited for that accounting of her actions before throwing her aside and seeking the arms of another.

In the moments just before despair and hopelessness took control, she felt the anger of the old Marguerite growing within her. It strengthened her resolve that Orrick would hear her before throwing away the precious gift she had given him.

Damn him! Why did he now act like all other men

when she needed the differences she'd grown accustomed to in him? His lack of faith was not what she would have expected from him and he should answer for it.

Tossing her cloak over her shoulders, she left her chambers and the keep determined to follow him and confront him. She had never considered that the guards would bar her way.

"Move aside," she demanded as three guards stood between her and the gate.

"My lady, we cannot do that," the tallest one said. "Without Lord Orrick's expressed consent, no one leaves the keep at night."

"I am your lady and I order you to stand aside."

"Lady, they cannot do that."

She whirled around to face the Scot. He towered over her but she held her ground. "I will leave, Gavin."

At the stalemate, she decided on the direct approach and simply ran at the guards, hoping to push her way through. With little effort, they pushed back and she stumbled to the ground. 'Twas the Scot who lifted her to her feet.

"My lady, please do not force us to restrain you," the shorter one pleaded.

"They carry out the orders of their lord and if you force them to hurt you, they will also bear his wrath. Go back to your chambers, lady."

She turned to him and grabbed at his tunic, bringing his face down nearer to hers. "I must speak to Orrick. I know where he is and I would go there now."

"Are you certain of that? Do you want to see what you fear to find?"

"Do you defend his inconstancy? You would— you are his friend in every way."

The Scot's face hardened and she feared she might have overstepped his control. Even the guards gasped at his glare and they probably thanked the Almighty it was directed at her and not themselves. "I am not with him, am I? Mayhap I do not approve?"

"Then tell them to let me go. I would have my last say before I leave in the morning. I deserve at least that." He looked as though he might agree. "You can console yourself with the knowledge that, after the morrow, I will be gone and all will be as they were before I came here."

He took in a swift breath. "Gone?"

"We both know that Orrick will never take me back if I answer the king's call. And, Gavin, I think you know that I must. So, tell them to let me pass."

The Scot took another deep breath in and let it out. Looking over her head to the guards, he nodded. "Let the lady pass."

They stepped aside now at his assurance and she ran through the gate, down the hill and onto the path she knew led to Ardys's cottage. The light of the three-quarters moon lit her steps and in a few minutes she stood before the door. The window's shutters were closed against the cool night air and wisps of smoke floated out of the roof.

Marguerite stood there for some minutes, unable to take the next step. So many things needed to be said. So many things needed to be answered for. So much needed to be explained. She reached for the knob and pushed it open.

Do you want to see what you fear to find?

Gavin's words came to her as she saw the woman Ardys wrapped in her husband's arms. Orrick kissed her over and over and his hands moved over the woman's well-endowed body even as they had on her own. Trying to convince herself that he did it simply to show her that he could, did not ease the pain and shock of it. He raised his head and met her gaze with passion-filled eyes.

Passion felt for another and not for her.

Feeling her world crashing down around her, Marguerite staggered away from the cottage. Looking around, she realized she had nowhere to go.

"You are more mean-spirited than I ever thought possible, Orrick." Ardys pushed him away. "Did you not see how much you hurt her?"

Orrick stepped away from Ardys and closed the door of her cottage. He did not know where Marguerite went and did not care.

He did not care.

Those words might not be true yet, but he would put all his efforts into believing them until they were. He walked to the table and drank deeply from a cup of ale there.

"You must seek her out, Orrick, and speak with her. Tell her this was all a false display. The lady loves you," Ardys said, taking his arm and tugging until he faced her. "She loves you."

"Apparently that is not enough for her to refuse

the king's advances. If you had seen the look of joy on her face at the news of her return to him, you would not being taking her side in this.''

The slap to his head surprised him. Ardys had the strong swing of a practiced man and he stumbled back.

''I thought you different. Now you are being stupid and I cannot abide stupidity.''

''Mayhap I need to remind you that striking your lord is a punishable offense?'' He did not like that she used their comfortable, easy relationship to attack him now.

She walked away. ''Only if he is not being stupid and does not deserve it. If he is not acting responsibly, then it is up to those of us who can to do what we must to remind him.''

He laughed at that. Saluting her with his now-empty cup, he laughed again. She had a quick mind and a quick wit…and a quick hand. But that did not change his mind or his heart in this.

''If she loves me as you say,'' he began. Ardys cursed under her breath, but he continued. ''*If* she does, why is that not enough to keep her at my side and out of the king's bed?''

''Have you asked that of her, Orrick?''

He had not. When faced with her reaction to the king's call, he had walked away. The joyful look on her face and the smile she had reserved for him alone spoke louder than any words she could say. Marguerite wanted to go back to Henry.

The cup was ripped from his hand, his cloak thrown in his face and he was pushed bodily out the door. Ardys stood with her hands on her hips glaring at him.

"Mayhap, *my lord,* when you begin thinking with your head and not your cock, the answer may come to you. Do not return here while there is still turmoil between you and the lady."

Orrick stood outside Ardys's cottage and stared at the door, now shut in his face. She should not dare to speak to him like that. She should fear his wrath.

He left his horse tied at the side of her house and walked up the path toward the keep. He would have to speak to Marguerite before she left. His mother had pleaded her case. Ardys had pleaded her case. But neither of them had seen Marguerite's own words against him.

The king had sent back to him the letters written by her in those first months and, in spite of knowing her condition at that time, the words tore him apart. The lies she had written about him were the worst and they grew darker with each letter. None of them would defend her if they knew how she had really felt about him and about them. By the time he reached the keep, his righteous anger surrounded him and he was ready to face Marguerite with her sins.

Chapter Twenty-Two

She sat in the seat she'd come to like, and waited. She was not certain whether she waited for Orrick to come or for the morning and her departure from Silloth, but she waited in the silent darkness.

Gavin had followed her into the village and stood waiting when she ran from Ardys's cottage. If he had given any sign of pity or even sympathy, she would have broken down, but he did not. He simply offered her his arm and escorted her back here and now he stood as a sort of guard outside her door.

She'd almost expected the crashing of the door or shouting to herald Orrick's entrance. Instead, one moment the opening between their rooms was closed and the next he stood in it. He walked in, but did not approach her. Marguerite would rather face him standing; however, she felt her legs shaking and knew they would not hold her.

"So, the preparations were made for your trip back to the king?"

"It should be our journey, Orrick. We were both summoned."

"I find that the thought of accompanying you back to him, back to his bed, is not to my liking," he snarled. "Although the king may think it amusing, I will not be your whoremaster and your cuckold at the same time."

"I do not go to his bed, Orrick. Why will you not believe me?" Marguerite shook her head.

"The king wrote that, in light of my obvious disdain for his gift as demonstrated by these, he would welcome you back."

He raised his hand and threw the collection of letters at her. They scattered as they flew and landed on the floor around her. Her letters. Even in the dark she recognized them as the ones she wrote and sent off to the king in the hopes that he would take her back. She had written so many untruths in her desperation during those early months here. Before she discovered the truth. Before she loved Orrick.

"I was desperate then. You know that."

"So desperate that you gave your body to me to placate me. As you have said you would do with the king now. Your pattern of lies and deceit has not ended after all."

So, Lady Constance had told him everything she'd said.

"I do not want to give myself to him, Orrick, but if it will save you and all that you hold dear, I will."

"Even knowing it will destroy what we have between us?"

She nodded. She hoped it would not come to that.

She hoped that she could call on the king's mercy and avoid paying that price. But Marguerite loved Orrick so much that she was willing to risk all to save him. "Come with me. Do not let me forget the person I am now and go back to the one I was before."

"Such a noble sacrifice." He spat out the words without looking at her. "I suspect that you would not find it such a hardship to accept his generosity again. To return to the position for which you trained so many years." He turned his hard gaze on her to finish. "Flat on your back in his bed. Or does the king take you as your barbarian husband did, against the door of your chambers?"

She gasped as he tried to turn what they did into something ugly and dirty. Whatever she had expected from him, this venom was not it. This was an Orrick she had never seen before, one who would not listen to reason at all.

"A few months ago, I might have wanted that, Orrick. But that was before learning the truth about him and before I knew that I loved you."

"I saw the joy on your face at his call," he accused. "I saw the exultation in your expression that he wanted you back."

"I am guilty of feeling that."

"Hah! Finally you speak the truth to me. He has but to send for you and give you some paltry gift and you run to him." He came closer now and she could see him clench and release his fists. "You sell yourself too cheaply, lady."

She did rise to her feet now and walked to him.

"I confess to you that, for a short moment, I did feel triumphant at his call. 'Twas but a momentary lapse in reason."

He shook his head and stepped away from her as though he could not stand her presence. This was what she had feared when she went to him that night in Abbeytown. That, if he knew all of her faults and sins, he would turn away from her. As if she had predicted it would happen, he did exactly that.

"For more than half of my life, my intent has been to possess and keep the king's attention. My father forced me to live his desire for power and even accept his dream as my own for years, until I believed it and pursued it to the exclusion of all else."

Marguerite moved closer to him again and looked at his hardened expression. "So, even though Henry tossed me aside, even after he took my sister to his bed, even after he took everything from me that I could give, I felt a moment of victory.

"I do not want him, Orrick. I do not want his gifts or his touch. It was simply a moment when I allowed all those years to crowd out all that we have now."

She could see that he battled within himself over whether or not to believe her words. "Come with me. Let us face the king together. Trust me."

Orrick gazed on her now with an expression of such wanting and need that it shook her to her core. "Do not go, Marguerite. Trust me to handle this as I know it must be handled."

"But you do not know the king as I do, Orrick. I have lived in his court and seen many men more powerful than you be destroyed at his whim or because they chose the wrong way to confront him. I do trust you, Orrick, but in this you must trust me.''

She waited, knowing that this was the most important moment between them, more important than when she professed her love to him. He turned away, telling in a gesture more than he said in words. Marguerite watched as he walked to the hearth and leaned against it, staring into the fire.

''If you trusted me, you would have told me about the one thing that ties you more to Henry than you will ever be tied to me.''

''He took my virginity, Orrick, but that does not signify now.''

''The babe,'' he whispered. ''You gave him a child. That cannot be changed.''

She staggered back and fell against the bed. He knew about the babe. ''You know?''

He still would not look on her. ''I have known for months and have waited for you to love me enough, to trust me enough, to share this final secret. I cannot compete with the king, Marguerite. I cannot compete with my king over the power and the riches he gave you, and now I find I cannot compete with the man over being the first in your body, the first in your heart and the first to give you a child.''

''You think this a competition? Over me?''

''Is it not?'' he asked. ''And if you answer his call now, the king has won.''

She clasped her hands in her lap and realized that she had no way to convince him but to reveal what she had not dared to think on for a long time. But in her efforts to make him understand, would she lose him?

"I have not been able to confess the sins from that time, Orrick. I did not even think I had sinned in being with Henry. 'Twas just the way I was taught to live, but you taught me so much more. And although I could bear the disdain from those in Henry's world and even those in yours, I could not bear to think of the way you would despise me if you knew the rest of it."

"Marguerite, bearing a child is not your fault. Why do you think I would hate you over that?"

"This is not about trust, Orrick. It is about facing my sins and my fears. I did not tell you because I could not. If I told you about the babe, I would have to tell you... I would have to tell you how I prayed she would die."

"Die?" His face blanched as he said the word.

"I was so selfish, Orrick, so evil that once I knew I had not borne him a son, I wanted nothing but to return to the king without the burden of his bastard daughter. Babies die so easily, and when she did not, I sinned again in turning away from her and not allowing myself to even think of her existence."

"You could not raise her yourself, Marguerite. Surely..."

"The couple raising her believe her to be Dominique's daughter and I never told them the truth of it. Not thinking on her and denying her existence was still easier than remembering my fervent prayers for her death and my disappointment that she lived. 'Tis easier not to think about her at all than to be forced

to confront that I was so stupid and selfish and misguided that I could want the falseness of the king
even more than a child of my own flesh and blood.''

She shivered as she thought of her arrogance during those days. When Dominique made the off-
handed remark that she could pass the babe off as
hers, Marguerite had seized it. She wanted nothing
that would interfere with her plans to return to Henry
and regain his love and her power. Nothing.

Including the child she'd borne.

The pain of it paralyzed her now. Before being
exposed to Orrick and his people, she thought nothing of her actions. But learning about goodness and
fairness and real love from him made her see the
terrible errors of her past. If she could not forgive
her own trespasses, how could he? He did not ask
any other questions, so she stood to face him and
find out the true cost of baring her soul to him.

''Now that you know my darkest sin, will you still
profess your love for me as you promised?''

The look of horror was all the answer she needed
from him.

The journey would take about a sennight. The
slowest part was reaching Abbeytown through the
heavily-wooded land. Once past there they would
meet the old Roman road that led into Carlisle from
the west. Since most of the road would be traversing
his lands, Orrick had no doubt that they would arrive
safely. The troop of ten soldiers led by four of his
knights would guarantee it.

For the past two days and nights, he had paced the

confines of his chambers trying to force from his mind the sight of her standing before him confessing her sins. He had hated her in those moments, for her words made him realize that he had failed her.

He did not hate her. It was more about hating himself for not being the man she needed. Through the months when she wanted to return to Henry, he had convinced himself that he was patient and knowing and strong enough to wait it out. Orrick knew from the moment the king offered her as wife to him that she was not going back. So, being older and wiser, he allowed himself to feel pride over his control of his reactions to her behavior.

And he had played her as much as Henry had.

He did not sit idly by while her character was torn down and rebuilt; he manipulated her with her needs and fears just as the king and her father had. Then he had enjoyed all the fruits of his work as she gave herself—body and soul—to him. He used her for her talents and benefited from it.

Just as Henry had. And as every man in her life had. For all his supposed goodness and mercy and patience, he was no better than those before him. Even when he was able to convince himself that he did it for love of her, his guilt haunted him.

And instead of revealing the secret he knew burdened her heart, he stood back sanctimoniously and expected her to trust him enough to divulge it to him.

Orrick turned back to the rolls now before him and tried to concentrate on the figures he was supposed to be examining for Norwyn. The harvest had been a good one here in Silloth. Counting up the columns and comparing them to those of the year past, he was pleased with the increase.

His pleasure lasted for a minute and then he shoved the parchments across the table, not caring if they fell. He was not fooling himself. He could not do this without her. He did not want to do this without her. But, when she begged for his help and his trust, he'd refused her.

He was no better than those before him.

Without warning, the door opened with such force that it crashed back against the wall. Gavin came in and slammed the door closed. He carried a jug and two cups and thumped them down on the table, too.

Before he could ask, Gavin filled the two cups, shoved one in Orrick's hand and then downed the contents of his own. With a glare, he motioned for Orrick to do the same. He drank it in a couple of mouthfuls and put the cup down. Gavin repeated filling and drinking his and waited while Orrick did so, as well. The Scot paused after two, filling the cups again but not drinking his.

"If ye had just tupped or beaten her into submission, this wouldna be happening." Gavin's English tended to slip as his intake of ale increased. These cups had not been his only ones.

"Stay out of this, Gavin," he warned.

"But no, ye had to prance around, acting all high and mighty instead of doing what ye should have."

Orrick let out a breath. "And that would have been what?"

"Tupping or beating her until she accepted the

marriage. Ye have too much monk in ye, Orrick. Too much monk.''

"You think it would have made her settle in better?"

"Aye. She would have known where she stood and ye wouldna have needed to bribe her with books.'' Gavin did drink the ale now. "Books? Daft Englishmen!'' He swayed a bit on his stool. "Ye know what this was really aboot, dinna ye?''

"You are going to tell me?''

"Whose is bigger?'' Orrick frowned, not understanding. "Ye or Henry. Who has the bigger cock?''

He should have punched him right then and there, but Gavin could fight better drunk than anyone else could sober, so he indulged him. "And that's the answer to my problems?''

"She didna tell ye, did she? So, every time she says she's wanting to go back to him, ye're worrying it is because his is bigger. When she tells ye she's happy here with ye, ye're worrying 'tis because yers is bigger. Damn it, Orrick! Go to Henry and just get it over with.''

If Gavin were not so serious and so drunk, he would have ignored it. If it were not true, he could have. In his forthright way, his friend had named his deepest fear although not in the way he thought it. He'd allowed himself to name it only a few times and tried to cover it with a veneer of learning and superior detachment.

It was all about insecurity of the male persuasion.

When she wanted Henry, he did worry that it was because he was not worthy or rich or handsome or powerful enough. When she wanted him, he worried that it was because he was too learned and patient and good-hearted and not more his manly attributes.

"If it were only that easy," he said.

"If ye would stop trying to reason everything oot and just start acting on what ye feel for her, ye would see this as I do. Ye want her. Ye love her. Ye go and bring her back. King be damned."

"Talk like that is treasonous, friend."

Gavin waved him off. "Henry wasna man enough to keep her in the first place. Go and get her."

"And if she does not wish to come back?" He had been a fool. Marguerite did not deserve to be mistreated again.

"Ye are her husband. Go, get her, bring her back," Gavin told him. "And tup her until she canna move." He paused and frowned. "Or is that beat her until she canna run? Whichever isna important. Just go and get her."

He tried not to laugh. 'Twas too important to him, but his friend's drunken assessment, as it was, made him see his mistake. He had either thought or felt, and each of the wrong time. When he should have reacted physically, he was deliberate and considered and calculated every action before he took any. When Marguerite needed his thoughtfulness, he could only feel. Orrick knew that even though he expected complete change from her, he did not expect to change at all to be the man she needed.

"Daft Englishmen!" Gavin blurted out again.

"Tell me, friend, how many wives have you had to beat into submission?"

An expression of horror settled on his face. "We Scots dinna need to beat our women. And I would never raise a hand to mine."

Orrick stood, knowing now that he could not allow Marguerite to face the king alone. "'Tis time, Gavin. Are you with me?"

Gavin stood now and nodded. "Do we go and get her?"

"If she'll come back with me."

"Have ye not heard a word I've said, mon? Ye bring her back."

"Oh, aye. 'And tup her until she canna move.'" 'Twas easier to agree with him when he was this drunk.

"Now ye have it. I'll see to the horses."

Chapter Twenty-Three

With François and her new maid at her side, Marguerite made her way through the castle at Carlisle to the chamber assigned to her. The dedication ceremony had been overlong, hot and tiresome. All she could think about was seeking a time of rest in her chambers before her presence was required at the feast to mark the king's visit here.

The corridors were lined with toadies hoping to catch the king's eye or hoping to press their case with one of his ministers or favorites. Watching the desperation in their expressions, she wondered how she had endured it for all those years.

Of course, she thought, turning another corner, 'twas easier to bear when you were holding the power and not seeking it. Hearing her name, Marguerite looked around to find the source. Recognizing the abbot, she waited for him to catch up and curtsied to him.

"Abbot Godfrey, I thought you might be here,"

she said, genuinely glad to see someone she knew. "I looked at Mass but could not see you."

"When the king comes, we must all attend," Godfrey replied. She watched as he surveyed those nearby, and when he did not find the person he sought out, he turned to her. "Where is Lord Orrick? I thought to speak to him before the festivities." She noticed that François shook his head at the monk's glance.

"Lord Orrick is in Silloth. I have answered the summons of the king without him." Bold words, but she did not feel so bold now. Truthfully, she felt sick without Orrick at her side.

The monk frowned and mumbled under his breath before taking her hand and leading her to a more private alcove. At her nod, François and the girl stepped away and stood between them and anyone who might approach.

"My lady, I find myself concerned about your presence here without Lord Orrick. Surely there are some who will…some who will…" He seemed to search for words that were not there.

"Some will take the wrong meaning from my attendance here without my husband?" she said.

"Respectfully, my lady, yes." Godfrey looked at her with pain in his eyes. "I thought that you and Lord Orrick had settled things between you. He seemed quite happy when last he visited the abbey."

"Things have changed, good abbot." She sighed. Weariness was overtaking her and she felt light-headed. "Can we speak more about this later? Mayhap after the feast tonight? I seek my chambers now.''

''Are you well, my lady?'' He took her hand and touched her cheek. ''You are pale.''

''My thanks for your kind concern, abbot. The journey was longer and harder than I expected.'' Marguerite pressed a linen square to her sweaty brow. She felt the perspiration trickling down her neck and back, as well. ''We arrived late last night and were not assigned rooms immediately. I am certain that I will recover with but a short rest and a good meal.''

''François,'' he called as they stepped out into the corridor. He pointed at her maid and nodded. ''See to your lady.''

As she walked to her chambers, she wondered if Godfrey would press her about what she might have to do. She felt his disapproval already. What would his reaction be if he knew she would be summoned to the king's private quarters this night?

When she reached her door, Marguerite waved off the help of the maid. Edmee had stayed behind at Silloth and, although Marguerite understood the reasons, she was not yet comfortable with the manners of Jolie.

She loosened the wimple and barbette that covered her hair and mopped her neck with the linen. Untying the laces at her neckline, she took in a deep breath and tried to refresh herself. When the profuse sweating stopped, she lay back on the raised pallet and, in only a minute, could feel sleep pulling her down.

Was she taking ill? Did some sickness attack her now?

As she fell asleep, she remembered the last time she'd felt these symptoms. Her resulting laugh was one of desperation and not humor.

Her maid woke her so that there was enough time to dress for dinner. Marguerite had purposely brought the beautiful blue satin-and-silk gown she wore when she married Orrick, to remind Henry and those who would be witness that she belonged to another man. Although her hair was braided, she wore a veil that matched the dress exactly and a circlet of gold to hold it in place.

She did not have a looking glass with her, but François's glance and then glance again told her that the work on her appearance was successful. And it must be, for to display anything but strength or beauty before those in attendance was an opening for attack. Marguerite knew the tactics and measures used by those who lived in the shadow of the king, and although out of practice, she remembered her lessons well.

François led the way to the dining hall, and as she walked down the corridors, many surreptitious glances, smiles and smirks were sent her way. One younger woman stepped in front of her and waited for Marguerite to face her. This must be Henry's newest conquest.

"Marguerite," the girl said with a nod.

"Adelaide. You look well," Marguerite said.

"I would think you too humiliated to show your

face in his court again," she murmured in a voice that was filled with sweetness and venom. "Especially since your husband has abandoned you to the king's whim."

"Humiliated, lady? I think not. My husband is one of the great lords here in the north and was detained from arriving with me."

Adelaide's laugh ended with a snort—not a genteel one, but one that demonstrated her disdain and disbelief. "Come now, Marguerite. You have long lost the king's favor, and being summoned back to his bed now will not in any way diminish my place as his favorite."

"I do not seek Henry's bed, Adelaide. You may keep your place in it." She leaned over closer. "I have found great happiness with Lord Orrick and need not look to the king for anything."

"Your husband apparently does not share your convictions. He is probably too embarrassed to show his face here since he knows that Henry wants you in his bed." Adelaide laughed again. "Your husband…"

"Is terribly late and begs his ladywife's pardon."

Orrick took her hand and kissed it and somehow managed to force Adelaide to one side. Marguerite blinked several times for she was certain he was a figment in her mind and not truly here before her.

"Orrick?"

"Aye, love. I do ask your pardon for my tardy arrival and for so many other things, but there will be time for that later. Come, let us seek seats and you can tell me of the dedication ceremony."

He entwined his fingers around hers and began to walk toward the large chamber ahead. She pulled him to stop.

"We should talk now, Orrick. I have been given a chamber here in the castle and we could go there to talk."

Now that he was here, she wanted to work out the problems between themselves before any more occurred because of her coming without him. Part of her wanted to take him and ride back to Silloth without stopping.

"There are too many about, Marguerite, and there is too much to be said." He smiled and lifted her hand to his mouth, kissing it softly. "Come—" he tugged her hand "—let us eat and meet whatever is heading our way together."

She followed him into the hall where they were met by one of the masters of protocol who handled the seating arrangements for large banquets like this one.

"My lady, there is a seat reserved for you at the king's table there," he said, pointing to the front of the room.

She hesitated, for the man did not mention Orrick's place. "And where is my lord's place?"

The two looked completely confused. Finally the younger one explained. "My lord, we did not know of your arrival. We will find you a place at one of the other tables."

"That is not acceptable," Marguerite exclaimed. "Lord Orrick of Silloth is one of the king's most important vassals in the north and will be treated with the respect he deserves. If he does not sit at the king's table, then I will not. Then the king will not be happy...." She let the threat hang out there.

Men like this—most men in fact—did not know how to deal with an angry woman. To add to the moment, she stamped her feet and huffed out a breath. Wide-eyed at her temper, one of them went running to the front of the room where he and another engaged in a heated discussion. Orrick wore an expression of vague amusement and she could only wonder what thoughts were behind it.

"You are scaring them, my lady. They do not know how to handle an angry Marguerite of Alencon."

"But their reactions tell me they have heard the stories."

Orrick laughed at her words, probably as he remembered a few outbursts from that Marguerite in her first weeks at Silloth. Now, she feared overplaying the role and truly angering the king. An angry Henry would be a resistant Henry.

"And how would you handle it, my lord?" she asked, watching the overseers scampering up and down the king's table, now rearranging some of the chairs.

"I am beginning to suspect that Gavin's methods might be best." She raised an eyebrow at him. "He recommends that women be either tupped or beaten into submission or obedience."

"And you support his methods?" They must have been drinking to come up with such a solution.

"We shared a few too many cups of ale when we

discussed the correct way of handling our problems and specifically you.''

''I can hardly wait to hear the rest of this, but it appears our places are now secure at Henry's table.'' Marguerite watched as the men waved them to the front dais.

''Gavin has suggested that when I speak to the king about you, I remember that the basis of our dispute is really not about you but about...'' Orrick laughed again and she enjoyed the sound of it. ''He argued that 'tis all about the size of our—the king's and mine—private members.''

Marguerite stopped completely now and only moved when Orrick slid his arm around her and made her walk. How did men come up with these ideas? Ah, too much ale and too much time. As they reached the front and were about to climb the steps, Orrick leaned over so that only she could hear.

''He suggested that when we meet the king, we should present them and decide whose is larger. After that, I should take you home and, well, I have told you the rest of it.''

Somehow, between his outrageous words and his guidance, they had managed to take their seats without her beginning to worry about what was to come. And from the look of concern in his gaze, she suspected he did it apurpose. She took in a deep breath and offered up a silent prayer of thanks that he was there, at her side, for she would rather not deal with Henry alone.

The king's herald called out to the crowd and everyone stood as Henry and his entourage entered the hall. Marguerite recognized his closest advisors and ministers as they followed behind in a near run to keep up with the king's energetic pace. As they climbed to the dais, Henry's gaze caught hers and she trembled. Not in attraction this time, but in fear, for his commands this night could destroy any chance of happiness for she and Orrick.

Orrick must have felt it or seen it. He touched her back gently to let her know he was there and then whispered to her, "You could end the anticipation now by simply telling me whose is larger."

She laughed out at his preposterous words and wanted to throw herself into his arms, but the king's voice interrupted.

"Something amusing, Marguerite?"

Henry stopped in front of them and she dropped into a deep curtsy before him. When she raised her eyes a discreet distance, his hand was held out to help her rise. Giving him hers, she stood before him and prepared to take her first close look at her former lover since she'd discovered the truth about him as a man.

Marguerite saw him now through the eyes of a woman in love, in love with her husband, and not overwhelmed by all the king offered. His innate sexuality and power could not be denied, but her blood did not boil nor her heart quicken as their eyes met. Had he always been this old? Still in his prime at two score and five, he appeared older now than when she last saw him in the summer.

"What was so humorous?" His eyes narrowed

and she knew he feared they had been finding amusement at his cost.

"My lady was reminding me of my deplorable table manners, Sire," Orrick said, bowing deeply to the king.

"I did not expect you here, my lord. I'd been told that you were absent from the dedication this morn."

Marguerite noticed he had not released her hand yet, and as he addressed Orrick, he raised it to his mouth and kissed it.

"I confess to being tardy, Sire, and beg your pardon for it. But, as my lady so quickly pointed out to me, I could never miss such an important obligation as this."

Henry looked stymied, for to do more, while so many nobles and clergy watched, would risk the approval of those he needed to rule. Taking the unmarried daughter of an ally as his mistress with the consent and encouragement of her father was one thing. Taking the wife of a faithful vassal in his presence and over his objections was quite another. Orrick's attendance would make things difficult for the king.

When he could say nothing else, he let her hand drop and continued on to his seat in the center of the long table. Once he was seated, everyone took their places and servants began to circulate with the bowls of water and cloths so diners could clean their hands before sharing in the meal. As they shared the silver plate and cup between them, Marguerite began to relax.

"I may not have completely agreed with Gavin's

assessment of the situation, but I think his idea may have some merit.'' He turned to her and offered her the cup of wine. ''I am sure, however, that not accompanying you was the wrong thing to do, and I will ask for your forgiveness for that and many other things when we have some private time.''

Her heart swelled at his words. Orrick was at her side and would be there for whatever came to pass. Dinner passed quickly for she wanted nothing more than to return to their quarters and settle the discord between them. She was so happy that she forgot what she should have remembered.

One of the gentlemen of the king's bedchamber delivered the message before dinner finished. He approached from behind as though speaking to the man at her left, but whispered in her ear instead.

''Eleven of the clock, lady. Alone. A sign of his esteem.''

She tried not to startle as the man's hand grazed her thigh and left a small package on her lap. 'Twas the way it was done. She did not have to open it to know what was inside—a jeweled trinket, perhaps a ring or bracelet, to suitably impress her and ease his way.

If Orrick saw it, he gave no sign. They continued to eat from the many courses, but the meal was ruined for her now. She struggled to give him no sign of her worries. Finally, the king jumped up and strode from the table without warning, a usual practice for him, but one that left those unfamiliar with it aghast.

With the king's presence ended, everyone was free

to pursue their own entertainments for the rest of the evening, be they in the castle, on its grounds or in the city itself. In spite of the size and importance of its cathedral, Carlisle was a city centered on commerce of all kinds, and many of the men attending the king would seek out the basest of all entertainments offered. Even Henry was known to visit a whorehouse if it caught his fancy.

But this night, as Marguerite clearly understood, the king's whore would come to him.

Chapter Twenty-Four

"You were right, Marguerite. I did not trust you."

Orrick waited for her to sit on the small stool and then crouched next to her. He took her hand and held it in his. She was trembling and pale so he knew that she'd received some kind of message. "I am trying to show my trust in you now. You asked me to come with you. I am here."

He leaned back and sat on the raised sleeping pallet to her side. He had missed her so badly over this past week. Knowing that he'd caused her pain tore at him, but he was unsure of how to broach it with her.

"You surprised me, Orrick. Both in how you reacted to this summons and to everything that followed. Everything in the past had been approached in such a thoughtful, deliberate manner, that your reaction had me doubting what I knew of you."

"I was doing much the same thing that you had done, Marguerite. I ignored all the signs around me and thought I could look on you and your past as something far and detached from me. When the courier delivered those letters and I was confronted with all of your feelings about me and about my family and people, the feelings I'd kept at bay all came rushing through.''

''They were not true, Orrick. You know that, do you not?'' she whispered.

''I told myself they were not true and that I understood how you had come to write them. But when faced with the substance of them, part of me inside tore apart. Then, seeing that look on your face when Henry called, all the jealousy and lust and wanting poured through. For days I could not think about the truth or what we should do. All I could do was feel the pain inside me.''

''Orrick, you do know that I have been faithful to our vows? I freely admit that it is your love that has allowed me to become the person I am today.'' Marguerite moved to his side on the pallet. ''The Marguerite who walked halls like these before did not have that. She knew only the days and nights granted to her by her father's plots and the king's passions and she did nothing that they did not allow.''

His stomach turned as he realized he must complete his confession to her about the rest. He was no better and she needed to see him in that light before they could move on.

''Marguerite, I have used you, too. I plotted and bribed you to gain your consent. How is that any different than the others in your life?''

''You love me.''

He looked at her, feeling the overwhelming guilt

within him. "I am using you as a man does a woman, as a husband does a wife. 'Tis still taking something of value from you."

"And giving me love in return, Orrick. You have no idea of how important that is. You grew to manhood in a family that loved and accepted you. You had friends and even teachers and mentors who loved you. I had none of those things. My father does not realize and never will, that I would have done anything he asked of me if he'd loved me first. But there was no softness of heart or affection for me."

He began to tell her that she was wrong, when she stopped him with a finger to his lips.

"There are certain ways in which men and women deal with each other in this world, Orrick. You know the laws of God and of men. I knew that I was valued for what I could bring to a man in marriage, or what I would bring when it was accomplished."

She leaned her head on his shoulder and he wrapped his arm around hers, bringing her closer to him. "The difference with you, with us, is that instead of being diminished or my value lessening by turning over lands and wealth to you, I am made more. I have the chance to use all I have learned and all that I know and all that I feel in our marriage. If I had not your love to rely on, I would have been destroyed by what I learned of Henry. Instead, I find it has strengthened me and allowed me to see him for what he is and what I was."

"Now I think it is you who has been thinking too much," he said. Kissing her forehead, he whispered, "So what comes now? The king has called you?"

She hesitated, but then shook her head. "Aye, the message came at dinner."

"I would go with you. You are my wife and I should be at your side as you are at mine."

"I will not sleep with him, Orrick. Please trust me?"

"When do you go to him?"

Again a hesitation in her reply. "At midnight. Alone."

He leaned back and waited for her to meet his eyes. Tears filled hers and began to spill over. "I trust your actions, ladywife. 'Tis the king I do not trust, so I would be at your side."

A knock at the door interrupted their conversation. François stood outside bringing a request from Godfrey to come to speak to him as soon as possible. Although he did not want to leave her side, he knew he must.

"Godfrey calls. He asks to speak to me now, but I can send word that I will meet him in the morning. What say you?"

"I am tired, Orrick, and would like to rest a while. If you would like to speak to him, go. He seemed anxious to see you when I spoke to him earlier today."

He went to her and kissed her. "I will return before you go to him. Wait for me."

She would not meet his gaze, but only nodded her assent. Leaving François before the door, he walked off to find the monk, knowing that she'd lied to him.

A few hours later, after holding a long conversation with Godfrey, he made his way to the corridor leading to the rooms where Henry stayed. Just before the final turn in the hallway, there was an alcove that was perfect for his purposes. Anyone going to the king must pass him.

He knew she would go alone, believing that she could manage the king. He knew that she did not want to give herself to Henry again. But he also knew that she would do anything to protect the love and the life she'd come to know with him. And if that meant believing more of the king's lies, she would do it.

As her husband, he meant to stop it.

Hours passed and he waited. Once the tide of visitors to the king slowed, no one but a few servants entered this wing of the castle. 'Twould seem that Henry was trying to be as discreet as he could in bringing Marguerite to him.

Then the soft pit-pat of a woman's gait echoed quietly down the hall and Orrick peeked from his hiding place. Her head was bent and she wore the plain cloak of a servant, but he would have recognized her anywhere. Marguerite continued past the curtained alcove, around the corner and on toward Henry's room.

Orrick paused, the pain in his heart growing. He'd been correct—she'd lied. She planned on seeing this through herself. Well, he would have to feel sorry for himself later. No, he needed to allow her the time and the room to make this mistake on her own. Orrick only hoped that when Henry proved himself unworthy of her yet again, she would know that she could return to him.

He was stepping out of the alcove when she came back around the corner and saw him. Since she'd passed only moments ago, she could not have reached the king's chambers yet. Puzzled, he frowned at her.

"What are you doing here, Orrick?"

"I knew you lied about when he expected you and I knew you would go to him alone and unprotected," he said. "I just thought to be here when you returned, in case you needed me then.

"Why are you back so soon?" He held his breath until she spoke.

"I did not want to face him alone."

He gazed into her eyes and neither one spoke. The love in her expression and the shame made his throat tighten. Then, with a gasp, she began crying and walked into his embrace. He held her within his arms, rocking back and forth, while she cried. Not wanting to draw attention, he pulled her into the curtained alcove, sat on the stone bench there and tugged her onto his lap. After a few minutes, she quieted and leaned against his chest.

"I do not want to go to him, Orrick. I want to go home with you and be your wife only," she whispered, her breaths hitching as she cried.

"Marguerite," he whispered back, kissing her forehead. "All will be well. Fear not."

"I cannot ignore his summons, Orrick. He will punish you if he thinks you kept me from him this night. I have seen him do it before."

He wiped the tears that fell onto her cheeks and then kissed her mouth. "I will stand at your side.

Come, dry your tears and do not let him know of your fears. He will play on them if he thinks he can.''

Orrick helped her to stand and she used the edge of her sleeves to dry her eyes and face. He pushed the curtain aside and they stepped into the corridor.

''And if he…if he wants…''

''He is king and can do whatever he pleases, Marguerite. But I will do all in my power to stand in the way of his desires if it is you he wants.'' He held out his hand to her and, without hesitating, she placed hers in it. ''Come, let us go to the king.''

Chapter Twenty-Five

"**Y**ou did not come alone, lady."

The king's words chilled her soul, but she felt Orrick squeeze her hand, giving her the support she needed. When she stepped forward, he did and when she released his hand, she felt him at her back.

"My husband thought it his place to escort me, Your Grace."

She saw Henry's eyes narrow as he examined both of them. "You are somehow different, sweet. Not just your appearance, but something about you. I cannot point to it though."

"I am not the person who shared your bed, Your Grace. The king's whore no longer exists."

He hissed at her words. "'Twas never like that between us, Marguerite. I was never unkind to you and never mistreated you. Did I make you feel like a whore?"

"But, Your Grace, when I wanted more, you threw me aside like one who asked for too many shillings for her services. Was that kind?"

Henry stalked around the room and then threw himself on a couch. "'Twas badly done of me. What would you have now to return to my bed?"

"I would be wife."

He sat up and glared at them. Orrick shifted behind her.

"I have a wife and need not a new one."

"And I a husband and want not another in his place."

Henry stood now and approached them. "This is not the picture you painted with your letters. Each one was worse than the one before. I thought this marriage would be good for you, but I began to doubt my wisdom when the letters arrived."

"Your Grace," she began, pausing to look at Orrick, "when I wrote those letters, I was terribly unhappy and angry at what I saw as punishment by you. I wanted to return to your side, never knowing all that transpired while I was away from you last year."

"You know of your sister?" A fleeting wave of guilt passed over his ruddy features as Henry asked. Nodding at Orrick. "Does he know of that time?"

"He knows I gave birth to a daughter."

"What say you to that, my lord?" Henry called out.

"'Tis a fact, Sire, that cannot be changed," Orrick said softly. "I know of the child and of the arrangements made for her upbringing. And soon, God willing, we will have a child to fill the empty place in my lady's heart and life left by her daughter's absence."

Tears threatened at his declaration. Even knowing

how badly she fared with her first, even knowing of her sins, he wanted her to bear his children. Henry huffed and turned away, walking to a table and pouring himself a cup of wine.

"I must admit, Marguerite, when I began receiving those letters last month, I…"

"Last month? But Your Grace, I began sending those to you shortly after my marriage, and stopped…more than a month ago."

The timing was not right. The letters had been delayed by a few months. Her uncle most likely discarded the ones sent to him since he supported anything her father told him to support. But her friend Johanna? Why would she seek to bring her back to court now? "Who gave these to you, Your Grace?"

"That woman who was companion to you. Joan?"

"Johanna. I did not think on it until just now. Your new…mistress is Lady Adelaide?"

Henry looked completely ill at ease at her question and she laughed. "My lord Orrick has encouraged my new manners. And, Henry, I know about the others who have shared your bed and your heart."

"Lady Adelaide has gained some favor with me." He answered her in an aggrieved voice as though his honor and not hers had been insulted.

"They are cousins and Adelaide sought to have Johanna sent home just before I left. This is Johanna's way of undermining Adelaide's power." She explained it more for Orrick's benefit and then realized that Henry gaped at her explanation. "If I return to you, Adelaide's place is in danger and she cannot affect Johanna."

"I do not like being played!" he shouted. "I will have them both removed. They will learn—"

"Nothing. They will learn to be more devious than before and you will never see their machinations."

Henry startled. "You would have me do nothing while these plots are hatched around me?"

"They are their own worst enemies, Your Grace. They will cause their own downfall in time." As she had been.

He looked to Orrick. "These women could teach the men a thing or two about how to get things done."

But Marguerite was still puzzled. She knew now how the letters came so late to Henry but not why he chose to act. "Your Grace, why did you seek to intervene now? You made it clear by your choice of husband for me, his distance from your court and your lack of contact that I was gone from your life. Why summon me back to you now?"

Henry drank deeply from his cup and then sat down, motioning for her to sit next to him. She looked to Orrick first before following the king to the couch. Once seated, he placed the cup on the table and took her hand. No sparks shot through her as their skin touched. No desire pulsed through her as he pulled her close. Amazed that there was no response within her to the touch of a hand that used to bring her to ecstasy, she allowed him to hold it.

"I know you will not believe this, but I did love you. But the love of a king is not the same as others and I could not give you all that you hungered for. Or should I say, all that your father plotted for."

Marguerite looked to Orrick and he nodded. 'Twould seem that Henry had recognized her father's actions for what they were—a bid for power.

"When you said you carried my babe, I knew it was time to send you away. I did not want you back in your father's control, so I sought the counsel of those I trust and they recommended yonder lord of Silloth as a possible husband for you."

Now it was her turn and Orrick's to be surprised.

"I did not want you harmed, so I made the arrangements for your marriage, and when the time came for you to return, it was accomplished." He laughed at what must have been the shocked expression on her face. "Not what you expected to hear?"

"No, Your Grace," she said, shaking her head.

"Come now, surely after all we've shared you can call me Henry."

"I am surprised…Henry."

"When I received your letters, I feared I had made a mistake in judgment regarding you, Orrick. I summoned you both so that I could decide whether or not to take her from you for your mistreatment of the gift I gave you."

Her husband looked past her and directly at the king as though the words meant something more to him than they seemed. A message seemed to pass between the two men in that moment. She would ask Orrick about it later.

"And now, Henry? What happens now?"

She braced herself for his answer, for he was still king and what he ordered would happen regardless of her change of heart or her husband's objections.

"This new Marguerite is indeed even more intriguing than the old one and I confess that there is no lack of desire on my part for you. However, I do not wish to fight to the death with your lord husband, as he will probably demand it as the price for your honor," he said.

Henry stood and waved Orrick to her side as he filled two more cups with wine. "And I have been warned recently that if I again break God's commandment concerning adultery, my soul is in danger of eternal damnation and I will burn in hell." He handed a goblet to each of them. "So, instead of taking you to my bed as I had planned to do, I will offer wishes for the health of your firstborn, Lord Orrick, and urge you both back to Silloth to await his or her birth."

They stopped before the wine touched their mouths and stared at him as one. "What mean you by those words?" she finally asked. She held her breath for none knew her suspicions yet. Her courses should have been on her during the journey here, but as yet, no symptoms heralded their approach.

Henry walked over to her and outlined with one finger the cut of her gown under the cloak she wore. "The skin on your breasts changes to a most attractive shade of pink when you are *enceinte,* sweet. It did it the first time and it changes so now. I saw it in the hall tonight when you curtsied to me."

Her hands went to her breasts as his words made them tingle. Could it be that she carried a child for Orrick? She looked at him and saw that he was more startled by the king's words than she. Then he smiled and everything was good.

She threw her arms around him and screeched her surprise and her happiness. Orrick pulled her to her feet and answered with a kiss that took her breath away. When he touched his mouth to hers again, the king interrupted.

"I think you should seek your chambers now."

"Aye, Your Grace," she said, curtsying to him as Orrick bowed.

Henry took her by the shoulders and did kiss her then, on the mouth, but it lasted for only a moment. The suspicious glint in his eyes made her think it a last test on his part.

Orrick took her hand and they walked to the door of the chamber. Just as they were about to pull the door open, Henry called to him. She waited for their private discussion to end, and the laugh that brought it to a close was another surprise. Orrick took her hand and led her back to their room. She had a celebration of her own in mind for the husband she had missed so badly.

"What made Henry laugh?" she asked as they made their way through the maze of corridors.

"He asked me what I would have done if he said he wanted you to stay the night with him."

"And what did you say that made him laugh?"

"I told him that I never doubted him since I think him to be a good man and a better king than one who needs to steal a man's wife. He said he'd heard almost those exact words and laughed."

With only another turn and not many yards left to

reach their room, Orrick picked her up in his arms
and kissed her as he carried her. If François was surprised by the sight, he did not show it, only opening
the door and pulling it closed behind them.

"I know that a jug of wine and an old friend is
no substitute for a warm and willing woman, but 'tis
all I have to offer, Henry.''

Henry accepted the cup and sat at the table waiting
for Godfrey to join him. He lifted a small bag of
silver and gold coins and tossed them across to the
man who had guarded his back too many times to
count.

"Is it difficult always being right?" he asked.
"Will you be humble as befits a man of God or will
you lord it over me for years to come?"

"That depends on how many coins are in this,"
Godfrey said as he picked up the sack and weighed
it in his hand. "If your gift is generous, I may just
forget about this time."

"Bah! You will not forget it. And sometimes I
wonder if your information on the queen's where-
abouts all those years ago was a blessing or a curse.''

It had been Godfrey of Poitiers, a knight in the
household of Eleanor, duchess of Aquitaine, who had
served as intermediary in the marriage negotiations
between the House of Anjou and the just-annulled
Queen of France. His efforts and his gift for secrecy
and discretion won Henry FitzEmpress the queen and
all of her lands to add to his own. In his fight against
Stephen and the years-long wait for the English
throne, that wealth had made the difference.

And in spite of all that transpired between the king and queen and princes, and in spite of his decision to take vows to serve God, Godfrey remained his true friend and the one Henry could count on when all others failed him.

"Would you say no if you could go back and change it?" Godfrey asked. "That is the truest test."

"I have asked myself that question often, sometimes daily, in the face of her perfidy, but the answer remains the same. Although there are many things I would change, I would do it all again."

"Will you release her from custody?"

"I know that your first allegiance was to her, Godfrey. I know how it pains you, but only God knows when the strife between us will end." They finished their wine in silence, for the subject of Eleanor was too painful to both of them.

"Is there anything else I can do to serve you, Your Grace?"

If Godfrey was addressing him formally, their time as simple friends was done. But first, something did bother him, something he had not mentioned to Marguerite. "About Marguerite's sister…"

"Dominique?"

"Aye. I do regret her. I thought that I accepted what was willingly offered and did not know the extent to which her father acted as procurer. If you know of some way that I can…" He stopped, not sure of what he wanted to do for the girl.

"You are a good man, Henry, and a better king," Godfrey said.

Henry stood and patted the monk's back. "Someone else told me that tonight. And I suspect he heard it from you, as well.''

Godfrey tied the sack to his belt and nodded. ''I will look into the matter of Dominique for you. Go with God, Henry.''

The door leading to the side chamber closed and Henry sat back down. 'Twas times like this, now fewer and farther between occurrences, when he did feel like a good man.

Epilogue

November, in the Year of Our Lord 1179

"My lady? Lord Orrick is back," Edmee said, looking out the window of Margaret's chamber and then back at her. "Should I take the babe with me?" The maid frowned.

Margaret looked at her son asleep in the cradle and smiled. He could sleep through almost any noise, but after Orrick's absence of more than two weeks from Silloth, she could only imagine what might happen. She had still not explained the damage to the door that used to hang between their rooms.

"Aye, Edmee. Take him to Lady Constance and apologize for my absence from the solar." Her mother-by-marriage was visiting from her dowager estate in Ravenglass.

The maid gathered up the babe and nearly ran from the room in her haste to avoid Orrick on his return. Apparently the sight of a naked and aroused lord of Silloth on his return the last time was something Edmee did not want to see again. Orrick had caught them unaware and did not realize that the young woman was tending to the babe in Margaret's room. It may have been the same time the door was knocked from its hinges, but Margaret did not want to think on that now.

There was no time.

She loosened her laces with a speed she'd developed over these past months. Tugging the gowns over her head, she slipped off the soft leather shoes and rolled down her stockings as she sat on the bed. She heard his shouting as he climbed the steps to their chambers. Her body was already shivering in readiness as she pulled the wimple and barbette from her head and climbed into the bed in her room.

'Twas safer to meet him like this than standing.

"Go away!" he shouted at the fools who must have followed him, expecting his attention. She cringed at the volume of his voice. The door slammed and she waited.

"Wife?" he whispered as he entered her room. "I want you now." His head and hair dripped of water. He'd washed on his way, probably dunking his head in a bucket on his way through the yard. His innate consideration had warred with expediency and lost in this instance.

Her breasts ached for his touch, and the core of heat inside her grew with his every step closer. The smile on his handsome face was wicked and he licked his lips as he reached the end of her bed. Faster than even she, he removed his tunic and used the undergown to remove some of the dripping water from his head. Then, still wearing only his stockings tied to the belt that held them up, he reached down and pulled the sheet off of her.

Without moving his gaze from hers, he began to crawl up her body. His tongue and teeth and lips teased her heated flesh and by the time he reached her mouth, she was begging. She opened her body to him and in one movement of his hips, he entered and filled her.

"Home," she heard him sigh as they fell over the edge of pleasure together. When they could breathe again, he rolled off of her, taking her with him and holding her close.

"Welcome, my lord," she said, laughing.

"My thanks for such a warm welcome, my lady. How do you fare?"

He said the same thing each time he arrived home. And in the same order, for they never had time for words until after he claimed her body again. And she had no objections to that.

"I am well, as is your son."

Orrick raised his head and looked at the empty cradle. "Edmee took him?" She could only nod and laugh again. "I tried to apologize, Margaret. Truly."

"Mayhap if you were clothed when you attempted it, Edmee might have accepted it?"

"'Tis Gavin's fault. He was the one that told me to tup you into submission." Orrick sat and pushed back to the headboard of the bed. "Speaking of him, I received a letter from him. Let me get it from my sack." He climbed from the bed and went back into his chambers.

Margaret pushed her hair out of her face and covered herself with a sheet. Orrick came back and sat next to her. He rummaged through the bag and found the letter. She opened it and read it, laughing at Gavin's description of his wedding night and his bride.

"Serves him right!" she exclaimed. "I am glad that his bride is no mealy-mouthed girl, but one who can handle him."

On their return to Silloth from Carlisle last year, she and Gavin had forged a friendship of sorts. That did not keep her from wishing a marriage for him or rejoicing when he was summoned back to his family for that wedding. His bride's name was Nessa and she was leading Gavin on a merry chase.

"I know this is late to mark the anniversary of your birth, but I hope you like it. I think it suits you."

He held out a small leather case and her hands trembled as she opened it to find a necklace of small stones and gold beads. It was perfect, the colors were her favorites and not so large that she would fear wearing it as she did with her mother's necklace.

"My thanks for this. I will cherish it."

"Ah, but that is not the real gift. This is." He held out a bigger package, one wrapped in waterproof canvas.

Tears filled her eyes for she knew what this one was. When she had declared her intention of being his good English wife and adopting the English version of her name, he had promised something special to mark the occasion and her choice. Unwrapping it revealed a new Book of Hours with her name, Lady Margaret of Silloth, embossed on the first page. But the words below her name were the ones that made her cry—Beloved Wife of Orrick.

"Here now, you are supposed to be happy. If you cry each time I bring you something home, I will have to stop."

Orrick held out the edge of the sheet to her and she dried her tears. He took the book and placed it on the carved reading table he'd had made for it. Opening the leather box, he lifted the necklace out and laid it around her neck. She held up her hair so he could fasten it in place. When he leaned back and looked on her with such love, she cried all over again.

"I have nothing to give you when you are so generous," she said, touching the stones of the necklace that now warmed on her skin.

"Not true. You have given me a son. A most splendid one at that," he said with fatherly pride. "Which reminds me…" He turned the bag upside down until another parchment fell out. "We have spoken of her, but I have news for you."

"Genevieve?" Margaret asked. Her daughter by the king was a year older than her son and she had not seen her since the day of her birth. There was no possibility of raising her so she remained with Margaret's sister at the convent where Dominique served God.

"Godfrey tells me that a new Gilbertine convent has opened to the east of Carlisle and that Dominique has been appointed as the assistant to the reverend mother there.''

"But she is so young!''

"Apparently she has the support of someone important enough to influence those who make the decisions.''

Henry. The king was somehow behind this.

"And they have a lay community there, as well, just as their other convents.''

She looked at him, trying to figure out his message. The importance of his words struck her. "Genevieve is there?''

"Aye, she is there now.''

"Could I…?'' She could not get the words out. Her throat tightened and her eyes burned once more with tears. "Would you allow me to…?''

"As a kind and God-fearing husband, I would see no reason against a yearly or so retreat to the convent there. So long as you promise to say a prayer for my wicked soul.''

"Wicked soul, my lord? I think not.'' She wiped her eyes again and looked at him, hoping he could see in her gaze the love she felt for him.

"If you had any idea of the impious thoughts going through my mind in spite of this talk of convents and prayers, you would be praying for my soul.''

"Or just praying that you—'' She pulled him to her and whispered in his ear all her wicked thoughts. He lifted the sheet and settled on top of her as she continued to describe all the things she'd missed while he was away. And she poured her love into him even as he poured himself into her.

The lord and his lady were heard but not seen until two days hence by those living in Silloth Keep.

And all was well in Silloth.

* * * * *

If you enjoyed THE KING'S MISTRESS,
look for a brand-new short story
by Terri Brisbin set in Silloth Keep,
coming in April 2005!

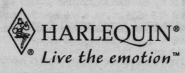

If you enjoyed what you just read,
then we've got an offer you can't resist!

Take 2 bestselling love stories FREE!

Plus get a FREE surprise gift!

Clip this page and mail it to Harlequin Reader Service®

IN U.S.A.	IN CANADA
3010 Walden Ave.	P.O. Box 609
P.O. Box 1867	Fort Erie, Ontario
Buffalo, N.Y. 14240-1867	L2A 5X3

YES! Please send me 2 free Harlequin Historicals® novels and my free surprise gift. After receiving them, if I don't wish to receive anymore, I can return the shipping statement marked cancel. If I don't cancel, I will receive 6 brand-new novels every month, before they're available in stores! In the U.S.A., bill me at the bargain price of $4.69 plus 25¢ shipping and handling per book and applicable sales tax, if any*. In Canada, bill me at the bargain price of $5.24 plus 25¢ shipping and handling per book and applicable taxes**. That's the complete price and a savings of over 10% off the cover prices—what a great deal! I understand that accepting the 2 free books and gift places me under no obligation ever to buy any books. I can always return a shipment and cancel at any time. Even if I never buy another book from Harlequin, the 2 free books and gift are mine to keep forever.

246 HDN DZ7Q
349 HDN DZ7R

Name	(PLEASE PRINT)	
Address	Apt.#	
City	State/Prov.	Zip/Postal Code

Not valid to current Harlequin Historicals® subscribers.

Want to try two free books from another series?
Call 1-800-873-8635 or visit www.morefreebooks.com.

* Terms and prices subject to change without notice. Sales tax applicable in N.Y.
** Canadian residents will be charged applicable provincial taxes and GST.
 All orders subject to approval. Offer limited to one per household.
 ® are registered trademarks owned and used by the trademark owner and or its licensee.

HIST04R   ©2004 Harlequin Enterprises Limited

Harlequin Romance®

From paper marriage...to wedded bliss?

A wedding dilemma:

What should a sexy, successful bachelor do if he's too busy
making millions to find a wife? Or if he finds the perfect
woman, and just has to strike a bridal bargain...?

The perfect proposal:

The solution? For better, for worse, these grooms in a hurry
have decided to sign, seal and deliver the ultimate
marriage contract...to buy a bride!

Coming Soon to

HARLEQUIN®
Romance®

featuring the favorite miniseries Contract Brides:

THE LAST-MINUTE MARRIAGE
by Marion Lennox, #3832
on sale February 2005

A WIFE ON PAPER
by award-winning author Liz Fielding, #3837
on sale March 2005

VACANCY: WIFE OF CONVENIENCE
by Jessica Steele, #3839
on sale April 2005

Available wherever Harlequin books are sold.

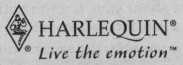

HARLEQUIN®
Live the emotion™

Harlequin Historicals®
Historical Romantic Adventure!

TRAVEL BACK TO THE FUTURE
FOR ROMANCE—WESTERN-STYLE!
ONLY WITH HARLEQUIN HISTORICALS.

ON SALE JANUARY 2005

TEXAS LAWMAN by Carolyn Davidson

Sarah Murphy will do whatever it takes to save her nephew
from dangerous fortune seekers—including marrying lawman
Blake Caulfield. Can the Lone Star lawman keep them
safe—without losing his heart to the feisty lady?

WHIRLWIND GROOM by Debra Cowan

Desperate to avenge the murder of her parents, all trails lead
Josie Webster to Whirlwind, Texas, much to the chagrin of
charming sheriff Davis Lee Holt. Let the games begin as
Davis Lee tries to ignore the beautiful seamstress who stirs
both his suspicions and his desires....

ON SALE FEBRUARY 2005

PRAIRIE WIFE by Cheryl St.John

Jesse and Amy Shelby find themselves drifting apart after
the devastating death of their young son. Can they put
their grief behind them and renew their deep and abiding
love—before it's too late?

THE UNLIKELY GROOM by Wendy Douglas

Stranded by her brother in a rough-and-rugged Alaskan
gold town, Ashlynne Mackenzie is forced to rely on the
kindness of saloon owner Lucas Templeton. But kindness
has nothing to do with Lucas's urges to both protect the
innocent woman and to claim her for his own.